THE HEALERS

THE PRIDDEN SAGA: BOOK TWO

Disclaimer:
All characters in this book are fictitious, and any resemblance to actual persons, living or dead, is purely coincidental.

Cover Art by Deranged Doctor Designs
Substantive Editor: Laura LaRocca

Library and Archives Canada Cataloguing in Publication

ISBN: 978-1-7389742-4-5

Printed in United States of America
Published by JMT Publishing, Canada
www.jmtpublishing.com
Second Edition, 2019

THE HEALERS

J. M. TIBBOTT

DEDICATION

To Rob for constant encouragement, even now…

J. M. Tibbott

ACKNOWLEDGMENTS

- Special thanks to:
- my writing group members for their suggestions and critiquing help
- my beta readers who caught loads of things I missed
- John Truby for his incredible training on writing a novel
- Ed Greenwood for showing me how too create a vital and believable world, and for his continued kind comments
- and all the positive feedback from the many who purchased Book One

J. M. Tibbott

MAP OF PRIDDEN

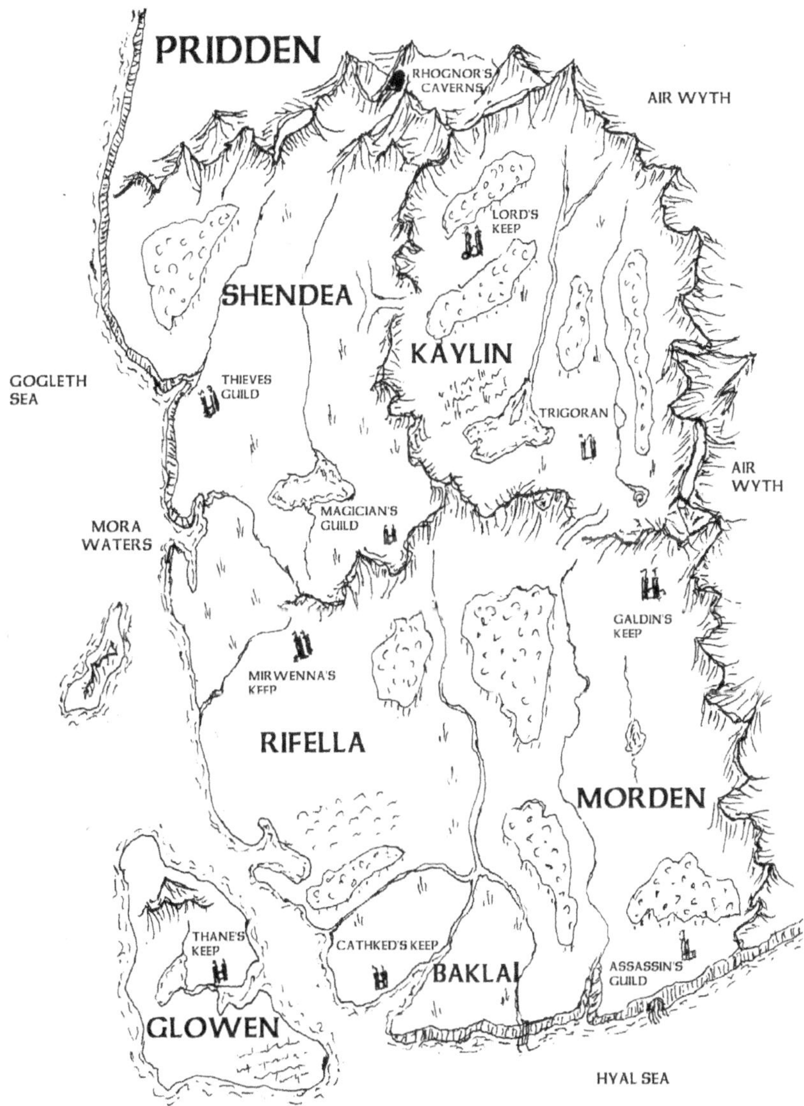

J. M. Tibbott

MAP OF SHENDEA

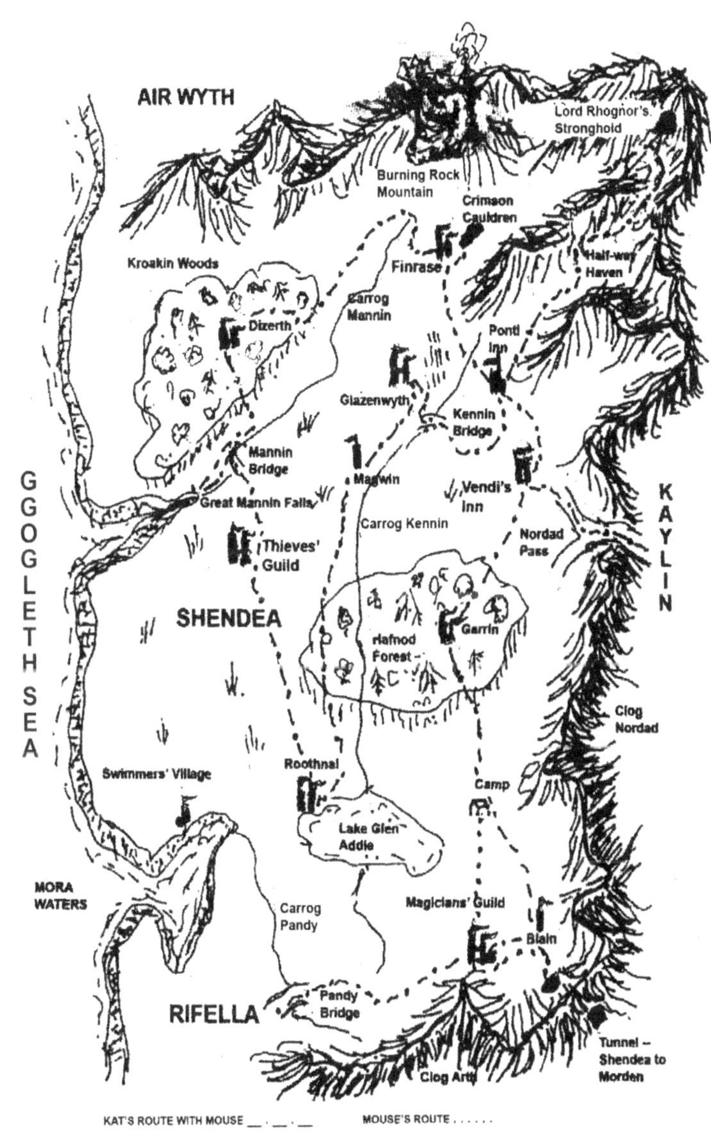

J. M. Tibbott

WHAT HAS HAPPENED SO FAR.

Kat, a brilliant, solitary video game designer, discovers she is in danger of being fired for her avoidance of working in team situations. Given the option to consider her future with the new management's style, she takes a sabbatical on the Island of Tortola in the British Virgins. Hiking in the bush behind her hotel, she is caught in a storm and takes shelter in an abandoned building. Opening an odd looking door, she is caught, without warning, in a vortex and is transported to an unknown world.

Kat awakes in a strange new land, and initially believes she is caught in a dream in one of her games. She is befriended by a Healer, Wynneth, and meets Eduardo, who is the lord of this land. After discovering she is not dreaming, Kat asks for help to return home, and Eduardo offers a trade. She must help him determine who is causing challenges between the peoples of Pridden, which could lead to war. In doing so she is to discover those who, when their talents are combined, will have sufficient power to return her home.

She decides to record her experiences so she might transfer them to a new video game when she returns to her own world.

She understands she is now in the world of Pridden, which consists of six lands. Currently in the land of Kaylin, whose inhabitants are so strait-laced, they forbid close relationships between men and women before bonding for life, Kat needs to learn the social requirements and customs here.

She is reminded of this forcefully when she accidentally exposes her legs to Haydar the Horse-Master, and thus is denied the use of a horse. She also manages to annoy Brith, the seamstress, who refuses to create comfortable clothing for her, deciding it is too revealing.

To find help, Kat meets with two incredibly attractive Rifellans, Praetor Bardu and his wife Irina. Their pheromones, without the calming affect of a tea called Karri-san, impacts Kat markedly.

To begin her journey, Eduardo assigns his counselor, Drainin, whom Kat distrusts, to accompany her through the land of Kaylin. During her travels, she enjoys a dalliance with the enticing Liandock, the Metal-Smith, who designs a unique pendant for her to allow her to discern between friends and enemies, and then meets with Penrow, the bear-like, but joyful Master Builder. In Trigoran, she encounters men from Morden whom she challenges, causing Drainin to chastise her.

Later, Drainin attempts to seduce her using the Kaylin equivalent of 'roofies' and Kat refuses to travel with him again.

When Eduardo's promise of a horse to travel to the next land lags, Kat, frustrated, attempts to 'borrow' one from Haydar. Eduardo saves her from the death penalty for this action, by taking on the responsibility for her thievery.

Eduardo now introduces her to Mouse, a seemingly timid little man from Morden, as her guide through the rest of Pridden.

In the meantime, Kat is lured to creepy Old Town and is kidnapped by the Assassin's Guild, who contracted to ferry her to Galdin, the Thane of Morden, who needs her help to allow him to rule over Pridden. Drainin is shown to be an ally to Galdin, and helps with the kidnapping.

Many of the people Kat has encountered ride to her

rescue, and free her, but in the ensuing battle, a young wagon driver called Bannon, and Bardu's assistant are killed. Most of the Assassins, and Drainin also die during the violent skirmish.

Kat realizes her prejudices about many of the people, because of their decidedly different customs, were unfounded, and asks forgiveness from those she misjudged. She establishes that Eduardo, who is a Wielder of Power, will be the person from Kaylin who will be one of those who will help her return home.

Kat, with a pen made from a cathnog tooth, a cute furry messenger pyrock, and the odd little man known as Mouse, sets out for Shendea.

J. M. Tibbott

CHAPTER 1

The path from Kaylin to Shendea through the Nordad pass, was disturbed only by the moaning complaints of the wind. The clop of the horses hooves on the hard rocky surface, together with the hypnotic rhythm and sway of their mounts, lulled Kat and her companion. The pack animal, tied to Kat's saddle, followed silently. As they exited the pass, they paused at a fork in the road, when the sudden cold from the green stone hanging between Kat's breasts startled her. *What now?*

A guttural roar shattered the silence. Kat's horse reared, and all three animals danced backward, neighing frantically. With a further screech, an enormous cat-like creature sprang from the bushes beside the pathway and leaped for the pack animal. Huge fangs bared, the animal's vicious claws raked the horse, who reared and screamed in pain and fear, and attempted to run. Secured to Kat's saddle he pulled against the bit in his mouth, unable to free himself.

"Cathnog!" Mouse pointed to the path on the right. "Run, Kat." He whirled his horse to the left with a wild scream and headed toward the thick wood of evergreens. The massive cat vaulted after him.

Her skin still prickling from the unexpected encounter, and furious with Mouse for abandoning them, Kat and the pack animal galloped up the right fork. *He ran and left us. The coward.* The stone on her pendant lay like a block of ice against her skin.

The cathnog roared again, fainter, as he followed the fleeing Mouse. Abruptly, a challenging deep-throated bellow joined the melee.

At the sight of a small building beside the road, Kat reined in her fleeing mount. *This will do. The poor pack-horse needs tending.* She dismounted, and led both horses into the shelter. The pack animal's eyes rolled in terror and the creature's entire body trembled, as Kat struggled to control the horse and secure the baggage animal to a post inside the small structure. She retrieved the first aid kit supplied by Wynneth from her pack. In the kit, she located an ointment and avoiding the thrashing hooves, applied the soothing mixture to the wounds on the horse's flank. At once the animal ceased its trembling and nickered as if in relief.

Kat still caught the roars and bellows of the battle in the distance, between the enormous cat and the mysterious second creature. *What will I do if my cowardly guide is killed? Will I be able to find my own way to the nearest inn?* She soothed her own horse. *Wait. Wink.* She removed the woolly covering from the traveling cage tied to the back of her saddle, and peered in. Two tiny bright eyes appeared from a ball of fluff, along with a grumpy peep. "I'm so sorry, Wink. I had to run, and I forgot you would be bounced around." With a sleepy chirrup, the pyrock's eyes closed and she became a roll of fur once more. Kat rewrapped the cage.

Unexpectedly a high-pitched scream, and a bugle of triumph from the unknown animal, hinted the cathnog met his match.

The ensuing silence was absolute, and Kat waited, unnerved. *Should I stay here or make a run for it? I'm not sure if the pack horse can keep up. Is Mouse alive?* The sound of hoof-beats persuaded her to wait.

Mouse appeared outside the shelter, his robe ripped and his horse quivering in the aftermath of the battle. He dismounted and entered the building. "Are you alright? I saw the cathnog leap toward you."

Kat's words were laced with icy disdain. "I am, no thanks to you. I thought you were supposed to be my guide." *I suspected he wouldn't be any help in the protection department. I'm right.*

"Lady Kat, I did not abandon you. I screamed to persuade the cathnog to follow me so I could draw him away from you."

Kat raised her hands to her mouth. *Ohh crap.* "My bad." *Uh oh, Mouse seems confused.* She lowered her hands. "What I mean is… I… I misunderstood. I thought you were running for your life and leaving me. I apologize."

"A natural assumption on your part."

"I must ask you. Although I rode fast, I heard some horrifying shrieks and bellows. What went on?"

"Fortunately for me when the creature almost caught me, a hydodd appeared, an animal who is the sworn enemy of the cathnog."

"Oh yes, I remember Wynneth telling me about them."

"This hydodd was powerful in the extreme, and larger than most. He managed to dispatch the cathnog speedily." Mouse grimaced as he waved his hand to indicate the size of the victorious hydodd.

"Mouse, forgive me, I may have misjudged you." *I hope I misjudged him, and he's telling the truth.* She glanced at the blood seeping down the arm of his torn robe. "You're wounded. Here." She grabbed the ointment again. "Wynneth's ointment will help. Let me see your arm."

Mouse exposed the slash on his arm, and grimaced again with the effort.

Kate applied the salve to his upper arm. *Wow, he's got muscles. How odd. He looks so small.*

"Thank you, Lady Kat." Mouse's face relaxed.

"You're welcome. Our poor pack horse also got slashed, and she most definitely appreciated the relief this liniment gave her."

Mouse walked over and examined the slash on the horse. "This wound is not overly bad. She will recover. We should continue on to the nearest inn. She will receive a chance to rest, and we will spend the night. In the morning, we will exchange our animals for pontis, one star turn sooner than anticipated. You will be happy to know, cathnogs rarely appear this high on Mont Diffenna, so we are unlikely to encounter another."

"Mont Diffenna? Is this where Rhognor lives?"

Mouse frowned. "Yes he does. But Lady Kat, it is fine you are less formal when speaking with me. But be sure to use Lord Rhognor's full title in the presence of others."

"Okay, okay. I'll remember. But perhaps when we are alone, you will, without the necessary guile of politics, call me Kat."

"Okay." Mouse grinned. "Wynneth told me this word means, all is well. I too will be less formal when we are alone, Kat." Still grinning, Mouse mounted his horse and the three headed up the roadway.

***

Mouse led them up the path of Mount Diffenna cutting through a forest of deciduous trees which rained withered leaves on the three of them, and left bare branches like bones rattling against each other. The dried leaves pattered across the roadway, pursued by frigid winds sweeping down from the mountain.

Mouse glanced back at Kat who followed close behind. *Thank Caleesh I defeated the cathnog out of her sight. If she had seen me take on the mantle of a hydodd, she would with-*

out delay, jump to the conclusion I have the power to return her to her world. I cannot achieve this on my own, and Eduardo would be upset if I interrupted her task to visit every land in Pridden.

"Mouse. How long before we reach the inn?"

Her words interrupted his thoughts. He turned in the saddle. "Lady… er Kat, we will arrive momentarily after the midturn meal. However, they will still be willing to serve us, as I imagine you are hungry."

"Exactly why I asked. I'm starving."

Mouse chuckled. "I do believe you will not perish before we reach our destination. You will soon be fed, and we will stay at the inn for the rest of this turn and over the night. Had we not been interrupted by the cathnog, we would have stopped for a quick meal and travelled to the next inn to sleep. We are traveling with less speed than I expected, and once we change to pontis, the way will be slower than on horseback." He groaned internally. *I am not looking forward to an extra day on a ponti. I find them most uncomfortable. I suspect Kat will experience the same discomfort.*

Mouse rode on, caught up in his own thoughts. *Interesting. I have not found Kat to be as difficult as I imagined. Perhaps this journey will not challenge me as much as I anticipated.*

J. M. Tibbott

CHAPTER 2

Kat's stomach grumbled in empty annoyance, at the same moment as the inn appeared at the edge of the trees. The building was extensive and constructed of stone. The substantial iron door opened and a portly man peered out as if he anticipated their coming. He beckoned for them to enter quickly.

Kat suspected he wished to keep the heat in the inn, and not warm up the outside scenery. *Food. At last.* She slid from her horse, grabbed her pyrock cage, and staggered through the doors, stopping briefly to inhale the delicious warm aromas from within.

Mouse, right behind her, hurried over to the proprietor, and spoke to him.

The elderly man nodded at Mouse, hobbled over to Kat, and led her to a table. "Your friend advised me of your encounter, and of the change in your plans. Istra will bring food and drink to you before long, Lady Kat."

"Thank you." *He probably heard my belly complaining from miles away.* "By the way, what is the name of this inn?"

"We possess no names for the inns in this area of Shendea. They are only known by the names of the owners. Most call this one Vendi's inn."

"Interesting." *Shendeans are less formal than Kaylins. Yay.*

Within minutes, an apple-cheeked girl, with dark ginger hair, appeared carrying a tray laden with bowls of steaming soup, a large plate of crusty bread, and flagons of a beverages with tendrils of heat rising from them.

Neither Kat nor Mouse, when he joined her, spoke a word, but shoveled in spoonsful of thick luscious wullawerth stew, which soothed their hunger. In between mouthfuls of fuel, they slaked their thirst with flagons of near-ale.

Plates and bowls empty, Kat leaned back in her chair. "I think the meal went down well, but I was so hungry, I hardly tasted much." She managed to conceal a burp of pleasure. "So what do we do now?" *At least I'm decently fed while I'm waiting to return home.*

Before Mouse could answer, Vendi sidled up to him. "Pardon me, Sire. I regret we are unable to receive the Pontis here in time to meet with you. You will need to travel to the next inn to make the exchange as previously arranged. We will, however, lend you a healthy pack animal, and keep this one here until she recovers from her wounds. My stable-master is switching your goods to the new horse as we speak."

"My thanks. What is the distance to the next inn?"

"Less than half a star turn. If you depart soon, you will arrive comfortably before the night falls."

"Excellent. If you send out two of your apprentices, at the place where the Nordad Pass splits, take the right road toward the forest. There you will find a cathnog who met his end from a hydodd. There is meat for smoking, which should supply your inn for four or five star turns."

The old man beamed at him. "Blessings to you Sire. Meat is often in short supply, and we appreciate your generosity. Please accept your meal as our thanks."

Mouse bowed his head slightly. "Our thanks to you." He rose from the table and turned to Kat. "We must be on our way to arrive at the next inn before night falls."

Kat stood and grinned at Mouse. "This gives new meaning to the phrase, eat and run."

Mouse glanced at her, puzzlement in his eyes, as they departed the inn.

I can't be bothered explaining another expression.

Waiting at the door to the establishment, their horses stood patiently, freshly watered, and accompanied by a new animal laden with their baggage. Kat tied her pyrock cage to the edge of her saddle and using a nearby stone, mounted.

Mouse surprised Kat when he raised one foot high enough to rest in a stirrup, and almost threw himself up into his saddle. *I didn't think he would be tall enough to get his foot so high. He's quite a bit more flexible than I suspected, too. How odd.*

Mouse nudged the horse and they rode steadily toward Rhognor's Stronghold, carved from the high peaks of Mont Diffena.

The horses continued to walk briskly beside each other when a thought occurred to Kat. "The old man rushed us out of there. Why?"

"You must understand, in these mountains each inn has specific obligations. Vendi's never boards pontis unless in an emergency, and is not prepared to board horses for any length. They only keep a few for their own use. He knows we need to reach the next inn before dark, because the place has long been established as a horse/ponti exchange center. When we complete our visit with Lord Rhognor, and return this way to visit the lowlands of Shendea, we will return their pontis, and reclaim our own horses."

"Makes sense. These Shendeans are quite logical. I can live with their ways."

"You will find Shendeans are far more pragmatic than Kaylins, and as a believer in logic you will no doubt relate to them well."

As the trail narrowed, Mouse took the lead, glancing back occasionally to check on Kat's progress.

"Mouse, a question?"

"Yes?"

"Did you also leave the cathnog's teeth for the innkeeper's apprentices?"

He stopped his horse and turned in the saddle to face her. "I did not. I removed the important fangs, and when we reach the Stronghold, I will clean them and you can present them to Lord Rhognor as a gift."

"I hope he won't think I'm some supernatural being who killed the beast by myself."

Mouse chuckled. "I'm sure he will not. However, do feel free to discuss the demise of the animal at the hands — or horns for that matter — of the hydodd." He faced away and continued up the trail.

The Kaylin saddles were comfortable, and the motion of the horses, hypnotic. Kat nodded in the saddle as she rode, caught up in thoughts of home, of Liandock and of her adventures thus far. She perceived no awareness of the passage of time, when Mouse spoke up.

"The inn is around the next bend of the road, and we will stay for the night."

As they neared the inn, Kat observed the formal, but foreboding building constructed entirely of finely dressed stone. The building bore no resemblance to anything with which Kat was familiar, and had additions tacked on apparently without thought or plan. *Whoever the builder, he must have been on steroids when he designed this place.* Kat chuckled to herself. He's *no artist though, because the structure is butt ugly.*

She and Mouse stepped down from their horses, and Kat grabbed the reins of her mount and began to lead the animal toward the smaller edifice, attached to the side of the inn.

A stable hand appeared from a smaller building. "Please, my Lady, I will take your horse." He already held the reins of Mouse's mount.

"It's fine, I can do it. You don't need to."

Mouse stepped forward. "Kat let the man do his job."

"I'm perfectly capable of leading a horse into a stable. I'm not helpless, you know."

"I know you are able. But you are The Lady Kat, and you are not allowing him to perform a service for you." Mouse's lips were drawn in a thin line. "Let him do his job."

"Oh." She relinquished the reins to the young man, whose eyes bore an expression of trepidation, but grabbed her pyrock cage, which was attached to her saddle.

He began to lead their mounts away, but stopped, turned, and addressed them both. "We have been expecting you." He swallowed visibly. "Your luggage will be sent to your rooms, and on the morrow, once you finish your morning meal, one of our helpers will collect your bags and load them on the ponti who will serve as your pack animal."

Mouse moved forward. "Thanks to you, apprentice." He passed a small chit over to the man, who lowered his head in thanks, and apparently relieved, entered the stable.

What happened? Do they truly believe I need servants? Do they think I'm helpless? They want me to solve problems for them yet seem unable to accept that I can take care of myself.

Ignoring her, Mouse walked to the substantial door of the main building, grabbed at the handle and pushed it aside. He motioned Kat to precede him.

As Kat entered she shoved the door wider and the weight startled her. *Wow, heavy. Mouse is stronger than I realized. Weird.*

A blast of cheerful and welcoming heat, and a din of laughter enveloped them as they entered. Despite the odd exterior, the inside of the inn, furnished with nut brown tables and comfortable chairs covered in deep red cloth, beckoned them to relax in the cozy setting. The innkeeper spotted them, hurried over, led them to a table, and snapped his fingers at a serving girl. She left the room, but returned almost at once with two huge mugs of heated spiced wine.

After checking the heat level with her tongue, Kat drank, and the wine flowed down her throat, warming her from the inside. She peeked inside the pyrock cage to make sure Wink slept peacefully. After two sizable gulps of wine, she felt recovered enough to glance around the room. The dining area, crowded with people, throbbed with noise and laughter. To her right sat a table of gorgeous bronze Rifellans in fur and leather uniforms. *Glad I brought plenty of Karri-san.* A pair of pale, black-haired Mordens occupied a table almost hidden in a corner, and on the opposite side of the room, laughing animatedly, perched a number of red-faced, flashy, fleshy men who were, she guessed, Glowens, from the state of their obvious inebriation. Near the roaring fire, sat a table of five smaller men. *Gotta be Baklai. They're bundled up despite being right beside the fire.* The balance, Shendeans, robed in a rainbow of bright and brilliant colors, conversed gaily with each other. The only glum faces in the room belonged to the pale-faced, dark-haired Mordens.

"There don't appear to be any Kaylins here, Mouse. Why not?"

He sighed. "Kaylins tend to remain at home. Most of them are not curious about the rest of the people of Pridden. The ones they've met in the past tend to flout their rules, and they are not as outgoing as the majority of males and females in this room. They would be uncomfortable in this company."

"Ah, of course they would." Kat stretched and yawned. "I managed to eat a little, but the wine has gone to my head, and I'm beat." She caught Mouse's quizzical glance at her. "I mean I'm really tired. I need my bed."

"I understand, Lady Kat. I shall follow presently, but first, I will confirm our mounts for the morrow.

***

The following morning, by the time Mouse and Kat saddled up and were mounted on the pontis, the first flakes of snow whirled about the travelers, and danced in the brisk wind sweeping down the mountain.

Kat bundled herself in her fur-lined coat. She chastised Mouse. "I think you're making a mistake not putting on a thicker robe. My coat will keep me much warmer than the one I wore yesterday. I hope the weather gets no colder." No sooner had she finished her sentence, when another blast of frigid flakes eddied around them, and promptly flew in her open mouth. Kat spat them out, and reached into the backpack attached to the side of the saddle, where she extracted a thick wooly shawl with which she wrapped her head and shoulders.

Mouse withdrew into the hood of his robe, and shook his head to dislodge the icy crystals.

Unlike the pontis she travelled with before, these creatures appeared odder than those in Kaylin. They were adorned with masses of hair around their heads, and sported long eyelashes, which acted like shields over their eyes, allowing them to plod sure-footedly up the narrow trail, without being blinded by the snow. *I'll bet they breed these ones to handle the blizzards in these mountains.*

Despite some obvious ice covered patches in the path, the pontis performed admirably over the treacherous track.

After traveling for most of the morning, Kat's backside ached abominably. The pontis who now supported them along the rough track leading to the crags of Diffenna, unlike the comfortable saddles of their horses, appeared built for the more padded posteriors of the Shendeans, not for the butt of a jogger, endowed with little fat and, *oh agony*, more bone. The mountain-hold of Lord Rhognor gave the impression of being no closer, and Kat's stomach again began to protest a lack of food. Appreciating these little animals' sure-footedness became difficult, when every muscle she owned screamed in protest at each bump during the last hour of the journey. To make matters worse, despite the fur around her face, her nose, she was sure, had turned into a block of ice.

She yelled over the wind to attract Mouse's attention. "Do we stop for a midturn meal?"

"A short way ahead, Kat. If you look carefully, you can glimpse the gates to Half-Way Haven."

When she raised her head to peer through the blizzard, she spotted an iron barrier. *Oh thank god. I can rest my butt at last.*

At the portal gates, more than halfway up the mountain, Kat almost fell from the saddle, and barely managed to stay upright. So grateful for what she viewed as the end of the journey, Kat found herself almost compelled to kiss the groom who took the little beast from her aching hands and led it to the stable.

He smiled at her. "I'll bed your ponti for you, lady."

"I thank your kindness" *If I follow their specific rules of politeness, I usually get what I want. Doesn't happen where I work... .*

She hurried up the path and through the doors of an elegant building, with Mouse close behind.

Once inside, Mouse paused to speak to a woman at the entrance to the dining area. He caught up to Kat as a young waitress showed her to a table near a fire. The flames jumped and danced around a massive pot suspended over the blaze.

"Lady Kat… ?"

Lady Kat, hah. I'll never get used to being called lady. Mom would have rolled on the floor laughing if she ever heard this honorific applied to me. I believe she despaired of me being anything other than another tomboy. She rubbed her forehead. *Boy, haven't thought of her and dad for a long time. They both had a sense of humor, not like the foster ones.* Kat sighed. *It's been so long, but I still miss them.*

"Lady Kat… ?"

Startled by his words, Kat realized he still spoke. "Sorry what did you say?"

"I said, our guide, Anwen, told me when we reach the entrance to the mountain hold, a room will be arranged for you to prepare for the audience and dinner with Lord Rhognor."

She smiled at Mouse gratefully. "Lead the way. I want to stand for a while before I need to sit again for a dinner. And… we agreed you would call me Kat."

He coughed. "Mmm, Kat, This is not Lord Rhognor's hold. We are only part way. First a brief meal, and then we climb the right crag called Bar Braich without the use of our Pontis."

Kat glared at him. *Oh Shit.*

***

Kat lifted her feet in the climb up Bar Braich, each foot seemingly attached to a block of stone, which she dragged along a narrow track created by the cold grey rock on either side. Her breathing labored, and despite her normal fitness, this mountain demanded more than she had trained for. The two young men who carried their luggage did not appear to find the climb as difficult.

Wynneth warned her, visiting Lord Rhognor would be a physical challenge. *This trek sucks. I hope this is gonna be worth it.*

As the Lord of Shendea, Rhognor's Stronghold, located almost at the peak, could easily be defended from the only entrance which appeared to be remotely passable.

She gazed up at the sharp stone ridges, thrusting upwards, like knives slicing into the cold, grey sky, and shivered, not with cold, but at the desolate landscape.

Anwen, their guide from Half-Way Haven, appeared to catch her grimace at the dark clouds surrounding the peak. "This is our resting time of year, when the light is shorter, and before the rains come to replenish the fields below us. But up on Bar Braich, many of these rains turn solid and are too fierce for any Shendeans to venture far outside of the Stronghold." She smiled. "Many offspring are brought to thought in this season of our path."

Kat raised an eyebrow. "I can imagine few would want to venture far from this place at any season, and especially in the cold and damp." *A warm bed is the only place I want to be.*

Anwen gestured at Mouse. "Your servant is not happy with this cold. He shivers."

"He's not my servant. He's... a ... well, my companion."

Kat noticed a grimace from Mouse at her words. She

pulled a small thick blanket from her knapsack and tossed it to him. "I told you to wear a more substantial robe." *At first, I thought he was stronger than he looked. Well, he's decidedly a mouse now. Damn. He's my guide, not someone I should be required to look after.*

"I did not prepare for the weather to be so foul and frigid up here. I never traveled in Shendea at this time of a path before." He glared at her and turned to Anwen. "How long before we arrive at the Stronghold?"

Kat frowned. *Path? What's a path?*

Anwen pointed at the rough road. "See the trail as it disappears around the ridge? On the other side is the entrance."

Kat and Mouse both sighed, relieved.

Mouse, fire in his eyes, pulled Kat aside. "I am not your companion. Companion in many of the lands, when referring to the opposite sex, means 'lover.' You should call me 'friend' instead."

Kat, more amused than embarrassed, nodded absentmindedly, but she needed Mouse to continue as her guide. "Fine. I will clear everything up with Anwen as soon as we arrive at the hall."

Mouse snorted.

"I said I will." *Can't believe this. Some men would appreciate being thought of as my lover.*

J. M. Tibbott

CHAPTER 3

Rhognor's Stronghold loomed ahead, an enormous opening in the mountain, with two massive ironbound doors, which flanked the entrance. Both creaked as wheels and gears groaned to open them sufficiently to allow the three people, plus two luggage bearers, access to the main hall, a massive room with arched ceilings and stone carved walls. Along one wall, rows of hooks, attached to the walls, bore many cloaks, shawls, and hats. A lower shelf supported piles of hand coverings of thick wooly material.

An enveloping blanket of heat surrounded Kat as she entered, and she almost moaned aloud with pleasure. Anwen shed her long woolly coat and thick blue hand coverings, and held out her hands for Kat's heavy fur-lined coat and the smaller one belonging to Mouse.

He still glared at Kat.

I think he's grumpy. I better clear this up now. "Anwen, I come from a land where words have different meanings. What I should have said is, he," she gestured at Mouse, "is not my companion, but my friend."

"Thank you, Lady Kat, for making that clear. It helps to know the correct relationships our visitors have with each other."

Kat glanced again at Mouse. He no longer scowled at her and his face had lost the pinched air, and color had returned to his skin.

She nudged him and pointed. "Look at those incredible tapestries. Most of the this room is covered in them. You can hardly see the stone of the walls."

"Mmmm." He appeared too busy absorbing the warmth of the hall to even take notice.

Anwen stepped to her side and pointed to the closest one.

"These tapestries are hundreds of star turns old. This one tells the history of Shendea — how we established our homes in these mountains and overcame all the challenges offered by this land. Each tapestry takes many turns to complete, and may involve at least three generations of weavers. The material for the threads comes from the brynosh plant and we work the fibers until they are soft and pliable. Only then can they be used to create these views of our life."

"They're beautiful. The sheen on them reminds me of ones from my home which are made from silk. Can I touch them?"

"Of course, the fibers are extraordinarily tough, and many hands have caressed them over the years, and yet they never seem to lose their color, or age in any way."

Kat walked over to the history tapestry and ran her hand down the fibers, which possessed the furry softness of newborn kittens. She kept stroking, and could almost imagine the fabric purring under her touch. Lost in a sense of peace and calm, and a hypnotic feeling of well-being, visions of people working and playing danced in her mind.

Anwen's voice cut through the illusions. "You will have time later to talk with the tapestries. We have prepared quarters for you, and someone will bring you refreshment there." She tilted her head at Kat. "May I ask what is *silk*?"

"Silk is a type of fiber we have in my home, but your brynosh is much softer, and much stronger."

"I would like to view this silk, nevertheless."

Wait, what does she mean by talking to the tapestries?

About to ask the question, Kat stopped, noticing Anwen appeared uncomfortable.

"What is the problem?"

"Lady Kat, do you wish your friend given quarters near you, or sequestered with the rest of the servants of the Hall?"

Catching the venomous glower Mouse aimed at Anwen, Kat pretended to consider this request.

"Ah, yes. I think the best thing would be to give him quarters near me." She glanced at Mouse. "Do you agree?"

This time he directed the frown, only slightly less malevolent, at her.

"That is settled then. Lady Kat if you and your… friend would follow me? Later you will be meeting with Deleth, who is the leader of the Healers' Guild in Shendea." Anwen walked to one of the passageways leading from the huge entrance hall.

As she strode behind Anwen, Kat glanced back at Mouse, mouthed the word 'friend' at him, and grinned mischievously.

The look he shot back contained promises of anticipated retaliation.

I really think he's lost his sense of humor… if he ever possessed one.

***

Entering her assigned room, Kat headed to a small table and set up the cage for Wink. She reached in the travel cage and extracted the small ball of fur, which squeaked sleepily, and opened one eye at her. Once in her more permanent cage, Wink yawned widely, and gave a hungry chirrup. Kat hurried to pass her small tidbits of food, which Wink chewed and swallowed. She circled her cage once, returned to her ball version and slept.

With Wink settled, Kat surveyed the room more completely. All the walls were covered in green fabric with a variety of designs cut into the nap. The room reminded her of the interior of a glorious tent in the middle of a forest. Even the air held the faint scent of fir trees.

The bed positioned in the exact center of the room caught her attention. The covers and fluffy comforters were a deep midnight blue with a sheen, which changed appearance when Kat moved her eyes.

Squatted in the middle of the bed, appeared to be an animal the size of a tiny rabbit, with light-brown fur, and blessed with sharp bright eyes and an expression of mild benevolence. The creature sat as if on a throne, like some Egyptian idol. The odd animal boasted a round yellow nose and barely visible ears. The stubby legs and a short blonde tail reminded Kat of a ferret which one of Nick's kids owned.

She heard Mouse as he walked down the passageway and she poked her head out her door. "What's this on my bed?"

He peered into her room, and chuckled.

"The animal on your bed is a boradai. They are very rare and are only supplied to significant guests, so they must consider you of some importance. It will tell you its name in due course. Or perhaps it will not. Boradai are picky about who they bond with."

He turned to leave. "I will come for you in one hour of time, to take you to the dining hall. I will not be invited to dine with you and the Lord."

She had no chance to ask him why he would be excluded from the dinner, because he disappeared around a corner without another sound.

She sat on the bed beside the small animal and put out a tentative hand to stroke its pelt. As she touched it, her mind flooded with images and a glorious contralto voice. *"I am Breen."*

She drew her hand back in alarm.

"Did you say something?"

Silence.

She placed hand again on the mound of fur.

"I can only speak in your mind when you make contact with me. I told you I am Breen."

Fascinated, and warmed by the touch of the fur, plush and silky, Kat's mind flooded with a sense of peace and tranquility. Her necklace warmed against her skin. *This Breen holds no danger, only serenity.*

"My name is Kat"

"You do not need to make the noise of your name aloud. I cannot understand the loudness, but I do comprehend your mind-words Kat. You and I will be a pair from this day on. Whatever you experience and think, I will too."

Kat withdrew her hand. *Wow — this is… is major cool.*

She stroked Breen's fur again.

"Why is it you are cold?"

"Cold? You can pick up my thoughts even when I don't touch you?"

She sensed Breen raised the equivalent of an eyebrow. She realized she spoke aloud, and thought - *"oops sorry."*

"I can always hear you now. So, why are you cold?"

"I used an expression which means you gave me an interesting fact. What you told me is, I can only hear you when I'm touching you. Am I correct?"

"Yes, your brain is not sophisticated enough to pick up my meanings without your touch. Only a few Shendeans are able to achieve that."

Kat felt so cozy and comfy, she lay on the bed and drifted off to sleep, still stroking Breen.

***

"Wake Kat. Now."

Kat sat up, her hands still on Breen, not quite sure where she was. "What's going on? Who is it?"

"Be calm. You need to get ready for your dinner with Lord Rhognor. Your friend will be here to take you to the dining hall."

"Of course. I almost forgot. Oops, sorry, I am talking aloud again." She could almost detect a chuckle in Breen's voice in her head.

"I understand. It will take you some time to get used to speaking with me without the noise you feel you need to emit. Eventually you will discover you can speak to me silently, and use your noise with the other people here."

Kat rose from the bed and as she glanced around the room, realized as she slept some wonderful person had unpacked her bags for her. She hurried to the closet to locate suitable clothing for her dinner with Rhognor. The emerald green dress with gold thread wound throughout the fabric, caught her eye. *Brith had been right. This is perfect for an important dinner.*

She strode back to the bed and put her hand on Breen. *"Do you agree?"*

"Indeed. You will give the impression of Rifellan royalty in the outfit you chose. Most appropriate. You do know it is important to use Lord Rhognor's title when you are at the dinner?"

Kat returned to the closet and took the dress from the hanger, calling to Breen. "Everyone keeps reminding me." *Oops, did the noise thing again.* She placed the dress on the bed, and removed her warm layered underclothes. She donned light silky underwear, which whispered as it slithered over her body. She remembered Brith mentioned this would make the dress drape better. She then carefully slid into the dress. *Great, it fastens up the front. I'm far too stiff from all the climbing to do up any buttons at the back.*

She tucked her feet into light green slippers, and headed to the chair in front of a small dressing table. Evaluating herself in the mirror, she grabbed a brush and worked at the mass of wild tangles, creating a shining halo of burnished red curls.

Surveying the pots of facial paints on the table, she chose a simple bronze shadow for her eyes, and a golden red gloss for her lips. Her cheeks, thanks to the trek from Half-Way Haven, required no further embellishment. She gazed at her reflection. *You look good, kiddo. Dressing up is sort of fun. The heroine in my new game could dress like this — like a glamorous warrior.*

A knock at the door indicated Mouse waited to escort her to Rhognor.

She opened the door and captured an expression of surprise in his eyes.

He bowed his head. "You will be a welcome sight at the dinner, Lady Kat. Your appearance is excellent."

"I thought we agreed you would call me Kat."

Mouse smiled. "Normally yes. Now, however, you are definitely Lady Kat."

I think he just paid me a compliment. Well, I 'll be… .

***

At the door to the great hall, Mouse knocked. When the guard answered, Mouse announced, "This is the Lady Kat."

As the guard led her in, she glanced at Mouse as he turned and departed down the corridor.

Her escort announced her to the crowd of people seated around a number of massive tables in the dining hall. A woman rose from her seat and headed toward her from a long table set with crystal goblets and a variety of eating implements in gold. *Well, in some ways, they are more formal than the Kaylins… or is this just Rhognor's doing?*

The woman, clad in an emerald green robe, who took Kat's hand in both of hers, seemed very familiar.

"I am Deleth, and I have been most anxious to meet you. We have much to discuss. But first we will seat you with Lord Rhognor. He insisted you should attend him there." She led Kat to the seat four places away from his left side at the elaborately appointed table.

As she sat, Rhognor peered down at her from under light-brown bushy eyebrows. He sat tall and slender in his chair. His face and hands were pale but well groomed, and the midnight blue robe he wore, adorned at neck and wrists with silvery white fur, suited a leader. "Hmph. So you are the Lady Kat about whom Lord Eduardo has been sending me so many pyrocks."

He frowned and gazed about him. "This does not work, I wish to have you at my side when we talk. Speaking from this far away is uncomfortable for me." His voice, cultured and pleasant, captured the attention of all at the table. He spoke to the man on his immediate right. "Hesginn, you must relinquish your normal place. Lady Kat should be seated where you are." He frowned again. "Come on man, move."

Hesginn rose lazily, humor etched on his face. He held the chair out for Kat to sit.

Kat tried to apologize to him, but he whispered to her. "When Lord Rhognor requests something, it is actually an order. Do not trouble yourself about this. It is his way."

Kat found Deleth seated beside her. She murmured. "Whew. Lord Rhognor is intense."

"Lady Kat," Rhognor pointed at the man who had seated her, "this is Thaumaturge Hesginn. He is my right hand in all things."

Hesginn, still standing, represented a stately presence of power in the room. Like all Shendeans, he stood over six feet, but his brown hair, blunt cut to his chin, reminded Kat of highly polished walnut. His eyes bored through her, a gorgeous pool of melted chocolate with a dark blue ring around the iris.

Whew, this guy's hot. I'll bet he enjoys his pick of women.

"Lady Kat." He bowed his head. "I have been most anxious to meet you. Lord Rhognor has mentioned you often. We will have much to discuss regarding your stay in Shendea."

Oh glory. His voice rises from a deep, dark abyss. Pick of women? I think he has to fight them off. "Thank you Thaumaturge." *I hope I pronounced it correctly.* "I'm sure we will need to meet." *What the heck is a thaumaturge anyway? Wish I could Google.*

Hesginn sat, and the staff began serving, and brought flagons of near-ale and pots of various teas to the table.

Thankfully, Kat reached for the Karri-san. *There might be Rifellans here and I must keep my reactions under control... and perhaps I will also need some to handle Hesginn. Interesting he wears the same color as Deleth.*

On Rhognor's immediate left sat an exquisite woman, with honey-gold hair, alabaster skin, and the faint blush of roses on her cheeks. She reminded Kat of the delicate fairies in a childhood book.

She appears so fragile a stiff breeze could blow her away. "Deleth who is the woman on Rhognor's left?"

"She is Lady Halfin, and is Lord Rhognor's bonded mate. They have been bonded for many years, but to their sorrow have not yet produced any offspring. When Lord Rhognor passes from this life, there will be difficulty replacing him. He is the last of his line."

"Won't she rule in his place?"

"No. Bond mates cannot inherit a Lordship or ascend to the post of a Thane."

"I guess having a child is very important to those who rule the lands."

Deleth regarded her curiously. "Are you sure you are not of Rifellan blood? Referring to offspring as a child is a common Rifellan term. Particularly from those of royal blood."

Kat shook her head. "I'm not from Pridden. So, no Rifellan anything."

The young apprentices served the main course and vegetables to all those in the dining hall, and the scents of roasted meats and subtle spices enticed a gurgle of hunger from Kat's stomach. Watching Lord Rhognor she began to eat when he did, and the taste of the first dish, reminded her of the wullawerth stews of Kaylin.

Whenever Rhognor ceased questioning Kat, Deleth fed her information about some of the people at his table. "Seated next to Hesginn is Tapestry Master Godrith, and we will meet with him on the morrow. Next to him is Hesginn's sibling, Walden. Usually he would sit at a table for assistants, but as sibling to a guild head, he is permitted to be here."

During most of the meal, Rhognor flung a slew of questions at Kat. Where did she come from? How did she fare in Kaylin? What sort of people lived in her world? The problem? He seldom waited for an answer, before aiming another question. As she watched him, he appeared more concerned with keeping his eating area neat and organized. He continually re-arranged his eating utensils, and took care to return his cup to the exact place from where he previously removed it. *He's the ultimate fuss-budget. He can't keep still. I don't believe he's an effective a leader as Eduardo is.*

Finally Kat gazed helplessly at Deleth, next to her. *Oh frick, the man's a tsunami, and I'm drowning under his interrogation.*

Deleth must have taken pity on her. "Lord Rhognor, you are not giving poor Lady Kat time to eat and relax after her journey here. Perhaps we could arrange another session where you can question her at greater length."

"Ah, of course. You posses much wisdom, Deleth, as usual. Arrange a meeting with the Lady Kat for the morrow." He turned toward Kat with a smile. "My pardon Lady Kat, but I am so curious to know everything about your world and your travels, I forgot you may be travel weary." With this he rose from the table. "I must deal with the challenges of the Stronghold, so I bid you all good evening." Before he left, however, he re-arranged the utensils at his place neatly, once more.

All in the hall rose from their seats and bid Rhognor good evening. As he left the hall, they sank back into their chairs, almost all breathing sighs of good-natured relief.

Kat leaned across to Deleth. "You remind me so much of Healer Wynneth of Kaylin. Are you by any chance related?"

Deleth's faced beamed. "We are indeed. Wynneth and I are womb-mates. We share many qualities, and although her abilities with compassion are well known, I enjoy the gift of prediction. I am the most talented healer on Pridden who understands the complexities of upcoming events. I am also the head of the Healers' Guild in Pridden"

"Of course. Now I know why you both resemble each other so much." Kat unable to help herself, barely managed to contain a yawn.

"You have travelled much today, and I see how weary you are. Lady Kat, please feel free to attend your bed."

They both rose.

"Thank you Deleth, I will." *Fabulous. I'll give Wink some treats, indulge in a warm shower, crawl into my comfy bed, and cuddle a bit with Breen. Hesginn makes me miss Liandock's ministrations. He's one forceful dude. Perhaps he'll be the one from Shendea to help me.*

CHAPTER 4

The trill of an unknown bird penetrated Kat's consciousness. She woke in a green forest, bright with the first warm glow of dawn. *Wait a minute. I'm in the middle of a mountain. Forest? Dawn? Birds? What's going on?* She reached out and touched something furry. *Ah, Breen.*

"Relax Kat, you are in Lord Rhognor's Stronghold. The forest is the decoration of the room you fell asleep in at end of day. The globe lights in our rooms are enchanted to resemble the changes of light emitted outside the caverns. The birds? Many aviaries are located in various places within the Stronghold. They react to the light and help those who live here feel they reside outdoors instead of, the middle of a mountain, as you mentioned."

"Oh." Kat sat up and stretched, glancing again around the extraordinary forest-like room. "Thank you… um… " *"Sorry. Thank you Breen. I'm sure I'll get used to this."*

"You will. When you wish to call for a meal, tug on the tassel in the corner. One tug will indicate you wish to request something of your apprentice. Two tugs suggests you wish to have tea and a snack, and three tugs signifies your desire for a meal. Your apprentice will bring appropriate foods, which may change as he or she becomes used to your preferences."

"Thank you." Kat gazed around the room as she left the warmth of her bed. A door in the left corner suggested a personal, so she headed for it. Success. Similar to the one at Lord Eduardo's hold, Kat soon enjoyed the luxurious soap and water shower and with a final rinse, grabbed a towel from the bench outside the shower door and wrapped herself

in the rich absorbant material. From the drawers and closet, she clothed herself in the full-length, culotte type skirt and top Brith designed for her. She passed on the robe the Shendeans seemed to prefer. Once dressed, she gave three tugs to the tassel.

Soon a knock at the door, which elicited "Come" from Kat, presented a young man clad in a pale green robe, bearing a tray of food and drink. Kat indicated he should deposit her meal on the small table in the corner, which sported two chairs. "What is your name?"

"I am Colwin, Lady Kat. If there is some food or drink you wish other than what I bring, please advise me."

"Yes, I do want you to bring me Kari-san tea with every meal and whenever I request tea."

"Healer Deleth informed about your wish for Karri-san, and I did include it with this meal."

"Excellent Colwin. Oh, and once per day would you supply me with the special food for my pyrock?"

His eyes sparkled. "You possess a pyrock, Lady Kat? How fortunate." He bowed and prepared to depart.

"Wait. One more thing. What foodstuffs do boradais require?"

"I do not know, Lady Kat. Borodais are rare. I will enquire in the kitchens, and will make sure you receive what you need."

Kat thanked him as he bowed again and left.

Before she sat down to eat, she walked over to Breen and touched him? her? *"So, what do you need to eat?"*

The boradai chuckled in her mind. *"I am of no gender, so you may refer to me as either him or her. You also do not need to concern yourself with my feeding habits. We take care of ourselves."*

"Oh, okay."

She turned and picked up a treat for Wink from the small bowl on her makeup table, and opened the door to the cage. Wink waited eagerly with her little mouth wide open, displaying needle-like teeth. Kat popped in two pieces of her food, and as Wink chewed, Kat reached in and gently stroked the small plush head. Wink butted at her and emitted a squeaky purr. With an enormous yawn, she turned around three times and curled once more into a ball. *Boy, pyrocks sleep a lot.*

The delicious aromas emanating from her morning meal enticed Kat to the table. She dug her spoon in a dish of what resembled porridge, and experienced something nutty and honey-sweetened. *Yes, I remember the name is journeyklim, except I can't remember who told me.* Unlike any oatmeal with which she was familiar, this tasted creamy and buttery. *These people enjoy their food. Everything is crammed with flavor. I adore home-type cooking — when someone else prepares it. Cooking for one — sucks.* She grabbed at her napkin. *Damn, my nose is running. Does it every time when things are so scrumptious.*

She drank the last few drops of her Karri-san when a knock attracted her attention. "Come."

Deleth popped her head around the door. "Wonderful. You are finished eating. Are you ready for a tour and another meeting with Lord Rhognor?"

Kat raised an eyebrow. "I hope he's not going to question me to death without giving me a chance to reply."

Deleth laughed. "I doubt he will. So excited about meeting you, he could not contain himself last evening. He's a man of extreme curiosity, which is why he can view what is ahead and plan well for our people. His knowledge allows him to anticipate challenges. He is the finest ruler of Shendea ever, and we are lucky he is our Lord."

"Really?"

"Indeed. I can see from your face you think he is fussy, but you will learn you may rely on Lord Rhognor like few others."

Oops. Perhaps I jumped to conclusions about the guy, and allowed my prejudices to surface again. I like Deleth, and I trust her, so I'll suspend judgment on Rhognor for now.

The healer eyed Kat's outfit. "An excellent choice of clothing. You will find we in Shendea, are not affronted by the bodies of people, but nevertheless, we are more comfortable adequately attired around each other. I have not seen a similar skirt before."

"Brith, the tailor in Kaylin, made my outfit for me. This skirt kept the Kaylins happy. They get quite agitated seeing ankles or legs, and their agitation can create problems."

Deleth laughed. "I am aware of their challenges with your clothing. Wynneth kept me informed." She caught sight of Breen on the bed. "I am pleased you received a boradai. The creature will prove useful, I am sure." She turned and left the room, beckoning Kat to follow her. "We will meet with Lord Rhognor, and afterwards I will take you through some of the Stronghold. But we will pick up your friend Mouse before the tour."

***

Kat and Deleth were shown to Rhognor's less formal meeting room. Kat wandered about examining the perfect order of everything. *His books are sorted — I think alphabetically. I'll bet if the covers were colored, he'd line them up according to their shades.* Every item he had positioned in perfect alignment with the edges of the furniture. *Man, this guy's obsessive.*

As Kat returned to her seat, Rhognor entered the room. "I am glad we could enjoy this additional time, Lady Kat. I am anxious to find out about where you came from, and what you have seen in your travels so far." His eyes bright and his movements short but swift, he sat behind his desk, but fidgeted, twiddling his thumbs, moving items and then returning them to the original position.

"I'm not sure exactly what you want me to tell you?" *He's a bit like a kid bursting to know the whole nine yards, almost hyperactive.*

"Everything, of course. But your time in Shendea is limited." He stood and paced the room. "And, you have a job to do." He stopped and faced her. "Lord Eduardo tells me you possess a knack for speaking to people." He laughed. "He also mentioned your knack is often for rubbing their hair in the wrong direction."

Thanks, Eduardo, you're giving me a bad rap without even being here. "Well, I think the latter came about because I misjudged some of the customs. I never meant to annoy anyone." *Well, hardly ever.*

"This unlikely to be a problem here. Shendeans are peaceful and calm people. We learn to be relaxed in any situation because we meet so many from other lands. Everyone comes here to meet our Healers, and to offer them employment in their own lands. Our Healers particularly must be at ease with all types of company in all types of places."

"Wynneth most certainly meets those requirements. She helped me."

"Excellent. Now I am aware you mentioned much of this to Lord Eduardo, but perhaps you would tell me about how you arrived in Pridden, and give me the highlights of your trip through Kaylin."

Kat began with her sudden appearance in Kaylin, after opening the door at the old building on Tortola. Neither Deleth nor Rhognor blinked an eye when she mentioned the Virgin Islands. *Well, well. Interesting. An island of virgins doesn't strain their sensibilities. Even Wynneth reacted. I guess she'd been in Kaylin too long.* She recounted the highlights of her trip through Kaylin, but omitted her night of passion with Liandock, and Drainin's attempt at seduction. When she mentioned the gornog hunt and the attack by kithras, they both gasped at her recounting.

Rhognor, beside himself with excitement, almost jumped in his seat. "Can you imagine hunting a gornog, Deleth? And fighting off kithras?"

"No, and I would prefer to never experience such a thing, Rhognor." Deleth appeared horrified at the thought.

Rhognor turned back to Kat. "So you are familiar with the spring bow, Lady Kat?"

"I learned to used it in Kaylin, and in my own world, I owned a long bow."

"Ah, so you were a warrior in your own land?"

Ha. Me? A warrior? I like that. Perhaps it's my gaming persona he sees. "No. We become proficient in weapons for fun, competing against ourselves. As a curious… er… offspring, I sought out all types of experiences."

Rhognor smiled at her. "Well, well. Young you are, but I am sure you are an unusual and capable female." He rose from his chair. "Now is time for my midturn meal, and since Shendea enjoys a flourishing marketplace within these caverns, I am sure Deleth will be delighted to give you a tour, and you can sample our foods. As a guest, anything you need will be covered by the Stronghold."

"Thank you."

"And one more item, Lady Kat. In a few star turns, I will meet with you and your guide, and we will discuss your route through Shendea. I too am anxious for you to reveal what you discover about our land."

Both Deleth and Kat rose, thanked Rhognor and departed his quarters. As they strolled down the hall, Deleth advised Kat they should find her guide and then tour the Stronghold. "So now you met again with Lord Rhognor, Lady Kat. Is your opinion of him changed?"

Kat sighed. "Whenever possible, would you please call me just Kat."

"Wynneth warned me you preferred informality. I will refer to you as Kat whenever we are alone, since you feel more comfortable omitting your title. However, you did not answer my question."

"Ah. Rhognor does want knowledge of all kinds. I'm not sure how he will put all this to use, though. He's not like any leader I've met before. As a matter of fact, if I hadn't been told of their various duties, I would assume Hesginn held the title, Lord of Shendea."

Deleth chuckled. "True, Hesginn is a strong and compelling man. He is much admired by the females in Shendea, and yet seems unaware of their attentions. However, when the passion strikes him, he is quite a satisfying lover, or so I am told."

Kat stared at Deleth. "Surely you're not promoting him to me?"

Deleth laughed out loud. "Not at all my dear. I am explaining his charm." She gestured with her hands, and shrugged. "I realize you think Lord Rhognor possesses little charisma, but he is kind, and his basic qualities make him a capable and excellent leader for Shendea."

Kat shrugged. *We'll see.*

CHAPTER 5

Later with Mouse in tow, Deleth led them to Tapestry Master Godrith's quarters in the lower caverns, which were as well lit as the main level. The lower caverns lacked stairs, but ramps let from one to the next, allowing the passage of carts of foodstuffs and materials for artwork. Deleth explained to Kat the ramps helped them supply with ease, most types of material to any level within the Stronghold.

After supplying information to Kat and leaving her to peer into rooms containing tailors, artisans, boot-makers and scholars printing copies of books by hand, Deleth and Mouse chatted as they strolled along. Kat, immersed in the sight of life in a cavern, couldn't catch what topic they discussed.

Interesting. Deleth appears to be familiar with Mouse. I wonder where she met him.

The entrance hall belonging to the tapestry portion of the Stronghold hummed with muted voices and the rumble of carts, which appeared from a tunnel directly across from her, all laden with long brown stalks of what she now knew were called brynosh.

A tall white-haired man in a soft beige robe came striding over. "Deleth, welcome. What brings you here?"

Deleth spread her arms and hugged him. "Godrith, I brought you a visitor. This is the Lady Kat."

That's interesting. She didn't use his title. Kat stepped forward. "Master Godrith, I'm most pleased to meet with you."

He turned to her, and clasped both her hands in his. "Oh fie, my dear. We do not stand on ceremony here. Call me Godrith."

Kat smiled at him. "Only if you agree to call me Kat."

He smiled and bowed his head in acquiescence.

Deleth cleared her throat. "Godrith. This is Kat's traveling friend, Mouse."

Godrith raised his brows. "Mouse. I am aware of much of your abilities as a guide. Welcome to Shendea."

Kat raised her own eyebrow.

Mouse bowed his head, but slightly, as if to an equal. "Thank you, Godrith. Your reputation flies ahead of you. Across all Pridden."

"As does yours, Mouse."

Kat caught a slight frown on Mouse's face. *I wonder why Mouse looked uncomfortable at his remark. Does he prefer to be unknown?*

Godrith put his arm through Kat's. "Come, my dear. Let me show you the wonders of tapestries." His eyes crinkled among the map of lines on his face.

"I would love a tour. Master Thontook in Kaylin told me you are the finest tapestry master on Pridden."

He laughed. "I should probably be humble about his words, but since Thontook is the finest weaver in Pridden, we each recognize extraordinary workmanship in the other." He laughed again. "Thontook is a man of considerable discernment."

Kat smiled at him. *I like him. He's another grandfather figure. I'll need to put him in the game too.*

Godrith led Kat through a series of rooms, explaining their functions as they went. Unlike Thontook's property, no clack of looms assaulted her ears. Instead, few spoke and a tranquil tune wove through the entire complex. In each section, the master of the area, plus at least two apprentices worked in concert.

"You've been shown how the threads are dyed to match the designs, and once they are dried, they are wound on these bobbins for the weavers." Godrith pointed at the tapered wooden bobbins, covered with a variety of colored threads. He led her to the next room. "We are preparing a loom for a new commission so you can learn how a tapestry begins. The strings of natural and rougher brynosh are hung within the upper and lower bars of the loom, and the apprentices tighten them to a precise tension. Those strings are called the warp, and the dyed threads the weavers use, are called the weft."

Kat, in awe of the size of the loom which rose from the floor and reached as far as the ceiling, could only nod.

"Come, my dear. The next room is to me, the most glorious." Godrith steered her by her elbow.

Kat gasped. Every shade of crimson, sunny yellows, robin's egg blues, and greens of new mown grass filled the room. Two weavers sat working a pair of looms, while a trio of musicians played in one corner. "I can understand why you find this room so compelling. Wow."

Godrith glanced down at her. "Wow'?"

Oh dear, how do I explain? "Forgive me. This's an expression I use when I can't find words to explain how I'm affected."

As he raised an eyebrow in apparent puzzlement, she hastened to clarify. "Not a bad expression, but one of excellence. Amazement. Joy. Um… well, just wow."

Godrith grinned down at her. "Well perhaps when I explain how the weavers work, you may say another 'wow.'

They moved to the nearest loom to watch the weaver creating part of a new glorious tapestry. The woman wove her bobbin filled with an apple green thread, over and under alternate warp lines. After about six lines, she used the sharp point of the bobbin to tamp down the green thread to form a complete band of color. Since the weaver worked from the back of the loom, many bobbins filled with a variety of shades, hung, waiting to be used again.

"How to they know what the front will be like?"

Godrith pointed to a mirror against the wall. "She watches through the warp and can inspect exactly what she has accomplished. And the original design hangs beside the mirror"

"You're right. Another wow."

Godrith smiled and patted her arm.

"Do the weavers come up with the designs?"

"No, Kat, they do not. I am the designer for all the tapestries. I meet with the person who wishes one made for the family, and based on their input, I produce the design, which they approve. However, since tapestries take so long to complete, neither one of us will ever view the finished creation. Tapestries are designed and fashioned for our descendants."

"We've got tapestries on my world, but I don't know if they take a long time to be finished."

Godrith took her arm again. "There is one more room I need to show you. These are works which were commissioned, but the current families have not yet accepted them." He led her into an enormous hall, lined with tapestries celebrating histories, families and customs, long since gone.

Kat, lost in a world of color and beauty, wandered among the designs, touching and experiencing the people and places of things past. "Anwen was right. They do speak. Somehow I glimpse life as it happened then."

Godrith nodded. "This is something we never understood — how a plant fiber, no matter how beautiful, can convey visions and emotions. They might come from the thoughts of those who were the weavers of the pieces. Whatever the reasons, we no longer question them. Allow yourself to wander among them." He moved across the room to converse with Deleth and Mouse.

Kat strolled from tapestry to tapestry, and experienced the soft touch of the threads, as she pictured the cultures they represented. *They're hypnotizing me.* She caught sight of an inky and mysterious scene hanging in the back corner. *What's that one?*

As she held her hand to the soft threads, she found herself slammed into a world of fear, and blood and violent conflict. Armor and weapons clanged and men shouted and grunted with effort, while wounded ones shrieked in pain. Horses neighed and the injured ones lay writhing and screaming. Kat, eyes huge, helplessly gazed at two men who fought until the one lost his footing and his opponent swung a huge sword and decapitated the unlucky loser. Lost, unable to extract herself, Kat watched in horror as a warrior, clad in soot-black armor and mounted on an enormous ebony horse, rode toward her swinging his massive blade. The sword came up in an arc, aimed for her throat. *Oh god, He's going to kill me.*

Someone pulled her away from the warrior. She fell back against an iron chest. Light suffused the room, and Godrith's worried face filled her immediate vision. "Forgive me, Kat, I forgot to warn you to avoid the touch of the dark one.

"I… I thought I would die."

Deleth held Kat's arm. "You are safe now."

Warmth and light enveloped her and Kat turned to thank Mouse. He stood yards away. *I'm sure he pulled me free. He had such strength and when I slammed up against him, I encountered hard muscle. Am I losing my mind? What and who is Mouse?*

She spun back to Godrith. "Who does the tapestry belong to?"

"The design, commissioned ages before my time, came from someone in Morden. No one knows who did so. No person in Morden made a claim, nor appears to want to."

Mouse moved toward the hanging. "I believe, Master Godrith, you would be wise to destroy the monster."

"Not so easily done. When you destroy a tapestry, the vibrations of all the emotions and events pictured, are released. The vibrations from this one, liberated within the Stronghold, would not be pleasant. I shall request a carpenter to build a cabinet to hold it. Preferably one with a lock."

Kat still trembling from her experience, nodded. "I agree." *My stone felt like a block of ice. What happened? I need to be alone.* "Deleth, Godrith, please excuse me. I would like to return to my room and perhaps drink some tea."

"Of course, Kat. You still appear shaken. If you wish a further tour on the morrow, please send a message via your serving apprentice."

"I will."

Deleth gazed at Mouse. "Sire, perhaps you and I might take a meal together?"

Mouse nodded at her. "Indeed."

They're familiar with each other. I wonder from where? Kat shrugged. *I don't care now, I only want to speak and cuddle with Breen.*

CHAPTER 6

Despite her weariness, the visions from the dark tapestry invaded Kat's mind and she slept poorly. By the time morning arrived, she'd tossed and turned so often, every muscle she owned, ached. She sat up and glanced around, but Breen was nowhere to be seen. *I guess he/she needs some down time too.* As she slid out of bed, she grumbled. *Crap, I hurt. A hot shower will help.*

On her way to the personal, she grabbed two treats from the dish on her dresser, and lifted the cover on Wink's cage. "Treats, kiddo." At her words and the influx of light, Wink lifted a sleepy head, and sniffed. A small squeak and a wide mouth, and Kat popped the offering down the little red gullet.

In the personal, she adjusted the water flow to hot, or as hot as possible. She stretched her body under the soothing pulse of the shower, and groaned in pleasure as the knots released from challenged limbs. So delighted by the pain relief, she burst into song, off-key, but happy.

***

Dry and dressed, Kat tugged on the tassel to call for her morning meal. Startled by the young woman who knocked, she raised an eyebrow. "What happened to the young man who came here yesterday?"

"Forgive us, Lady Kat. Colwin helped until the Stronghold assigned me to you. He normally apprentices with the cooks. I will be your permanent helper while you reside with us in Shendea. I am Kaydith and have not yet chosen a profession, so am still apprenticing."

"Fine. Did Colwin mention I wished Karri-san tea with every meal?"

"He did, Lady Kat."

"Oh, and please, while we're alone, call me Kat. Lady Kat is so formal, and I'm not a formal person."

Kaydith smiled. "As you wish."

***

Kat finished her meal, poured another cup of Karri-san, and brought out her journals, some blank pages and her writing utensils. First she added the information she received yesterday from Godrith to her game. She made a small drawing of him, so she would remember his face, lined by the smiles and laughter of years. *This's a fine idea to draw the people I want in my games. The drawings should give the guys back home even better information to code my characters.*

After adding to the game, Kat practiced copying the py-rock message writing. She sat back to ponder some excellent words to add to her word list, which she had not even thought of since leaving Kaylin. *Every day is getting harder to conjure up new ones. Damn, I need my computer. Wait. Godrith used discernment to describe Thontook. Not the best word ever, but okay for now. Perhaps I should create some of my own.* She penned the word, stood, stretched, and glanced around the room. *I think I've been at this for hours I'm stiff from sitting still for so long. Can't see Breen. I wonder where she is?* She snorted to herself. *Breen must be a she, because I can't get my head around her as an it.*

At her thought, the ferret-like creature scampered in from the hall, moving in the same rhythmic way an earth type ferret might. As she jumped on the bed, Kat reached out and touched her pelt.

"So where have you been, Breen?"

"Avoiding your noise, Kat."

"Oops, sorry. Keep forgetting about talking out loud to you. My bad."

She sensed Breen's chuckle.

"You are not bad. I cannot understand the loudness. I needed to leave you in the night because your sleep, disturbed by your restlessness, and your thoughts so confused created loudness in my mind. I must plead with you Kat, do not ever touch that particular tapestry again. Some people are far more affected by the talking of the tapestries than others. You are one of those, and the dark one is very harmful to you."

"I promise I will never go near the thing again. Such horror."

"No Shendean knows who commissioned the piece, and nor are we aware of the Master who created the design. It cannot have been a pleasant experience."

"Breen, Shendeans are such a calm and gentle people, how can someone even design such a monstrosity?"

"The Master would be unable to refuse the commission Kat. To do so would indicate disrespect. Shendeans always treat others with respect. This is their nature."

Kat broke contact with Breen. She did not want to relive the tapestry experience. The creature curled itself on her pillow and slept. Kat hurried over to the tassel and tugged three times. Kaydith appeared with her midturn meal, the scent of which, made her salivate.

"Kaydith, once I'm finished my meal, can you bring my friend Mouse to my room?"

"I will, Kat."

I need to learn some more pyrock writing, and I'm sure Mouse can help.

***

Kat, seated at the small table with writing supplies spread out, raised her head at the knock, and called out "Come." When Mouse entered, she smiled at him. "Good day, Mouse. I need your help." *Hah, I remembered to greet him first. I hope Wynneth appreciates me being social.*

"And the same to you, Kat. What do you need?"

"Wynneth taught me some writing to put into pyrock messages, and I need to know a few more words." At Mouse's puzzled expression, she explained. "My writing is not easy to read by the people of Pridden."

"Fine, let me determine what progress you made"

Kat presented the three pages of pyrock messages to Mouse who perused them, and as he continued, he began to grin. "You write in runes. Here you printed phrases in our writing and beside them, you indicated the same information in runes."

"You can read runes, Mouse?"

"Yes, but not many can. Wynneth showed wisdom to teach you Pridden writing."

"But does this mean, if I send a pyrock to you I can use my usual writing?"

"Of course."

Well I'll be… . Mouse is continually full of surprises. "I'm missing about ten words I believe I will need. I expect this will take us 'til close to the evening meal. When we are through can we go to the communal dining hall to eat?"

"An excellent idea."

Kat pulled the paper and pen toward her, and they bent their heads over the pages and immersed themselves in words.

***

They practiced for some time before Mouse led Kat through a series of hallways to the dining hall shared by the residents and workers of the Stronghold. Entering the hall, Kat gasped at the size of the interior, so huge, they needed an apprentice to lead them to an empty table. Situated perfectly for quiet conversation, the table for two, tucked in a corner, surrounded by masses of Shendeans, all clothed in robes of blue, green, yellow, and some in creamy white, suited Kat perfectly.

"I'm sure hundreds of people are here, but there's hardly any noise, Mouse. The Shendeans are far more soft-spoken than most of the other people."

"And the noise level is further reduced by the tapestries on the walls, which tend to mute the sounds."

An apprentice in an apple green robe, brought flagons of near-ale, and Kat requested Karri-san tea. He brought the tea, accompanied by a second apprentice who bore two platters of various foods, which he deposited on the table.

"Oh, the dishes smell divine. Shendeans sure know how to cook and prepare food in wonderful ways."

Mouse grinned at her. "You would never be aware they enjoy very little meat in their meals. Animals for consumption live mostly in the grasslands between Carrog Mannin and Carrog Kennin, and are not often sent to the Stronghold."

"What are Carrog Mannin and Carrog Kennin?"

"Two of the largest rivers in Shendea. Much of the trade within this land relies on travel via these rivers. Carrog is the word for river in the ancient Shendean language."

"Will we get a chance to visit both of them?"

"Of course."

"Great." Tummy rumblings persuaded Kat to ply herself to the meal, and she and Mouse ate in silence.

She pushed back her empty dish, and reached for the Karri-san. "So, Mouse, tell me about yourself." *If I use Mouse in the game, I'll need background. And he's a mystery.*

He shrugged. "I do not possess much to tell."

"Oh, come on, Mouse. Where were you born, for instance?"

Mouse seemed to shrink into himself. "I was brought to life in Morden."

Kat's eyes widened. "You were? Wow. I would never guess." She peered at him intently. "You're not like the Morden's I encountered in Kaylin. They're all so brawny and strong and aggressive. And they're arrogant as well."

Mouse smiled faintly at her. "The last trait is one you also share with Mordens, or so I am led to believe."

Kat glared at him. "I beg your pardon."

"There is no need to beg for anything, Lady Kat."

Kat stared at him, now lost for words. "You… you're kidding me."

He frowned. "Kidding? What does this mean?"

I must stop using slang. This takes so much time to explain. "The word just means you're making a joke."

"I… I did." He shook his head. "I am not comfortable talking about myself. I am ordinary. There is nothing exceptional about me."

I'm not sure what he's hiding, but I'm convinced he's lying. "Oh, Mouse. Your hair is brown and your skin is not as pale as most of the Morden's who've passed my way. You say you're not special, but you appear to be different from the rest."

"The Mordens you probably encountered are from the north, near Lord Galdin's keep. The country is mountainous and harsh and thus those people need to be strong and aggressive to survive. I hail from the area to the south. The southern Mordens are not as pale, and the conditions not as harsh, so we are milder in abilities and temperament."

"If true, you're the first southern Morden I've met."

Mouse yawned. "My apologies. This has been a long day for me. I need to retire."

Kat, unable to hold back a sympathetic yawn, nodded her head. "I didn't sleep well last night. I need my bed too."

***

Kat slipped into her bed, nudging Breen over to the side, and thought about her evening with Mouse. *There is more to Mouse… . He's a bundle of contradictions. Who and what is he? He revealed nothing about himself tonight. His conversation consisted of words, but without any information.* Kat yawned so widely her jaw creaked. *Tomorrow…*

CHAPTER 7

Mouse sat at the small table spread with dozens of maps, poring over them intently. A knock at the door and he cocked his head. "Come."

Deleth poked her head around the opening. "Good morrow… er… Mouse."

"Deleth, you are a most welcome sight. Thank you for remembering to use Mouse."

"I would be most remiss if I forgot. I know intimately the narrow path on which you walk." She strode over to him and when he stood, gathered him in a warm embrace. "I spoke to Godrith and requested he act in a more formal manner with you."

"My thanks. When he greeted me, I caught a flash in Kat's eye. I am positive she wondered at his words. She is an astute woman, and I would venture little escapes her notice. I imagine her past drives her to suspect all who come her way. She strives for control at every opportunity."

Deleth chuckled. "You are just as astute. I imagine the two of you will confront each other frequently."

"I fear you are correct." Mouse grimaced at his own words. "I mistakenly thought she would be more amenable to my guidance. A foolish notion, I now realize. She attempts to dominate every situation." He scowled at Deleth's vain effort to hide her grin. "I do not find this amusing. Every triumph she treats as a joke."

"I apologize. Your path is narrower than I judged."

"Indeed. Eduardo did me no favors when he requested I guide her through Pridden." He flung his arms out in frustration. "We are not yet part way through Shendea, and I am already contemplated six means of extracting revenge."

Deleth's smile vanished. "Mouse. You would not."

He sighed. "I would not. But I find comfort when I consider such things, without the need to take action. I cannot be myself. I must continually be clothed in the mantle of Mouse."

"It is important you remain so. Eduardo and you are stalked by strong enemies. None must suspect your bond. As you know, even Wynneth is not privy to this information. I pledge my help while you are in Shendea, and I will advise you by pyrock of others who you may trust during your further travels in Pridden." She peered at the maps spread out on the table. "Is the route you will take through our land settled?"

"Yes. I believe Kat will appreciate seeing the Burning Rock Mountain, and benefit from the wellsprings of the Crimson Cauldron."

"A wise choice. All women enjoy those thermal pools."

Mouse raised his eyebrows. "So I must treat her like a woman?"

Deleth laughed. "Perhaps not. She might discover she enjoys weak little men whom she can control, and you would find yourself the object of her attraction."

"The thought of such a situation terrifies me. She might eat me alive." He joined Deleth in her laughter. *If truth be known, having Kat as a lover would be… stimulating… but far too dangerous.*

"I cannot foresee such a happening. Remember, I possess the farsight." Deleth patted him on the shoulder. "Shall we order tea, and you can advise me of the balance of your plans."

"Excellent idea." Mouse strode to the summoning tassel and tugged.

Within minutes, a knock heralded the delivery of tea with small crisp sweets, which Mouse took from the apprentice and placed on a table in the corner of his room. Deleth joined him and when they sat, she poured tea for them both.

"So where to next?"

"Naturally we will travel to the Thieves Guild. You are aware I am a member."

Deleth nodded.

"After a trip to Lake Glenaddie, we will return to the Stronghold via the grasslands. Rhognor will desire a detailed analysis of our travels, and hopefully Kat's accomplishments in Shendea."

"He will indeed. But I am surprised. I perceive no plan to show her the Magicians Guild."

"We will call on them when we travel to Rifella."

Deleth stood. "I suggest we visit the market and partake of a midturn meal. I often hear rumors and tales of happenings throughout Shendea when I spend time at my favorite tea booth." She turned back to Mouse who rose to follow her. "Please take care, Mouse. I sense both you and Kat may face extreme peril in the star turns to come. Not only in Shendea. You may summon strange and challenging situations in all the lands. I hold a vested interest in your safety."

"Given our past relationship, I am aware of your interest. I could not function without the knowledge that both you and Eduardo are my closest allies." *What challenges can she perceive? I suspect Deleth, despite her abilities, is not acquainted with the details, but is conscious of evil lurking on the horizon. What part will Kat play?*

CHAPTER 8

Kat walked through the halls of the Stronghold. Night had fallen long since, and the lights were dimmed, creating sooty shadows, which wavered in the faint illumination of the globes attached to the walls. Instead of the gentle birds of the morning, the harsh cry of a raven echoed from one of the side tunnels. As she approached the dark opening, an enormous bird flew at her, with a screech and flap of wings and tar-black feathers. Kat instinctively raised her hands to protect her eyes, but the bird flew on, with raucous caws, and disappeared down the darkened hall behind her. *What the… .*

Her pendant lay like ice on her skin. *Uh oh, what's happening?* Other sounds issued from hallways leading away from the main passageway: a hiss, a faint scratch like fingernails on stone, a cough, and the slither of something unknown. All wove tendrils of ice up her spine. At the far end of the hall, a shape began to emerge. As the thing approached, it morphed into a man in a robe, black as obsidian, with only his eyes visible. Kat stared, caught like prey, seeing horror, pain, and torture in those eyes no living soul should view. Her limbs paralyzed, she attempted to call for help, but no sound disturbed the silence of the corridor. The creature moved closer and finally Kat screamed as the ice cold nose touched her face.

Her eyes snapped open. A furry face filled her vision and a wet, cold nose pressed up against hers. *Ohh Breen.*

"Wake, Kat. Your thoughts are filled with horror, fear, and despair. You also created a loudness which hurt my brain."

Kat sat up, dislodging Breen from her chest. *"A nightmare. Oh god. I couldn't move and I couldn't cry out."* She clutched at Breen again.

"But you did. I suffered pain."

"Sorry, I couldn't control myself."

A knock interrupted her discussion with Breen.

A call through the door. "Kat are you alright?" It was Mouse.

She hopped out of bed and hurried over. Opening the door a sliver, she caught the worried expression on Mouse's face. "Sorry Mouse. I experienced a nightmare. I didn't mean to disturb you. I'm fine, only a nightmare. Go back to bed."

"Are you sure?"

I want to be alone. I want him to leave. She snapped at him through the crack. "I'm fine. Go. Now."

Mouse, his face a mixture of anger and concern, waited a moment, turned, and walked back to his room.

Kat slammed the door. What *don't people get when I want to be alone?* She strode back to her bed and stopped short. *Something odd persisted about Mouse.* She clenched her forehead, experiencing the pull of the skin as she did so. She remembered when she saw Mouse at the door and glanced up at him. *Wait a minute. His eyes are normally lower than mine, or at least on the same level.* She shook her head and smoothed at the furrow between her eyes. *Hmph. Perhaps I stood bent over, legs unsteady from the dream.* She continued to the bed, lay down and curled around Breen, stroking the silky fur. Her pendant lay warm and comforting.

"You do not trust the man you call Mouse. Why?"

"I must trust him to a point. He is my guide through this land."

"I do not believe you rely on him."

"I learned in my life on my own world I can't rely on any man, and he's a small mousey little man, with little strength, and equally little courage." Kat paused and cocked her head, remembering the tapestry incident. *"I cannot imagine us fighting for our lives, back to back. I suspect he would turn and run to save himself before he would defend either of us from a dangerous situation."*

"I can read no other with whom I am not bonded, but he appears to be stronger than you perceive him to be."

"He's not, I saw him run from a challenge, even though he did appear to explain his actions. I'm confused by him. The truth is, Breen, I no longer know what to expect. I need to clear my head." Kat rubbed her forehead. *"I'll attempt to sleep some more. I must send a pyrock to Wynneth, but I should wait until dawn."*

"Sleep is what you need. I will hold soothing vibrations for you."

"Thanks, Breen, I... I... "

***

The gentle murmur of birds and the scent of a pine forest woke Kat from a sound and restful sleep. The little hollow on the bed where Breen slept, lay empty, but she heard a plaintive squeak from Wink. Kat slipped out of her bed and crossed the room to the dish containing Wink's food. Grabbing two small pieces, she moved to the cage, removed the cover, reached in and scooped up the furry little ball. As she returned to the desk, she fed the demanding creature. Wink still chirped expectantly, so Kat reached for two more pieces, and popped them into the waiting mouth. Wink chewed, swallowed, and emitted a purring squeak.

"Satisfied now, you greedy guts?" Kat stroked the small furry head, which butted at her finger. "Wait here, and I'll prepare a message for Wynneth." Kat reached for her cath-nog pen and a sheet of paper. She referred to her pyrock writing pages and advised Wynneth about the nightmare. "Okay, kiddo. Time to deliver a message."

Wink held out her foreleg, and Kat attached a small tube in which she'd encased the message. "Take this to Wynneth, and wait for a reply."

Wink raised wings, flapped them twice, lifted from the desk and winked out of existence with an audible pop.

Once the little creature left, Kat went to the summoning tassel and tugged three times.

Within minutes, a knock at the door disclosed Kaydith, bearing Kat's morning meal. Steam rose from the bowl holding what appeared to be oatmeal, but the smell reminded her of vanilla. When she dipped her spoon in, Kat tasted the nutty, creamy, buttery flavor, laced with the hint of cinnamon. She almost moaned with pleasure. *Boy, if foster mom number one, made oatmeal like this, I would never have run away so quickly. Her porridge, glutinous and nasty, never went down well. Mind you, the horrid stuff did match her personality.*

At that precise moment, a crackle indicated Wink's return. Kat left her half-consumed cup of Karri-san and hurried over to the desk. She removed the note and referring to her pages of pyrock writing, read the message from Wynneth. The healer suggested Kat advise Deleth of the dream, and ask her for advice. Wynneth added to the message. *I am too far away to be of help.*

Kat picked up Wink, already curled in a tight ball, and deposited the little pyrock in her cage. She moved across the room and tugged the tassel once more. When Kaydith appeared, Kat requested she guide her to Deleth's rooms.

"Certainly, Kat. I can take you there now"

Kaydith escorted her through the halls and left Kat outside Deleth's door. She knocked at the entrance, and glanced at the carving on the lintel. The symbol represented healing, which Wynneth revealed to her months before.

Deleth opened her door and smiled. "Good morrow. You are up early."

Kat tried desperately to remember to be polite as Wynneth taught her. "How are you Deleth?"

"Excellent. Please come in and I will order tea for us." She crossed to the tassel in the corner of her room and tugged twice, and turned back to Kat. "What brings you here?"

"I advised Wynneth of my nightmare… er… dream, and she suggested I pass the tale to you."

"I am curious to hear this."

Kat relayed her journey through the darkened tunnels, and the creature coming toward her, which generated such horror and fear.

Deleth's brow furrowed. "You received such dreams before?"

"Similar ones, yes."

"Curious."

Kat grimaced. "More than curious, more like horrifying. What does this mean?"

"I am not sure. Did you advise Mouse of these dreams?"

"No. I'm not convinced I can completely trust him." *My stone remains warm around him, but I'm sure he's hiding things.*

"I believe you are mistaken in your conclusion, but trusting Mouse is something you ought to learn in your own time and place. For now, I believe we should relay this information to Lord Rhognor."

"Oh Deleth, what can he do?"

"I am not sure. But it is imperative he is aware of everything which affects you, since you are, after all, touring Shendea on his behest."

"I never considered that." *Damn, he's going to demand every single detail of the dream? I'll be with him for hours.* "Deleth, perhaps you can give him the details. I would like to wander through the Stronghold." She held up her hand to forestall Deleth's objections. "I can tour the halls on my own. Plus, there'll be an opportunity to meet additional people. And that's what Rhognor wants of me. Right?"

Deleth scratched her head. "Perhaps." She pursed her lips. "Take care, Kat. We are not as formal as the Kaylins, but we also prefer to practice the rules of polite interaction."

"I won't embarrass you Deleth. I'll be circumspect. Trust me." *Poor Deleth, she appears worried about me pottering around on my own.*

"I do trust you, Kat."

"Thanks."

As she turned to leave, Deleth called her back. "If you need to purchase anything, advise the merchants who you are and ask them to record the sale to the Stronghold account."

"I will." *I better go now, before she thinks of something else.*

Kat strolled in the direction she assumed the market would be. *First person I come to, I'll ask to show me to Hesginn.* She snickered to herself. *Yup, the hot Hesginn is the perfect person to help me visit the marketplace. Who knows what will develop?*

CHAPTER 9

Goof grief, I must find someone for directions. I sometimes think I'm in a rabbit warren. Kat stopped a young man in a pale green robe. "Would you please deliver a message to the Thaumaturge." *I can't believe I remembered his title. I must ask him what the darn thing means when I see him.*

"Yes my lady. What do you wish me to say."

"I am hoping he will agree to show me through the marketplace. My name is Lady Kat." She gestured at the series of small structures ahead. "Is the flag in the corner the entrance to the market?"

"Yes, Lady Kat."

"Wonderful. If he agrees, would you ask him to meet me at this entrance?"

The young apprentice nodded, and hurried off to convey the message.

Kat sat on a bench near the booths, and indulged in her preferred past time of people watching.

***

A deep voice interrupted her musings. "Lady Kat?"

She started at the sound of the beautiful baritone voice of Hesginn.

"I did not mean to surprise you." He inclined his head.

"Oh, don't apologize. Only daydreaming. Please, can you call me Kat? The formality of Lady Kat makes me uncomfortable."

"If you prefer. We Shendeans are not as shackled to the need to be formal, as are the Kaylins."

Kat chuckled. "They are bound by formality."

"I suspect you encountered challenges in their land."

Kat nodded. "Sometimes, yes."

"Your message said you wish to tour the market?"

"I do. Marketplaces are always both interesting and fun."

Hesginn led her to the market, through the alleyways of stalls, and eating areas. Kat, struck by the bright, welcoming lights and colors, grinned at the displays around her. The area, filled with happy, smiling people, laughing and talking with each other in muted conversation, conveyed a sense of fun. Over the voices rose sounds from musical instruments, played by a quartet located in the open area with vendors surrounding them. The tunes they played, light and full of life, encouraged people seated at various tables, eating food, or drinking tea, to move joyfully to the melodies. Shoulders swayed to rhythms of the tunes.

Hesginn turned to Kat. "This is Deleth's favorite place in the entire market. Shall we sit and drink a tea, and perhaps enjoy a light meal?"

"Perfect." Kat headed to a table and the two of them sat.

A young man in a light green robe approached. Hesginn ordered for the two of them, and Kat requested Karri-san tea.

"You must be affected by Rifellans." Hesginn grinned at her.

"I discovered both the effect, and the cure while in Kaylin." She gazed around her at the people seated in the communal area. "Can you explain about the robe colors? I believe healers wear light blue, and apprentices wear light green. What do the other hues represent?"

"Simple enough when you are privy to the information. Deep, royal blue is only worn by Lord Rhognor, as our leader. Emerald green is worn by leaders of guilds, and Masters don ivory robes."

"Your robe is emerald, are you the leader of a guild?"

"Yes, of the Magicians' Guild. In truth, Lord Rhognor is the titular head of all guilds. Of course he would never find time to manage them all, so each guild retains a working head."

"What about the pale yellow?"

"The assistants to masters and to heads of guilds all wear yellow. General guild members wear grey or white."

"So everyone can be aware of what place each person holds in the Stronghold?"

"Yes. The embroidered crests on the left sleeves, indicate the final piece of knowledge. You will become used to them."

"Thank you Hesginn. You are most helpful. But, one more question."

Hesginn raised a queried brow.

"Lord Rhognor introduced you as Thaumaturge. What exactly is the meaning? I'm not familiar with the word."

Hesginn smiled. "The meaning is simple. The word has always been used for the head of the Magicians' Guild, and means a magician of advanced skills, who practices the grey magic. Most members of the guild only practice white magic."

No wonder he's so hot, he also carries out some frosty magic. Wow.

When they finished eating, Hesginn suggested they visit the less travelled parts of the market. "These areas deeper within the groups of stalls, often contain some unusual offerings. The shopkeepers behind the main portion of the market change often, and I enjoy perusing them every five or ten star turns. I never guess what I will discover."

"Sounds perfect." Kat did her best to appeal to him — touched his arm, and smiled at him. *I'm putting on my best flirt, but he doesn't react. I wonder why?* She continued to hold his arm as he guided her through the back end of the market.

Hesginn, still discussing the various stalls, eased his arm free of hers and increased the distance between them.

She attempted to move closer, but he kept the gap constant.

"Lady Kat, I am thirsty, and if you will seat yourself at the table beside the flag, I will bring tea for us."

"Fine." She sat, and made sure the other chair rested beside her.

Hesginn returned with two cups of steaming beverage, set them down, and moved the chair to the opposite side of the table.

Kat did her best to keep her surprise at his actions from revealing itself on her face.

"Lady Kat." He cleared his throat. "I cannot help but perceive a tendency on your part to exhibit attraction for me. I would prefer you not do so."

Oops, did I make a goof? "Ah, of course. You bat for the other team."

His face screwed up in obvious puzzlement.

"Sorry, an expression from my own world. The meaning is you prefer to… er… mate with men."

A expression of horror traversed his face. "What do you take me for? A Glowen?"

Oh shit, I put my fat foot in it. "Forgive me, I didn't know. Are Glowens the only people who bond with their own sex?"

"No." He practically spat the word out. He paused, breathed in, and exhaled. "People who enjoy such preferences live in every land. This is normal. Unfortunately Glowens are chaotic in their choices, and cannot settle on anything.

Their greatest sin is, they conceal who they are. We in Shendea believe in truth and honesty. We are proud of ourselves and of our preferences. Any who do hold a preference for a mate of the same gender, display an orange crest on their right arm." He showed her his upper right arm. "Witness? No crest."

"I wasn't aware of Shendean preferences. I intended no insult." Kat swallowed. "I plead ignorance."

Hesginn leaned back and stared at her. "I understand. I did not feel insulted because you thought I might prefer my own gender, but because you thought I might conceal my preference. You are not familiar with our ways."

"Your ways aren't unfamiliar. In my world, many express similar preferences. To be fair many on my world do conceal their preferences, because they fear others will misjudge them. If Shendea is so accepting, why do Glowens deliberately conceal their choices?"

Hesginn sighed, and shifted uncomfortably in his seat. "To be fair, I cannot assume they conceal anything intentionally. Glowens are convinced life must be pleasurable in every way. Since all they do is for pleasure only, they experiment with relationships. The constant change between their connections, creates turmoil for the rest of Pridden. A man you met before who mated with a woman, may now be with a man, or both a male and a female. I suspect if a relationship becomes confusing for a Glowen, they choose to switch to different one."

"Confusing and weird." Kat cocked an eye at Hesginn. "Are they happy?"

"To all appearances, extremely."

"So why did you become so angry when I asked about your desire? Surely you can accept the Glowens for who they are."

He ran a hand through his hair. "I do. However, I become frustrated because at my age and position, others question why I am not yet bonded. I find this unthinkable I might be mistaken for possessing frivolous Glowen tendencies. I am Shendean, and adhere to the truth in all situations." He coughed. "Kat, you are an attractive female, but my desires belong to another. When you are bound through emotion to one person, no other can be of interest."

"I understand." She paused. *Should I ask?* "Uhm… who is she?"

"Her identity is private."

"Oh." *Damn, a mystery, and the commitment, makes him more appealing. I suspect though, I would be unwise to step over this line.*

"I met your brother Walden, but haven't conversed with him. Tell me about him." *Not a subtle change of topic, but my mouth couldn't contain my foot any longer..*

Hesginn sighed and rolled his eyes. "Walden." He sighed again. "My sibling is the exact opposite of me. He is weak, lacks ambition, and constantly makes errors in judgment."

"Isn't he a magician?"

"Yes, but only because of my standing in the Guild. We permitted him to join as a white magician, but he is most incompetent, and without my support, he would never be accepted."

"White magician?"

"Yes. They are mostly novices, or those whose capabilities to absorb the skills are limited. The majority of those at the guild are white magician. The abilities of those of us who are grey magicians are far more advanced. This is why, of course, only a grey magician is qualified to head the guild."

"So Walden will never become a grey magician."

"Never!"

Did I catch a flash of anger in his eyes? "You must find having a brother who is not your equal, difficult."

"You used the word brother twice in our conversation. I find only Rifellans use such a term for a male sibling." His eyes bored into her. "Are you sure you are not Rifellan?"

"Others suggested the same, but I'm from a completely different world." Kat furrowed her brow. "If your sibling is such a challenge, why does he occupy a place in Rhognor's Stronghold?"

"I ask the same thing myself." He grimaced. "I sometimes question Lord Rhognor's judgment." He shrugged. "Of course, Walden may be tolerated because of my position."

Well, well. Hesginn also questions Rhognor's abilities. Kat stood. "Hesginn, you are most gracious, and I apologize again for my error." She hesitated. "I enjoyed the tour of the market, but I admit I'm weary. If you'll excuse me, I'll return to my rooms." *I suspect I committed enough errors for today.*

He tilted his head at her. "Of course."

Kat turned and briskly left him behind. *Boy did I goof. His hotness is not available for a taste test. Whatever.* She sighed. *Too bad Liandock's not available.* This time she grinned to herself, remembering the lusty Rifellan.

CHAPTER 10

Deleth sent a message via her assistant to Rhognor, to request a meeting.

Soon his apprentice appeared at her door. "Lord Rhognor is most happy to meet with you, Healer Deleth."

"My thanks. I will follow you to his quarters." *Rhognor is still the most formal of all Shendeans. Wynneth advises me Eduardo is slowly changing formalities with the citizens of Kaylin.* She sighed. *I hope I will be able to persuade Rhognor to do the same over time, because in all other things he is a fine and flexible leader.*

As they arrived at Rhognor's quarters, the apprentice knocked, poked his head in the door and announced Deleth.

Rhognor rose from behind his desk and as she approached, welcomed her with a hug. "Deleth, what brings you to my quarters? Not troubles, I hope?"

"No, simply a minor challenge for which I need help."

"Well, come sit, and I will order tea for us." He strode over to the tassel in the corner and tugged. "So what does this challenge concern?"

"Not a what, but a who, Rhognor. Our visitor, Lady Kat."

"Ahh. She is an interesting woman. With your permission, I would appreciate my lady Halfin's input as well. You and she are far better equipped to recommend solutions for other women than I."

Deleth nodded and Rhognor walked to the far end of his office, cracked open the door, and beckoned to someone.

Halfin appeared and smiled at Rhognor. "What is your need, my pet?" She caught sight of Deleth, and blushed.

"Forgive me, Healer, I did not realize you were attending my lord."

Deleth smiled at her. "Lady Halfin, I am always pleased to detect affection between mated couples. Both of you are a fine example to Shendea. We would not experience problems if all our people followed your lead." *Although Halfin is blessed with strength, she prefers to bask in Rhognor's shadow.*

Rhognor took his mate's hand and led her to a chair." We need your help. Deleth brought to my attention our visitor, Kat, faces challenges which confuse her. Enchanters possess empathy, and you may be able to bring some clarity to the situation. I ordered tea for us, and we may attack this problem with refreshments at hand." He motioned Deleth to a chair, and sat in another himself.

Halfin's laugh tinkled in the room. "You wish my empathy, yet you speak of attacking. Your words often conflict with each other." Her smile for him lit her face with warmth. "Perhaps if Deleth would give me more information."

Deleth nodded. "Kat is having frightening night-dreams. She calls them nightmares." She continued to describe Kat's dreams with detailed accuracy to Halfin.

"Are these dreams common?"

"Indeed. Wynneth, the healer in Kaylin, informed me of a number of such incidents."

A knock at the door indicated the arrival of tea, and Halfin served each of them and then turned to the healer. "Deleth, you are the one with the foresight. What do you believe these dreams mean?"

"I cannot foresee what is in her future. My abilities fail me with this young woman. I am sure she will face many dangers, but what they are, I am unable to perceive. I am hoping the three of us may discover a solution, at least for these dreams she is experiencing."

"How curious you find Kat's path is blocked to you." Halfin shook her head in apparent puzzlement.

"I agree. All I am able to summon when I attempt to envisage her future is fog and shadow."

Rhognor who had been fidgeting in his seat, sat straighter and gazed at the far wall. "This is obvious. Perhaps the danger we all sense is here in the Stronghold, and since we cannot determine what will happen, Kat should continue her journey through Shendea." He stretched over to Halfin and clasped her hand. "You, my love, must meet with her before she leaves and supply her with information for the balance of her visit in our land."

"I would like that. I find her company quite stimulating." She smiled at him, pleasure in her eyes. "I will approach her after the midturn meal."

Deleth coughed. "I spoke with her guide, and he will provide a journey for Kat through most of Shendea. After the interior travels, they intend to return to the Stronghold so she may report the results of her trip. Finally they will depart for Rifella via the Magicians Guild."

Rhognor clapped his hands. "Excellent. My lady and I intend to take our fourth season visit to the Magicians' Guild. A perfect opportunity for us to travel part way with them."

The love between these two is enchanting. But why is there a shadow surrounding Halfin? "Rhognor, I will advise Mouse he should prepare Kat for the journey."

***

After a circuitous route to her rooms the previous evening, and a satisfying and deep sleep, Kat rose the following morning, determined to spend time writing in her journal.

With a substantial breakfast easing her hunger pangs, she buried her nose in her game writings, and absentmindedly sucked on the tip of her cathnog pen. "Eew." She dropped the pen on the desk and hurried to the personal to wash her mouth. She peered in the mirror and stuck out her tongue. *Black. Gross.*

She rinsed her mouth until the vile taste disappeared. *I hope the stuff isn't poisonous.*

A knock on the door claimed her attention. "Come."

Mouse poked his head around the door.

"Mouse, what's in the Kaylin ink? Is it harmful?"

"Why?"

Without replying, Kat extended her tongue at him.

Mouse grinned. "The only animals in all Pridden who possess black tongues are the gondal lizards of Baklai. I do not recommend you attempt to disguise yourself as a gondal."

"Come on, this is serious. I accidentally put my pen in my mouth. Will the ink hurt me?"

"No — the ink is made from a bitter but benign plant."

"I'm glad I amuse you."

"I gather by the tone of your voice Kat, you do not mean what you say." He shook his head. "This is a type of humor uncommon in Pridden. I believe you use a word for this in your world. Sarcasm, I understand?"

"Yes." She frowned at him.

"Ah. I did not mean to anger you, but your black tongue is amusing."

Kat glared at him.

He hastily changed the topic. "I brought the cathnog teeth with me, so we might prepare them to present to Rhognor."

"I'd forgotten about the teeth." *This should be fun. I wonder how Rhognor will react to the gift?*

"I also brought all the equipment necessary to cleanse them. Can we use this table?"

Kat nodded.

"I suggest we each take two, and I will demonstrate what to do with the first one, and then you follow my lead with another." He grinned at her. "Okay?"

"Okay." Kat laughed. "You'll be speaking like a male from my world before you realize what you're doing." She picked up one of the longer teeth. "Ouch. Nasty and sharp. I'm bleeding." She grabbed a cloth from her makeup table and pressed the wad against her finger.

"My apologies, Kat. I regret I did not warn you to be careful in handling them. Please remind me when we present them to Rhognor to advise him they are not filed."

"Filed?"

Mouse picked up her pen. "This one's edges are smooth, so the tooth may be put to practical use. If the fangs are only to be displayed, they will not be rubbed down. Rhognor must decide whether or not to file them himself."

"Fine. I'll be careful. Now let's get this done, so we can present them to him. I'm dying to watch his face when we hand them over."

"I pray and hope when you observe his face you do not decide to join Caleesh."

"It's only an expression, Mouse."

He raised an eyebrow at her. "You have many expressions." He pointed to the supplies he brought with him. "Dip this soft cloth in the bowl of liquid, and gently rub it on the tooth in circular motion to remove any dirt or blood. Be careful of the sharp edges." He held up the fang. "See, as I polish, the yellowing disappears, and the tooth shines."

"Wow. You're right." She cocked her head at him. "What is the liquid?"

"A cleaning solution prepared by the healers, which works well on cathnog teeth."

The two of them cleaned diligently and presently all four fangs shone, leaving the natural coating untouched by any abrading material.

"A job well done, Kat." He handed her a box to hold the teeth. "Rhognor is expecting us, as I believe he wishes to discuss other matters."

"Fine. Lead the way." Kat paused. *Where is Breen?* She gazed around and located Breen curled in a shining fur ball in the center of her bed. *"There you are, Breen. Catch you later."*

The boradai lifted her head, opened one eye, and nodded.

Kat smiled to herself as she followed Mouse out the door and down the hall. *Wait a darn minute. How the heck did Mouse know about the word sarcasm in my world?*

CHAPTER 11

A young apprentice ushered Kat and her guide through the door to Rhognor's quarters. Rhognor rose from behind the massive stone desk, and ushered them to seats around a wooden table in the middle of the room.

"The timing is most opportune that you are here, Kat." In his own quarters, he relaxed in his chair, and sat calmly. Gone was the fidgeting of days before. "I do believe you need to continue your journey through Shendea."

"We are anticipating our further journey with pleasure, Lord Rhognor. However, Mouse and I bring a gift for you before we leave." She glanced sideways at Mouse for corroboration.

He nodded for her to continue.

Rhognor's eyebrows rose. "A gift? How kind."

Kat took the small box from her pocket. "On our way from Kaylin, we encountered a cathnog."

Rhognor's eyes widened.

Kat continued her tale. "Fortunately, a hydodd appeared as the cathnog chased us, and in the subsequent battle, the hydodd won. Mouse removed the fangs, and we prepared them for you." She handed the small box to Rhognor. *Boy, my formal-speak is improving. But it's exhausting, and I must get home so I can talk normally again.*

Rhognor opened the box and stared at the contents. "These are magnificent. You did a fine job preparing them for display. I will treasure them. Many thanks."

Mouse inclined his head to acknowledge the lord's appreciation. "Lord Rhognor, we are prepared to depart the

Stronghold in two star-turns, if we can rely upon your generosity to re-unite us with our original pontis."

"Absolutely, Mouse. They are housed at Halfway Haven stables. The stable master knows they are yours, and will help you prepare them for the journey to the Ponti Inn."

"My thanks my Lord."

"You are most welcome." He glanced over at Kat. "Before you leave, Kat, you should meet with my lady Halfin. She will advise you of the general customs in Shendea, which should prove advantageous in this current journey." He rose, walked to the far end of the room, and peered around the open door. Kat attempted to eavesdrop, but could not hear what he said, when Halfin appeared and took her mate's hand.

Rhognor adores Halfin. His face lights up in her presence. Maybe she relaxes him.

Halfin turned to Kat. "I am to educate you on our customs in Shendea."

"So you will reveal all the quirks, right?"

The other three in the room all seemed puzzled.

I didn't think the word qualified as slang. "We use the word to describe oddities in someone's nature."

Halfin nodded her head. "I understand. Perhaps we can move to the marketplace and enjoy a midturn meal while I advise you of our… our... quirks." She smiled at her own joke, and then swiveled to face Mouse. "Would you please accompany us?"

He nodded.

Halfin released Rhognor's hand. He appeared reluctant to part from her, but allowed her to usher the other two from the room.

Kat glanced back and caught the affectionate smile on Rhognor's face as he gazed at Halfin. *So that is what real love looks like.*

***

The three sat at a table in the middle of the square, with plates of food and plenty of tea spread in front of them.

"Halfin, Hesginn explained the different shades of robes Shendeans wear, but he didn't mention what your peach color represented."

"My robe is the only one of this color. As you know, my lord is the true head of all guilds, but in addition, each one claims an acting head. I am the acting head of the Enchanters' Guild. The challenge is, no new offspring were born with the talents of an enchanter for many ages, and I am the last of my kind. Rhognor and I are sadly not blessed with offspring, so the Enchanters' Guild will cease to exist when I join Caleesh."

"I'm so sorry, Halfin."

She patted Kat's hand. "There is no need for sorrow. This is how life moves. Caleesh determined the Enchanters' Guild is no longer needed." Her faint smile revealed a tinge of regret. "As for the rest of the guilds, Hesginn is the acting head of the Magician's Guild, Deleth is acting Head of the Healers' Guild, and Derwynn, whom you should meet on your coming journey, is acting head of the Thieves' Guild."

Kat's mouth dropped open. "Thieves' Guild? You're kidding."

Halfin stared at Kat. "Kid-ing?"

Oh crap, I did it again.. "We use this expression on my world to indicate when someone is joking."

Halfin still appeared puzzled. "I am not joking, I am only imparting information."

Kat shook her head. "Shendeans are so strongly attached to honesty, and yet you tolerate a Thieves' Guild?"

Mouse regarded Kat, a half frown on his face. "The Thieves' Guild are useful. I too am a member."

"You're a member of a Thieves' Guild?" *Perhaps I'm wise not to trust him.*

"Kat, I am not sure you understand how the Thieves' Guild functions, but we will visit them, and they will hopefully demonstrate their… our… talents. You will behold we are held in esteem in Shendea. Our services are valuable."

"Fine, I'll withhold judgment until we visit them." *How weird. Imagine a guild made up of thieves. Do they steal from each other? Or from other guilds? Whatever. It's gotta be confusing.*

Mouse offered to obtain dessert for them, which Kat accepted straightaway.

She addressed Halfin. "Even though no others exist to take your place, what functions do the Enchanters' Guild perform?"

Halfin gazed into the distance. "We are the guild of nature and earth and trees. We bring appreciation of the outdoors to all our people. We learned the ways of plants to provide solace and health to our people, and passed on this information to the healers. We spoke to the creatures in the wild, learned the secrets of the fauna of our land, and helped our citizens to use nature wisely."

"You say you spoke to the creatures. Do you include hydodds and cathnogs in your communication?"

"Of course. Cathnogs tend to be dedicated to hunting. I find their thoughts are often jumbled, and quite bloodthirsty. They are not easy to befriend." She beamed, as if remembering some incident. "But hydodds. They are magnificent and are definitely the lords of all the creatures in our land. They are revered by the small helpless ones."

Mouse joined them with a supply of sweet treats. "Did Kat tell you, my Lady, we encountered a cathnog on our way to the Stronghold. A magnificent hydodd saved us from the vicious claws and teeth."

Halfin clapped her hands in obvious glee. "I wish I could have seen your meeting. I am fond of hydodds."

Kat stared at Halfin, frowning. "As an enchanter, I would think you would prefer to live outdoors among trees and all the creatures in the wilds, yet you are indoors in the Stronghold. How can you bear such confinement?"

Kat caught a faint shadow in Halfin's eyes.

"I must live in the Stronghold. Lord Rhognor is my bonded mate. He is wonderful to me. He brought many things from the wilds to the Stronghold: birds, and small trees, plants and many small creatures, and I can still run living earth through my fingers from the flower gardens throughout these halls. We are from two different ways of living, but the place he created is a happy one for me. His kindness means I do not often miss the wilds."

"But is this why you will be the last of the enchanters?"

"I do not believe so. As I mentioned, our abilities with growing things are now passed to the Healers' Guild. I am certain Caleesh anticipated what our people wish for, and thus determined my guild is no longer needed. This is the way of life. Healer Deleth, who possesses the sight, confirms this for me."

Wow. She adores Rhognor as much as he loves her. I can't imagine giving up my dreams, my core beliefs for any man. For me, that would be the final loss of control.

CHAPTER 12

Kat rose. "I must go." She took Halfin's hand. "Thanks for the information. I want to record this while I still remember all you told me."

Halfin glanced up at Kat. "Are you sure you can find your way back to your rooms?"

"Yes. I've been back and forth with others enough times so I'm comfortable with the route by now." She turned to Mouse. "We can discuss the rest of our journey later?"

He nodded. "After your morning meal on the morrow will be sufficient. Lady Halfin and I will discuss any other items you and I may need on the journey."

"Fine." She hurried off toward her rooms.

Barely out of sight of Halfin and Mouse, Kat glanced back at them. *Do Halfin and Mouse also know each other?* She bumped into a solid male body. "Oof, sorry."

The man put out a hand to steady her. "You are the Lady Kat, are you not?"

She stared up at him. "Yes, I saw you at the feast. You're Walden, Hesginn's brother."

He stiffened. "I am the sibling to the Thaumaturge." He gave an awkward bob of his head.

"Do you always call him by his title?"

"When speaking with others, naturally. He is the head of my guild."

"Well when we speak, let's forget the title. I find it cumbersome and a colossal mouthful."

Walden laughed. "You are right. A mouthful indeed, but then he is… is drawn to unnecessary formality."

"Really? I didn't notice."

"Well, he can be, when anything concerns his standing within the Guild." Walden paused. "Shall we locate a seat and enjoy a meal?"

"I ate a short while ago so I'm full, but perhaps some tea." *My writing can wait. Walden may be a fount of information.*

"Perfect. I found a little stall where they serve a variety of our teas, and we can sit and I can answer any questions you may need answered."

Kat smiled at him. "Lead on."

Walden threaded his way through stalls unknown to Kat. He led her to some small tables and once she seated herself, he approached the stall owner for tea. He returned with two huge mugs of steaming beverage, topped with an ivory wax-like blossom.

"What is this drink called?"

"This is gwindle tea. Our people use this to keep their bodily health balanced, and their minds clear and focused."

The tea reminded Kat of lavender and peppermint with a touch of vanilla, and something else which she could not identify. "The taste is wonderful." She glanced around the area. "I'm unfamiliar with this part of the market. I never guessed at the size."

"This part evolves as some merchants leave to return to their homes, and new vendors arrive with different goods." He pointed to nearby stalls. "Those three are usually tended by Mordens, and change frequently."

"What do they sell?"

"They vend their flatbread which is tasty and nutritious. The bread keeps fresh for a lengthy lifespan and is excellent for those who travel long distances. Almost all people on Pridden use this bread." He pointed to another booth filled with boots and shoes and belts. "All the items in that stall are made from the skin of the drag."

"What is a drag?"

"They are the biggest serpents in Morden, growing to the length of ten horses. They encircle their victims and crush them to death."

Kat shuddered. "Ugh. The skins are attractive though, if they're the ones I admired at a Morden booth in Trigoran."

"Before you leave Shendea, you should purchase a pair of drag boots. They are strong and will serve you well in every land."

"Thanks for the suggestion, but I'm not sure I'll feel comfortable wearing boots of snake-skin."

"I understand." Walden rose, and held out his hand to Kat. "You're tea is finished so now I will take you to the Magicians' stall."

Kat took his hand and stood. "Wonderful. I'd love to watch magicians at work."

At the Magicians' stall, Kat stared at diagrams and illustrations of stars and what appeared to be a type of calendar. "Can you explain all this?"

"We magicians keep records of the seasons, which follow the movements of the night lights in the sky and of our star, which moves across the heavens depending on the seasons."

"You enjoy four different seasons, right?"

"Correct, and those four seasons create one path period. Our magicians determined our world revolves around our star, and this accounts for the seasons. A single path period, therefore, completes one revolution."

At last, I really understand what a path is. "What are those red marks?"

"Those indicate the appearance of Red Rash which first begins in northern part of Shendea, but eventually spreads to all Pridden. The Rash is a violent illness, which left untreated, results in death."

"How do you manage to save your people?"

"Our healers developed a potion which they distill from the syeth venom. This venom is Morden's best-selling product. Syeths are the smallest serpents in their land, and their venom causes paralysis in the victims, which also leads to death. Our healers discovered how to change the properties to combat the effects of Red Rash."

"When is this rash prevalent?"

"You do not need to worry, Kat. The illness only appears every seven paths. The last one appeared three paths ago. So the next outbreak will not be for another four paths."

"Good to know." She walked on to another vendor, whose stall attracted her attention, laden with necklaces, bangles, and rings containing gems ranging from blood-red rubies, sky-blue turquoise, pale yellow citrine, and polished black agate.

The shopkeeper approached her. "If you are searching for a gem to enrich your gown, My Lady, may I suggest this wristlet. This vivid gem is mined from the Clog Neran mountains, and is the precise color of the blue ice in the upper canyons. This is a rare find."

The stones reminded Kat of crisp cold days back home when snow fell to earth and sparkled like diamonds. "How beautiful, but… "

Walden standing behind her, interrupted. "You must purchase this, Kat. I insist."

Kat whirled to face him. "I can't. I don't carry funds of my own."

"You are a guest. The Stronghold will cover the cost." Before Kat could stop him, Walden advised the owner of the stall they would buy the wristlet. "Charge this to the account of the Stronghold."

The shopkeeper bowed in assent.

Walden plucked the bangle from the stall owner's hand and placed the jewels around Kat's wrist. "Perfect. The stones suit you." He smirked.

"What's so funny?"

"Hesginn is the keeper of the records for the Stronghold. He will see this item and be furious to find out I approved the sale. He does not understand what women want, which is why he is still without a mate. He became furious when I, his younger sibling, found a perfect mate before he did."

"Why would such a thing matter?"

"Because I accomplished something before him. You must understand, my sibling possesses little, if any, sense of humor, but is dedicated to being the first and the best at everything. He envies me my successful bonding. As punishment he forced me to join the Magicians' Guild. I wished another occupation, but he would not listen. As a result, I take every opportunity to annoy him and play tricks on him. This at least, makes my thankless vocation bearable."

Seems sibling rivalry is common everywhere. "Sorry to hear this. What did you actually want to do?"

"I longed to be an apprentice artist with the Tapestry Guild. I believe I possessed some talent. But as a youngster, joining the guild required permission from Hesginn. Now, unfortunately, I am beyond the age for me to apprentice with Master Godrith."

"He sounds immensely controlling."

"He is, but no matter. I find many ways to laugh at his expense. Life is meant to be more joyful."

"I hope he won't take your joke out on me. I need Hesginn's support with Lord Rhognor."

"You should not encounter a problem, Kat. Lady Halfin is fond of you, and Rhognor is exceptionally fond of her."

Kat eyed him. Walden did indeed appear to be a happy person. "Walden, my thanks for the tour and persuading me to purchase this bracelet. I need to prepare for the rest of my journey, so I must return to my quarters."

"Of course. My pleasure." He beamed as he bowed his head.

Kat turned and left the area. *Hm. So Hesginn is a humorless control freak. He didn't seem that lacking in humor to me. Probably just as well he resisted my charms though.*

CHAPTER 13

Kat exited the market into an unknown area of the Stronghold. She continued to guess the way to her quarters, but encountered fewer and fewer people. The dark gaping maws of other passageways led off the corridor she chose. They did not instill confidence. The lights grew dimmer in the section she traveled, and sighs and whispers echoed from the maze of halls. A chill invaded the air, and Kat shivered. *This is kinda creepy.* At last she observed a man coming from one of the side corridors. *Terrific. Finally another person.* "Excuse me. Can you tell me how to get to Healer Deleth's quarters." *Once I'm at her door I can find my own way.*

A rancid smell invaded her nostrils.

"What are you doing so far from well travelled corridors?" Clad in brown-stained work clothes, with a scraggly beard, and unkempt hair, he broadcast a sinister appearance.

Uh oh. "Um… I think I took a wrong turn."

He leered at her, exposing missing teeth, which failed to produce a sense of comfort in Kat. "You did indeed." With those words he pounced. He grabbed at the sparkling bracelet she'd purchased at the market.

As he pulled her closer, she gagged at the foul odor of him. She twisted her wrist to escape his clutches and aimed a vicious kick at his crotch. The split skirt allowed her to contact his body with force. He screamed, bent over, and holding his body, retched.

Without pausing, Kat fled back the way she'd come, seeking the safety of the market again. *Son of a… . Not a helpful Shendean.* In a few minutes, she heard him pounding after her. Relieved, at the sight of the lights of the entrance she'd left earlier, the footsteps behind her slowed and stopped. Kat did not. She continued to run, until she bumped into someone. "Deleth." She bent over, gasping for breath.

"Kat. Whatever is the matter? What are you running from?"

Barely able to speak Kat gestured back along the corridor she came from. "Man. Tried to rob me." She straightened up breathing deeply, willing her heart to slow down.

Eyes wide, Deleth gasped. "Did you go beyond the well-lit passages?"

"Yup."

"Oh my. Every place possesses some unpleasant people, and a number of criminal types live in the far reaches of the gloom. Rhognor spent many star turns dispatching his guards in an attempt to clean up the area. He did reduce the number of unfriendly people who inhabit those halls, but some still remain. Kat, the place is dangerous. Please, do not go there again."

Kat rolled her eyes at Deleth. "Duh."

"Excuse me. What does daa mean?"

"I never intend to go there again. I was expressing my annoyance you would consider me stupid enough to return to the area."

"Oh, Kat. My apologies. I never meant to indicate you are not capable. I just thought you did not realize the danger of the place. This is not an area with which you are familiar."

"Deleth I certainly did not expect the to find danger anywhere within the Stronghold, so I go caught unaware."

"No one thought to warn you. Those of us who live here are familiar with the less than honest few who live in the dark depths." She took Kat by the hand. "Come, I will take you to your quarters and we will order some calming tea for you."

Kat allowed Deleth to lead her to the familiar path back to her rooms. *Things like this wouldn't happen back home. I know which areas to avoid. Sometimes I worry I'll never get back.*

When they arrived, Deleth waited for Kat to open the door, then strode to the tassel in the corner and tugged twice. "Sit Kat. Tea will be here without delay. You received a fright and you need to regain your balance."

She sat.

Deleth moved a chair to sit beside Kat and patted her on the shoulder. "Is the attacker the only thing upsetting you?"

"The attacker isn't what's upsetting me. I am capable of defending myself. A foul smelling man and aggressive, but I'm well versed in self-defense. I kicked him… hard… in his junk. That took care of him."

"Junk? What is junk?"

Rats. Not again. "Junk is what people on my world some-times use to refer to the male… er… reproductive parts" *I hope she found my explanation delicate enough.*

"I understand." Deleth nodded. "But something else con-cerns you."

"I'm not happy." Kat stood and strode around the room. Eventually she returned to the seat and thumped down on the chair. "While I find much about Pridden to be beautiful and interesting, I truly do want to go home. Eduardo promised a return if I helped him with the problems in Pridden, but ev-erything moves at a snail's pace." She caught a questioning glance in Deleth's eyes, which she ignored. "I'm not sure exactly what he expects me to do. I'm excellent at solving things. But a whole world's problems?" She shook her head in frustration. "Dammit, Deleth, who do I trust? Mouse is not what he claims to be. Dangerous creatures and people are everywhere. Hesginn and Walden are so far apart in the way they describe each other. Which one of them is lying?"

Deleth sighed. "Kat, both are telling the truth. They view things from a different perspective. Shendeans are a truthful people. Our entire society has developed from the approach of honesty in all things."

A knock on the door interrupted their conversation.

At Kat's, "Come," Kaydith entered, and in silence, brought the tray of tea to the table. She quietly exited the room.

Deleth poured for the two of them. "You need to understand how we in Shendea behave. Unlike the Glowens who confuse us, we do not prevaricate. Plus we never knowingly withhold information. What you see in Shendea, is what exists." She drank. "There are many people here you can trust. Rhognor is a fine and honest man and a superb leader. Halfin, his mate, is beyond reproach in all ways."

"How can I trust either Hesginn or Walden when they perceive things from such different viewpoints."

"You can believe what they say. Both always keep their word. For myself, I find Hesginn somewhat tiring because he adheres to rules so closely. However, I am fond of Walden. He may not control the power of his sibling, but he exhibits a wonderful sense of humor, and he is a kind and generous man."

"Maybe, but I'm stuck with Mouse and I'm convinced he's hiding something."

"I think what you perceive in him, Kat, is his own inner conflict. Mouse's early days were more challenging than most. His birth parents were killed before he achieved his first path as a newborn, and his substitute parents joined with Caleesh when he reached only fifteen paths."

"I didn't realize this."

"He survived on the street, but now serves a cruel master. He must always be subservient, and only when he travels outside of Morden he is allowed a limited freedom to experience a less fearful life." Deleth sighed. "I have known Mouse for most of his living days, and he never once broke my trust."

"Deleth, you tell me all this, but I'm no further ahead to returning home than when I first arrived here. I trust you… but perhaps you're only spouting the company line."

Deleth's eyebrows appeared to be climbing up her forehead to join her hairline. "By your words I believe you are suggesting I only tell you what others want you to hear." She held out both her hands. "Kat, I am Shendean. I cannot withhold information. I also cannot foretell what your future holds, but I am positive everything will work out."

"I hope you're right. I want to go back to what I know -- to the people I know and understand. The longer I am here, the more I realize I don't belong in this world. I'm not in control here, and I don't like it."

"I do not pretend your task is easy, but Eduardo and Wynneth are both convinced you will persevere. Ask for help when you need some, and trust in yourself above all others."

Help? Humph. They all talk a good game. But their actions?

CHAPTER 14

Kat burrowed in her bed, grumpy and irritable. But, during the night, curled up with Breen and stroking the furry little body, her foul mood melted and she slept deeply. Plaintive squeaking from Wink woke her.

"Oh Wink, I forgot to feed you last night. I'm so sorry. I was overtired and distracted."

Her hand, resting on Breen elicited a droll comment. *"She does not understand you and your loudness hurts my brain."*

"Oops, sorry to you too."

Kat jumped from the bed and grabbing food from the container on her dresser, hurried to Wink's cage. She delicately scooped the creature from the warmth of her protective cage, no longer in a tight sleepy ball, but now legs and tail and wings flapping in distress. She walked to the table, and after setting Wink down, she popped food in the tiny mouth. Squeaks and distressed movements ceased, but the pint-sized maw opened again and Kat spent ten additional minutes offering food to the hungry animal. Finally, Wink settled in a pose similar to a crouched cat.

"Do I see a grin on your face, Wink?"

The pyrock chirruped.

Kat laughed and picked her up. She strolled to the cage, stroking the furry little beast. "You always make me happy and positive." She deposited Wink in her cage, where she rolled up in a ball and dropped off to sleep.

***

Once she completed her morning meal and dressed for the day, a knock came at the door.

"Come."

Mouse peered around the door. "Good morrow, Kat. Rhognor requested our presence. I believe he is planning our assignment for Shendea."

"Fine, I really want to get moving. I find visiting the various places in the Stronghold of interest, but I would much prefer completing whatever this assignment is."

"You do not appear to understand what you are to do, and yet you finalized your task in Kaylin."

"I don't know what I'm doing." Kat shook her head in frustration. "Supposedly I must discover the persons who are creating disturbances in Pridden. Eduardo informed me I showed some people a different way of acting. I have no idea of what he meant." She spread her hands in question. "All I want to do is go home, and he wants me to change people's minds. I'm no guru."

"What is a goo-roo?"

"Oh, just some man who says wise things."

Mouse blinked at her explanation. "Perhaps Rhognor will offer enlightenment on the subject. He is expecting us, so we should attend him."

Kat glared, her happy mood evaporated.

***

At the entrance to Rhognor's quarters, the two were ushered in, obviously expected.

Rhognor rose from a highly polished wooden chair, walked over and clasped Kat by the hand. "I am delighted you came so swiftly. Deleth and I discussed you both. In view of your unpleasant experience in the outer reaches of the Stronghold, we think it best you continue your travels in Shendea, sooner rather than later. Please be seated." He returned to his seat behind a massive carved stone desk.

Kat sat and gazed at sides of the desk. The carvings depicted scenes from life in Shendea, all created by incredibly talented craftsmen. "Your desk is stunning. I've never seen anything so elegant. Who did the carving?"

"You appreciate fine art." He stroked the gleaming surface. "Regrettably we do not remember the name of the artisan. This desk has been part of this office for many paths. My ancestors, as far back as our recorded history, all worked from this fine piece of furniture." He lined up two sheets of parchment. "I enjoy preparing my tasks from here and find this a constant source of pleasure and stability." His mouth twitched in a half smile, and he sighed.

Silence. The three of them sat without words, gazing at the desk, with Kat caught up in her own thoughts. *Pretty cool desk. It must weigh a ton.*

Rhognor blinked. "Mouse, my pardon. I am pleased you are guiding Kat. Eduardo is always excellent at his choices. He believes you are the perfect guide on her journey through Pridden. Based on your reputation, I concur with his choice." He beamed at Mouse. "Kat is in capable hands."

Capable hands? What is he aware of about Mouse? Curious.

"Thank you for your kind words Lord Rhognor." Mouse appeared to shrink in his seat. "You mentioned an unpleasant experience for Kat. Can you explain?"

"My apologies, I thought Deleth informed you of the incident."

"She and I have not met in the last star turn."

"Ah. Perhaps Kat can tell you what occurred." He aimed an enquiring eye at her.

"I became lost in a less travelled part of the Stronghold. A robber tried to steal my bracelet, but I managed to fight him off, and ran back to the marketplace."

"Did you recognize him, and how did you defeat him?"

"A filthy man and he smelled foul, but I'd never seen him before." Kat shrugged. "I fought him by delivering a well aimed kick."

Mouse raised both eyebrows. "A kick?"

"Yes." *Explain, Kat. Explain.* "In my own world, I studied a form of fighting known as karate for many… er… paths. I am well advanced in this type of combat."

Now Rhognor expressed curiosity. "Is your world so challenging, women need to study combat?"

"Women should always understand how to defend themselves, but I studied longer so I could use the information I gained in my profession."

"Profession? Are you part of a guild?"

"A type of guild, I suppose. I designed games."

Rhognor's face lit up. "Games. How extraordinary. People in many lands play games. Most of them are calm, but in Rifella and Morden they are physically challenging. Here in Shendea, our games are more thought provoking. You should request Deleth demonstrate one for you."

"Perhaps." *Please drop this. I don't want to dive into an explanation of computers and our technology.*

Rhognor turned to Mouse. "While you and Kat travel through Shendea, we will pursue the capture of this miscreant. I spent much time and effort in an attempt to cleanse the outer reaches of the Stronghold of these undesirables. My guards are excellent, but the Stronghold consists of many passages and places of hiding. My men achieved much, but there are yet elements we would prefer to eliminate. Shendea is a place of restful calm, and they do not belong."

"An excellent idea, Lord Rhognor. Your land has long enjoyed a reputation for peace and tranquility." He smiled at

Rhognor and addressed Kat. "Since Lord Rhognor indicated we may continue our travels, I suggest, after the midturn meal, we discuss the planned route we should take within Shendea."

"Perfect. Where?"

"Since your quarters possess greater capacity, I suggest we meet there."

"Fine." She paused. "Perhaps you would like your midturn meal in my quarters as well?" *Maybe I can discover more about Mouse this way.*

"It certainly would be convenient, but I need to prepare many things before I meet with you."

"As you wish." Kat faced Rhognor. "Thank you again for your time, Lord Rhognor."

He bowed his head at her.

So Mouse avoided dining with me in my room. And he became very formal when Rhognor remarked on his abilities. I wonder why?

CHAPTER 15

Kat spent time during her midturn meal deciding what word gaps existed in her English/pyrock writing list. *Deleth should be able to fill in these blanks, but I wonder… .* She glanced at the bed, and smiled at Breen curled in a glossy fur ball. She strolled over and stroked her.

"What do you wish, Kat?"

"Can you show me pictures of the writing which people do in Pridden?"

"Yes. What words would you like to know?"

"If I take you to my writing table, and keep contact with you, can you guide me through writing some words?"

"Yes."

Kat picked up Breen and positioned her on the table, so her hand contacted the creature. With the other hand, she picked up her pen, poised to reproduce the words.

"What does the word for danger look like."

Breen projected the picture of the written word for Kat, which she copied on her parchment. Once she copied the word, she concentrated on what she'd written so Breen could view the picture in her mind.

"How did I do?"

"Excellent. I notice you put the rune for the same word beside the written one."

"Apparently my writing resembles runes to people in Pridden. I do this so I will remember what each word in your writing means."

Inspired, Kat let Breen lead her through six additional words, until a knock interrupted them.

"Come." Kat rose and re-deposited Breen on the bed.

Mouse entered carrying three pieces of parchment. "Here is a list for you to pack, which I wrote in your runes, and some maps of our intended route. We can examine them together."

"Fine. Let me put my other work away." Kat gathered her parchments and stowed them in her writing pouch. She closed the ink container, wiped off her pen and put them aside.

"Excellent." Mouse seated himself at the desk, spread the maps out, and handed the list of packing items to Kat.

"This list is pretty much what I expected, so most of this is ready." She put the list aside, and took a seat herself. "I'm anxious to inspect our route, though." She rubbed her forehead. "I suppose we'll need to go to Halfway Haven to get the pontis, and to the Ponti Inn to pick up our own horses?"

"Correct. From the inn we'll take this route toward Finrase."

Kat pointed at the map. "Burning Rock Mountain? Sounds like a volcano. I always wanted to view one up close."

"The mountain continually ejects molten rocks, if you call such a mountain, a volcano. But Kat, getting too close is highly dangerous. You will need to admire the inferno from afar."

"Not a problem. I don't plan on becoming a crispy critter."

Mouse wrinkled his forehead, and shook his head. "You possess an interesting way of expressing yourself." He returned to the map. "You can, however, visit the Crimson Cauldron at Finrase. People stop at the Cauldron to immerse themselves in the heated mud, which the healers claim is therapeutic."

"I'll definitely take advantage of the mud. Traveling on horseback tends to make certain muscles ache. What will we do after Finrase?"

Mouse pointed at the map again. "We head for Glazenwyth, down to Magwin and to Roothlan on Lake Glen Addie. From there we will head to the Thieves' Guild.

"I suppose this is where you will persuade me they're beneficial?"

"Hopefully you will be able to view a specific ceremony." He peered at her with furrowed brow. "Once we leave the guild, we will cross the Carrog Mannin, head through the Kroakin woods to Dizerth. From there, back to Finrase toward the Ponti inn and finally back to the Stronghold."

"Why back here?"

"You will need to report on your progress, and any challenges you encountered to Rhognor."

"Ah, fine." Kat stopped. A sudden thought struck her. "Mouse, what sort of people will we encounter on this route?"

"All kinds. Few Kaylins travel anywhere, but we will encounter more Baklai in the warmer areas. Naturally we will meet Rifellans, because they fulfill Rhognor's need for guards, which they do in most of the lands." His mouth crinkled at the corners. "I would suggest you bring a sufficient supply of Karri-san with you."

Kat glared at him. "I intended to. Who else?"

"Glowens often visit Shendea, but the only Mordens we will happen upon are the few who come to trade in Syeth venom." He tugged at his ear. "Mordens, particularly those from the north, find Shendeans too spiritual for their satisfaction. Southern Mordens, however, prefer to keep to themselves, and generally only trade with Baklai."

"I assume once we leave the Ponti Inn, we will be in warmer areas. I consulted with Deleth, and she advised me what clothing to pack. Even so, I'm not looking forward to dragging my luggage down the mountain." *One thing I'm not is a pack animal.*

Mouse smiled at her. "You will be pleased to know the Stronghold will provide us at least two others to help us take our bags to Halfway Haven. From the Haven, of course, we will have Pontis and afterward, our horses."

"Yes. I remember two young men helping us with our baggage when we climbed to the Stronghold on our way here."

Mouse rose from his seat at the desk. "Leave your bags outside your door early on the morrow and an apprentice will bring them to you at the front gate. Once you complete your morning meal, make your way to the gate and we will depart on our journey. Be sure to dress warmly." He chuckled. "I will do likewise this time."

"Okay. I'll meet you tomorrow." *Well, Mouse does have a sense of humor. I only wish we could move faster so I can get home sooner.*

CHAPTER 16

Early the following morning, Kat deposited her travel bag outside her door, and prepared her backpack and what she now called her diplo pouch for travel. Her morning meal arrived during the final stages of packing, and Kat ate the hot journeyklim with gusto.

Wink, the little pyrock, well fed, snored happily curled up in her travel cage. Kat enveloped the cage in a plush pouch, lined with fur, which she attached to her backpack.

She moved to the bed and stroked Breen. *"Where should I place you so you'll be comfortable in our travels?"*

"The left side pocket on your backpack will be perfect. Insert some comfortable fabric."

"Will you be warm enough?"

"We boradai are not subject to extreme changes in temperature."

Kat shrugged and did as Breen requested. The odd creature bounded across the bed and leaped in the pocket of the backpack. Kat tied the strings to close the pocket, leaving sufficient room for Breen to poke her nose out, should she require it.

Kat gazed around the room to make sure she remembered everything. She left Wink's regular cage in place, because she would be back here before leaving for her final journey out of Shendea.

Donning her backpack and slinging her diplo pouch over her shoulder, she carried her fur coat and a thick scarf. The halls were too warm for her to wear her outer clothing until she reached the front gate of the Stronghold.

***

When Kat arrived at the gate, Mouse greeted her. "Did you pack all you will need?"

"I believe so. So long as unexpected problems don't arise." Kat dropped her backpack and her bag on a nearby table, shrugged into her thick coat with the cuddly fur lining, and wrapped the tight knit scarf around her neck. Once she slipped into the backpack and hung the diplo bag over her shoulder, she glanced back at the two apprentices, snugly dressed themselves. "Are we all ready?"

Both nodded at her, opened the huge gated doors, and proceeded ahead of her. Mouse followed behind. As Kat walked through the opening from the Stronghold, she slipped on the fur hood and donned her thickest gloves.

Soon all four of them were in the middle of whirling snow, which crunched underfoot. This time, however as they descended the mountain, the bitter wind howled at them from behind. The trip down the mountain seemed less onerous, and the only task facing Kat required careful footing through the icy patches on the path. *This is much easier than the trip up. I won't be as exhausted when we arrive at Halfway Haven.*

She glanced back at Mouse, bundled up in his own fur robes, who did not appear to suffer the descent. This time his face was relaxed, not pinched and frozen.

They reached Halfway Haven in far less time than the climb up seven days before, and the apprentices and the stable master at the Haven helped them load their baggage on one of the pontis.

Mouse suggested they partake of a brief midturn meal, for which Kat's stomach expressed gratitude. Once they completed eating, they headed back to the stable and their waiting pontis. Mouse helped Kat to mount one, and he climbed aboard the other. They set off down the trail toward the Ponti Inn, with Mouse in the lead.

Even riding down hurts the butt. Kat called ahead to him. "Pontis are not comfortable animals to ride. I'm going to need a hot bath to ease the aches and pains tonight."

He turned back in his saddle. "They may not be well padded, but they are the surest footed animals for these mountains. Plus Shendeans possess more padding in their seats, so they do not complain as much as you."

Kat glared at him through snow covered eyelashes." I'm not complaining. I'm only warning you. I'll need a properly heated bath."

***

The stable master at the Ponti Inn greeted them with smiles. "We are glad you returned to claim your horses. They eat much more than our small pontis, so we are most pleased our own animals are back in their place." He hastened to help Kat off her ponti, and for once, far too stiffened up from the ride, she failed to object. "One of my assistants will deliver your luggage to your rooms. He will retrieve them on the morrow, and load them on your own pack animal."

Kat managed a faint groan of thanks.

When Mouse opened the sizable door to the inn, the blast of heat and chorus of voices assaulted Kat and she stopped short. The aromas of roasting meats curled around her nostrils and pangs of hunger enticed her to enter the dining hall. The innkeeper, anticipating their arrival, spied them and rushed to seat these important customers.

"My Lady, Sire, we just began serving our evening meal, so I will set aside choice items for you both." He motioned to a serving girl and ordered her to bring hot flagons of near-ale to the table.

Kat, seated in a plump chair beside the roaring fireplace, lifted her cup and swallowed the beverage gratefully. "Oh, wonderful. This stuff is delicious." Her fur-lined coat, flung over the back of the chair, added another soft layer of comfort. "You know, Mouse, I think I'm going to live."

"I never suspected a stiff and sore body indicated death."

"You're being very literal."

A bemused expression crossed his face. "I intended to be humorous."

"Whatever." Kat, more relaxed, gazed around the room at the mix of inhabitants from most of the lands of Pridden. Six men from Glowen, given the huge glasses of Orenberry wine on their table, and their flushed faces, roared with laughter at a shared joke.

I wonder if any of them are bonded, given what Hesginn told me?

From the table next to them, one of the men, pale faced and more somber in his appearance, leaned toward the Glowens. "Do you have Orenberry wine for sale."

The man pulled two bottles of his wine from beneath the table. "Naturally we do." The two tables proceeded to barter with each other.

A noise at the entrance to the main hall attracted Kat's attention, and she watched as eight Rifellan men and women, dressed as guards, entered and proceeded to a special table the innkeeper reserved for them. They were expected guests. On the right shoulders of their outfits, they sported the colors of Rhognor's Stronghold. Grateful she had consumed plenty of Karri-san. Kat admired the strong lines of their bodies and their confident presence. *Man, oh man. They are gorgeous.*

Reluctantly tearing her eyes away from the Rifellans, she scanned the room and chuckled to herself, observing a table of Baklai who eyed suspiciously the group of Mordens seated on the opposite side of the room. The color in the hall came from Shendeans encompassing many professions.

At this point, Kat's meal arrived and the bouquet of cooked meats reminded her of heavenly foods experienced in the past. She and Mouse attacked their meals with gusto.

With two substantial flagons of near-ale, and fine food filling her belly, Kat had reached the stage of a relaxed and sleepy mood. "Mouse, I'm asleep on my feet. I'm going to skip the hot bath — I'll take a quick shower and tumble straight into bed.

"I understand. I, too, shall not keep my bed waiting."

Grabbing her coat from the back of the chair, Kat, with the help of an apprentice, located her room. Once inside, she withdrew food for Wink, fed her, and helped Breen from the side pocket of her back-pack. The boradai headed for the bed and curled up on the pillow.

A brief shower later, and Kat fell into bed, asleep within minutes.

***

A loud purr interfered with Kat's dreams of cathnogs stalking her. "Really Breen, you make more noise than a roomful of tigers." She stretched out her hand to pat the Boradai and still her snoring. As she touched the fur beside her, she froze. Something much bigger than Breen lay there. The purring increased in volume. Kat moved her hand up the warm body, terrified to open her eyes and glimpse what lay beside her. When she could stand the suspense no longer, she peeked from behind her lashes. A sliver of moonlight revealed two brilliant emerald green eyes, which stared back at her. Unable to move or call out, Kat, and what appeared to be an immense black panther, regarded each other. The panther opened an enormous mouth, revealing a capacious collection of sharp shiny ivory teeth. Instead of biting her, a long pink tongue reached out and licked her shoulder. Heart pounding, Kat forced herself to breathe. *Am I dreaming?* She reached for her stone and discovered the necklace warm and comfortable on her chest. Her hand landed on a smaller furry body.

"Breen. What is going on?"

"You may relax Kat. This is Shade. She is only here to protect you. I like her."

Kat opened her eyes completely and regarded the huge coal black animal lying beside her. Shade's coat gleamed in the moonlight, and the beautiful emerald eyes glowed. *Is this a coincidence? Her eyes are the exact color of my stone.* "Where did you come from?"

The cat purred, stretched out, settled the massive head on the pillow beside her, and closed its eyes.

She touched Breen again. *"Is she issuing an invitation to go back to sleep?"*

The furry boradai yawned, revealing a row of much smaller needle sharp teeth. *"I believe sleeping would be best for us all. You are safe Kat. Relax."*

The effects of the adrenaline rush slowly drained from Kat's body, and she sank back in the squishy down of her bed. With one hand on Breen and one on Shade, sleep overtook her and she drifted off.

* * *

A beam of early sunlight pierced her closed eyelids, and bird sounds penetrated Kat's brain. She sat up and stretched. *Sun. Goody, I think the snow has stopped.*

On a fluffy rug in the middle of her room streched a glossy ebony feline. Wow, *she's even bigger than the cathnog we ran into.* When Kat's feet hit the floor, the animal raised its head exposing those brilliant emerald eyes. The cat yawned, baring a set of substantial, alabaster teeth, which Kat no longer found alarming, since Shade, her protector, did not trigger a response in the stone lodged over her heart. Kat chuckled. Breen, curled in a ball between the cat's forelegs, with one small foot resting on a massive paw adorned with lengthy claws, seemed minuscule in comparison.

"You two can sleep, but I'm hungry and I need a shower." Throwing her nightclothes on a chair, she entered the stall and basked in a refreshing fall of hot water. Ponti induced aches melted and she stretched luxuriously under the steamy cascade.

Dressed in her Rifellan leather outfit, she fed Wink and headed for the eating hall to enjoy a morning meal. Before she could close Shade and Breen in her room, the powerful cat, with Breen curled up on her back, slipped out the door and padded beside her.

Entering the hall, Kat caught sight of Mouse signaling to her to join him. "I requested your Karri-san tea, but unsure as to your choices for the meal, did not order for you." Mouse made no comment about Shade.

Kat seated herself, and Shade sat beside her, tail curled over her paws similar to a house cat. "Don't you detect anything different?"

"Indeed I do. The leather outfit you are wearing makes you resemble a Rifellan. And one of noble birth too."

"No. I mean the cat,"

Mouse gazed at her, his expression blank. "Cat? Are you wearing some ornament with the depiction of a cat?"

Kat glanced around the room at the other diners, and the wait-staff apprentices. Not one person paid any attention to Shade. *Can't they see her?* Kat reached down and touched Breen.

"They cannot discern Shade. She is invisible to them, as am I when I am in contact with her."

Kat glanced at Mouse. "Sorry — I hoped you'd noticed my cat bracelet, but I realize I'm not wearing it, so I guess I left the thing in the room."

Mouse appeared thoroughly confused by her words, but said nothing.

She looked up at an attendant who requested her morning meal order. Kat ordered the thick nutty porridge she usually ate. "I believe the name is journeyklim?"

The attendant smiled and nodded. "You are correct, my lady."

"So, Mouse, do we leave right after this meal?"

He nodded. "When we are done eating, return to your room, pack your belongings, and leave your biggest bag in the hallway. You will need a much lighter coat, so meet me at the stables and we will leave on the next phase of our journey."

***

After the meal, Kat rose, followed by Breen and Shade, returned to her room to complete her packing. With her bag outside the door, about to don her back-pack, Kat put her hand on Breen. *"Do you want to jump into the side pocket of my pack?"*

"No. I shall travel on Shade. She is warm and comfortable and I like her."

Kat shrugged. "Fine, it's up to you. *I suspect this is going to be a most interesting journey."*

CHAPTER 17

By the time Kat arrived at the stables, the packhorse loaded, and this time attached to Kat's saddle again, she found Mouse already mounted, and apparently impatient. "We will enjoy time to relax, but not today. Reaching Finrase before dark is important. I suggest we depart. Now."

Kat climbed aboard her horse. *No wonder Rifellan women wear these outfits. I can move easily. Thank you Brith.* She glanced over at Mouse. *He's crotchety. I wonder what's eating him.* "If you'd warned me the previous evening, I would have hurried. I can't read your mind, you realize."

Mouse twitched his mouth, turned his horse around and headed down the trail, leaving Kat to follow with the pack animal attached.

The snow ceased overnight and now the sun peered intermittently through the clouds. Kat, comfortable even with a lighter coat, pointed her face to the sky and absorbed the warm caress of Pridden's star. Shade padded silently in front of her, sometimes taking the lead for both her and Mouse. *He doesn't spook the horses. Don't they observe him, or are they comfortable around him? I wonder?*

Mouse changed position from lead to tail end frequently. Both he and Kat rode without speaking, Kat immersed in thoughts of her games, and Mouse frowning. Kat assumed his unpleasant mood lingered.

The rhythm of the journey down the mountain, lulled Kat into leisurely thoughts of games and words, and a remembrance of home, disturbed only by the crunch of dry leaves and packed snow, and the occasional clop of a horse's hoof on the odd bare stones in the pathway.

Without warning, Kat's horse, now in the lead, danced in place and whinnied. Breen disappeared from Shade's back, and the fur along the cat's spine bristled. The three horses stopped and attempted to turn back along the trail. Mouse forced his mount to ride beside Kat, but the animal's eyes were rolling in panic. From the trail ahead a cathnog appeared, snarling, teeth bared, ready for battle.

"Kat, turn back."

Before Mouse could do or say anything further, Shade roared and challenged the cathnog. The attacking animal answered with a guttural cry. Shade, who outweighed the cathnog advanced on the other beast and bared vicious fangs.

While terrifying, the two reminded Kat of a couple of alpha males posturing for position. *I should be more afraid, but my stone is warm.*

Shade continued to advance on the cathnog, both of them claiming dominion over the other. But Shade's larger body mass and more aggressive stance slowly forced the cathnog to retreat, belly to the ground. Shade's final victorious cry forced the other animal to turn tail and run.

During this battle of wills, Kat fought to keep her horse from bolting, but as Shade returned to her side, the animal calmed and stood still. The packhorse ceased pulling at the line attached to Kat's saddle.

***

Mouse, as he battled for control of his horse, watched the cathnog disappear, and astonished, his mouth hung open as he stared down the trail. He remembered his attempt to force his way in front of Kat at the appearance of the fearsome animal, but his agitated mount proved difficult to control. Twice the horse turned to run back up the trail and twice, by sheer strength, he forced the animal to turn toward the approaching beast.

He failed to understand why the cathnog ceased his movements forward, but continued to roar and bare teeth. Every movement of the cathnog and his horse appeared to slow down and time became liquid. What astonished him more, was when the animal began to back away from them, dropped his belly to the ground, and his growls grew fainter. Without warning, the creature turned and raced back down the trail. *What the… . What happened?*

He pulled his horse beside Kat's "What happened a moment ago?"

Kat turned to him, her eyes shining. "Shade saved us."

"Shade?"

"Yes. Can't you see her?"

"What?"

"Shade. She's an enormous black cat, like a panther."

"I see no such cat."

"She's over there." She pointed at a bare spot on the trail.

Mouse stared at her, shaking his head. "Nothing."

"I'll show you. I'll ask my boradai to jump on her back again." She closed her eyes and pursed her lips.

Mouse observed the boradai climb from Kat's backpack, leap from the horse and just before hitting the ground, vanished from sight. *Am I losing my mind?* "Kat, your boradai disappeared."

"Oh. You can't see either of them?"

"No." Mouse rubbed his eyes. Still nothing. "Where did this invisible cat come from?"

Kat shrugged her shoulders. "I don't know. She appeared last night in my room. Breen, my boradai said she is here to protect me. She doesn't scare the horses, but I'm not sure if they understand she's here. I'm aware others don't appear to discern her, but I thought since you saw the cathnog's reactions, you might be able to."

"Describe her to me, please."

"Well, she's completely black, except her eyes are emerald green."

"Are her eyes the same color as your stone?"

Kat clutched at her clothes over her heart. "How do you know about my stone?"

"Wynneth told me. She decided I should understand about the stone warning you of danger, since I am to guide you through Pridden. She thought I should be aware of any protections you might possess."

Kat stared at him and shrugged. "I guess that makes sense."

Mouse gawked at her. He pulled on the reins of his horse and indicated he would take the lead. "We should continue on to Finrase. We must arrive at the inn before dark."

Kat nodded.

"I believe we would be well served if you would request Shade to precede us down the trail. Would you do so?"

"I don't talk to her. She only does what she does when she wants to."

Eduardo, you handed me a huge chore. And Kat, who are you? What other powers do you possess?

CHAPTER 18

"Crazy." Kat gaped in awe at the hot, red lava cone outlined against the deepening dusk of evening. "Volcanoes have always fascinated me."

Mouse eyed the fiery crimson oozing down the side of the pinnacle piercing the sky. "Shendeans do not use the word volcano. This is Burning Rock Mountain… the only one in existence in all Pridden."

"Can we approach closer in the morning?"

"Not much. Burning Rock is unpredictable. We rarely receive warning when explosions and rivers of fire will erupt from the peak, and occasionally, scorching streams will burst from further down."

"How beautiful, and how dangerous." Kat, transfixed by the flaming lava flow, dotted with blue flames in places, and melding with the yellow, pinks and mauves of the sunset, absorbed the play of color. She spied a sign to her right, painted with an icon representing a bubbling muddy pool. "Is the Crimson Cauldron located down the pathway to the right?"

"Yes, and the inn is around the next turn, so there is time to obtain our rooms and if you wish it, to avail yourself of a visit to the Cauldron before dinner." He grinned. "One should never visit the Cauldron after a meal. The repercussions are not pleasant."

They rounded the bend in the trail and Kat kicked her horse into a trot, eager to experience the hot mud baths. *A spa. Oh joy, oh rapture.*

The stable-master relieved them of their horses, and summoning an apprentice, informed them he would deliver their baggage to their rooms, and their horses would be well fed and watered. Mouse murmured his thanks, and led Kat through the doors of the inn.

A tall, portly man in a pale yellow robe approached them. "Lady Kat, Sire, your baggage is on the way to your rooms. Are you ready for your evening meal?"

Kat answered him. "No, we will visit the Crimson Cauldron first, and eat later."

"Ah, yes." The innkeeper turned to Mouse. "I should caution you Sire, evenings at the Cauldron are not well attended."

Mouse nodded.

As they headed to their rooms, he called out to Kat. "We will meet at the Cauldron. Follow the signs, because the mud pools are close to this inn." He stopped. "Oh yes, bring your spring bow. The innkeeper warned us few people are at the Cauldron, and on occasion, unpleasant characters are known to frequent the area."

I wonder what he means by unpleasant?

Kat found her way to her room, and once in, she fed Wink and deposited her back in her cage. She pointed Breen toward the plush bed covering. The boradai climbed on the bed, circled three times, curled up in a ball, and fell asleep within minutes. Shade disappeared moments before they entered the inn. Now clad in loose clothing, Kat set off for the Cauldron.

She arrived at a small building beside the mud pools, and as directed went in for instruction about how to obtain the best enjoyment from the mud experience. She chose a change room, and after hanging her own clothes from a peg, donned the suit she needed to wear in the hot mud. The suit covered most of her, but fitted like a second skin, so she threw a brown robe over the pool wear. The young apprentice told her to remove the robe at the edge of the mud pool, and to enter wearing only the suit. She chuckled to herself. *What would these people think if they saw how we use hot tubs?*

Exiting her change room, she found Mouse, up to his neck in the ooze, relaxing amid the slowly bubbling mud. The smell of sulphur stung her eyes and nose. *Ugh rotting eggs. But everyone claims there are health benefits from pools like these.*

"I shall keep my eyes shut until you enter the pool, Kat."

"As you wish." *Like I care if you see me in this suit.* She removed her robe, laid the plush covering beside the pool, and slipped into the heated mud, opposite to Mouse. "This is heaven, my muscles are loosening and my aches dissolving."

He opened his eyes and smiled. "Indeed." He closed his eyes again and lay back against the side of the pool.

Both remained silent. The mud bubbled like viscous chocolate, hot, but smelly. Kat could sense muscles turning to rubber and tension bleeding from her body. Even her brain quieted. *I will sleep like a child tonight — with nothing but sweet dreams and a body well rested.*

Time passed and the two travelers lay in mud, easing stressed bodies, and calming equally stressed minds.

"Kat. We can only remain in the pool for a limited time. We need to leave and return to the inn. I will exit first, and I request you do not open your eyes until I am robed once more."

"Fine." Kat kept her eyes shut, but ultimately couldn't help herself, and risked a peek. All she caught was a flash of a male body as Mouse put on his robe. *Darn, missed him.*

She waited until Mouse entered his change room, and then left the mud pool herself. *Best not to disturb his sensibilities.*

In the change room, she showered, placed the robe and body suit in the container provided, and dressed in her own clothes. She picked up her spring bow and armed it. *Now why'd I do that?*

She felt marvelous — clean and renewed, but her stomach emitted a faint grumble indicating a desire for food. *Odd. My skin is so warm, my stone seems cold by comparison.*

She emerged to find Mouse waiting on the path back to the inn. Without warning a hooded man with a raised sword appeared and charged him from behind.

As she yelled ,"Watch out," Kat raised her bow and shot the man in the chest, at the same time as Mouse stormed toward her, a magnificent jeweled dagger in his hand. She ducked to the side, and Mouse stabbed at another assailant whose club threatened to crush Kat's skull, and who dropped as he ran into the dagger clutched in Mouse's hand. Kat, aghast, breathing heavily, adrenaline racing through her body, gaped open-mouthed at Mouse. "Are you alright?"

"Yes. You?"

She nodded. "The lovely relaxed feeling from the mud bath? I think it's been replaced."

"Agreed." Mouse bent over the man Kat shot, and wrenched the arrow from his body. As Kat watched him, he strode to a stream of clear water and washed the point thoroughly. He handed the weapon to her and she returned the arrow to her quiver.

Kat folded the limbs of the spring bow against the barrel, a benefit she recently discovered, which allowed her to use less space to pack the bow in her luggage.

Mouse stepped to the other man and removed his dagger from the chest of the attacker, which he also cleansed in the stream. He inserted the blade in an ornate leather sheath, and hid them both beneath his cloak.

"What will we do with the bodies, Mouse?" Kat still breathed heavily.

"I will need to speak with someone at the inn. They will be taken care of." His glance at her seemed thoughtful. "What I want to find out is how they knew we would be here."

"You think someone targeted us?"

"I do." He glanced around the area. "Nothing here now indicates our presence. We should proceed to the inn for our meal. Let them seat you and I will join your in a few moments."

Kat nodded once again, and walked briskly along the path back to the inn, her breathing slowing, and the prickle of excess adrenaline abating. *Mouse stepped up and handled himself well. I never expected him to react so quickly. Did I misjudge his abilities? Again?*

CHAPTER 19

Kat, seated at a table near a group of Shendean healers, raised the flagon of near-ale to her lips and drank three sizable gulps. The apprentice advised food would arrive soon, and from the mouth-watering aromas, Kat suspected wullawerth stew. Next to gornog meat, this was her favorite.

She raised eyes from her cup and spied Mouse entering the inn's dining area. He showed signs of being smaller and greyer than ever. *He did handle himself well at the Cauldron.* He appeared challenged though, by the encounter with the two attackers.

He walked to join Kat and sat. "I solved the body problem. However, I am weary and will need to sleep much longer this night. I suspect you will wish to do likewise."

Kat nodded at him. "I agree. I need to rest my body soon."

"We shall stay in Finrase for an additional night, so you may delay your rising on the morrow."

"Thanks, Mouse, I'd appreciate the opportunity to sleep in."

The innkeeper, who appeared familiar with those who soaked in the mud baths, served them both a light meal, but despite a stomach, which demanded plenty of food, Kat ate sparingly. *I'm knackered. Too much to eat and I'll sleep badly and experience nightmares.*

Both their plates remained unfinished.

The young woman who cleared their table, smiled at them. "You attended the Cauldron, correct? You are wise to eat lightly after a visit to our mud pools."

Mouse glanced at her and murmured his thanks. He stood. "Kat, forgive me, but I must leave you before I fall asleep at this table."

Kat rose as well, barely able to keep her eyes open. "Absolutely. My bed's calling too. The relaxing mud, then the challenge after, took a lot of energy from me."

They left the dining hall and each headed in the direction of their rooms.

Kat entered her door, and with a groggy glance at Breen, staggered over to her bed, discarding clothes on the way. *"Move Breen."* She grabbed at the comforter, slid beneath the sheets, and slept.

At some point in the night, the bed creaked and warm breath, purrs, and a furry head rubbing along her jawline, woke her momentarily before she drifted back into dreamland.

* * *

The stamp of hooves on stone, men shouting at each other, and wagons creaking, penetrated Kat's conscious mind. Plus her back felt cold. She sat up and discovered most of the covers had been pulled off her during the night. Shade, lying in the center of the bed, raised her head and opened one green eye.

Kat shook her finger at the animal. "You're a blanket hog, you oaf. And there's no need to use the entire bed. Try taking my blanket again, and you'll sleep on the floor."

Shade yawned exposing prodigious fangs.

"Just because you've got colossal teeth, doesn't mean you can bully me, you obnoxious feline." *I hope she doesn't take offense. Her teeth are huge.*

Jumping from her bed, Kat strode to the personal, but stopped in mid thought. *I just remembered a word for my list.*

Brobdingnagian. I saw the word in a dinosaur book I gave Nick's kids. It meant something mountainous.

Grinning to herself she continued to the personal, where she luxuriated in the stream of hot water flowing over her. Dressed again in her Rifellan leathers, she collected her clothes from the floor where she'd discarded them the previous night.

Summoned by Wink's anxious squeaks, she stuffed food into the pyrock, and before heading for the dining area for her morning meal, paused long enough to add Brobdingnagian to her word list. She seated herself at an empty table, and ordered food and drink from the serving girl. *I don't see Mouse. I wonder if he's already eaten.*

She glanced at the entrance, in time to catch Mouse walking toward her. He appeared less grey this morning.

"Good morrow, Kat. You are now well rested. May I join you?"

Kat raised an eyebrow. "Of course, why would you ask such a thing?"

"You might not wish to be reminded of the dangers of last evening."

"Mouse. I'm not a shrinking violet, you know. And before you ask — merely an expression."

Mouse held up his hands. "I assumed the phrase originated from your world. I did not intend to question your words. Attempting to remember all your odd expressions is tiring." He paused to request food and drink from the young female who appeared at the table, and turned back to Kat. "I must handle some items, and prefer to spend most of the day resting. You may desire to visit the professionals who offer other relaxing treatments, or perhaps inspect some of the shops of Finrase."

"Possibly. I'm still experiencing the effects of the Cauldron, so I may also choose to do little. Plus I need to complete some writing of my own."

Two apprentices brought their food to them. Kat viewed the nutty porridge-like dish with pleasure and poured a creamy topping over the contents. She spooned a considerable amount in her mouth. *Oh this is so yummy.*

She glanced over at Mouse, tucking into a similar dish with obvious relish. "So tell me about the Thieves Guild."

"I am surprised you have not expressed more curiosity about the men who attacked us the previous evening."

"Neither of us know who they were, and until we find out more about our attackers, there is little to discuss."

"You ae correct." Mouse placed his spoon beside his bowl. "So you do wish to know more about the Thieves' Guild. This is difficult to describe to one who has not been privy to information about them before. I believe you consider thieves to be those who steal things from others?"

She nodded.

Mouse regarded her with a horrified expression on his face. "The Thieves' Guild do not steal anything. They reverse time."

Kat swallowed. "Time?"

"Yes. The Thieves' Guild helps to reverse time for those who chose between two options, but are now convinced they did so incorrectly, and regret the choice they made. Thus, they wish to take back the time, and decide to follow what they now consider to be the better option."

"Why would anyone want to change their past? Our past creates us and molds who we now are. Personally I would not wish to change anything in my past."

Mouse smiled, picked up his spoon and ate another mouthful of food. He swallowed. "You are speaking, Kat, from the position of a person who is reasonably balanced in her life. Many are not sufficiently happy with their lives, as they often lived without purpose, without direction, and drifted. They are the ones who wish to change past events."

"You wouldn't want to change your past, would you?"

"No, I would not. My life contains direction and strong purpose."

"What is your purpose?"

He smiled at her and shrugged. "I am not the subject here. These people are able to re-live their time from the point of their original choice."

"So, do they choose the best way for themselves, and do they use their new direction wisely?"

"To our regret, frequently not. Helping someone change a past decision is not done without challenge, nor frivolously. The entire Guild is required to be present. This is why we take care to research the applicant, the selection they made, and how they lived with their original choice. Only two or three people are selected to re-live their lives during a path of our star. Sometimes none qualify."

"Amazing. I wish I could attend a ceremony."

"You are fortunate. One man is approved, and they will hold the rite when we arrive at the Guild. You will understand what we do much better than I can explain in words."

Kat rose. "Thank you. I am going to check out the town, and perhaps locate a relaxing treatment as well. I need to complete some writing, so perhaps we can meet for the evening meal?"

He nodded. "Excellent idea."

***

Kat wandered through Finrase, admiring small shops, which sold potions, jewelry, clothing and a variety of shoes and accessories. She approached a tiny shop whose sign offered body manipulation, according to icon. *Sounds like massage to me.* She entered, and asked the young woman at the counter what services they supplied.

"Did you taken advantage of the Cauldron, my Lady?"

"I did. Last evening."

"The only service which we suggest for you is the complete back manipulation."

"Sounds perfect. Uhm… you should invoice the Stronghold for my treatment — tell them I am Lady Kat."

"Of course, Lady Kat. We are familiar with your name."

Kat raised her eyebrows in surprise. *Phones don't exist here, nor does the internet, yet somehow everyone seems to know about me in advance. Kinda creepy.*

Kat, directed to a small change room, received a long white robe to cover her. When clad in the robe, the woman directed her to another room, where a second assisstant waited to attend to her. She lay prone on a raised bed, and the young woman began the massage. Kat groaned in ecstasy. At one point the woman mounted the bed and walked up Kat's spine, treading with care. She experienced a series of cricks and crackles, and her entire spine became loose and flexible. Once the attendant completed the manipulation, she placed a warm blanket over the spinal area, and invited Kat to relax.

All rubbery and calm, she fell asleep on the bed, and woke when she recognized the sound of the attendant as she entered the room again. She heard the young woman rubbing something into her hands, and beautiful perfumes filled the air. Two well-oiled, warm hands began to massage Kat's feet. She drifted off again.

She woke again to the sound of the door opening, and the attendant removed the warm blanket from her. She suggested Kat sit up gradually.

She sat, her mind clear and alert, and her entire body soothed and calm. She breathed in the scents of the aromatic oils in the air. *Perfect. I can spend time writing for my games.*

Kat left the shop and headed for her room at the inn. *I'm not hungry now — somehow the massage removed my hunger, so I'll take a short nap, write some pages, and I should be in time to meet Mouse for the evening meal.*

***

Mouse departed the dining lounge, and headed for his room at the inn. *I must report to Galdin.* He rummaged in his backpack and produced the small packet holding the messenger moths Galdin handed him at their last meeting.

He slipped out a single moth, and placed his mouth close to the head of the creature. He attempted a slight tremble to his voice and whispered to the moth. "Master, I managed to pry the woman loose from the Stronghold. We are headed for the Thieves' Guild, and after leaving the area, should be able to journey to the Magicians' Guild. I am aware a passage exists through mountains which leads to Morden, located a short distance from the Guild. I will attempt to lure her to the passage and should be able to bring her to you."

With the message recorded with the moth, Mouse picked the creature up, opened his window, and threw the feathery messenger out. He watched the moth wing its way toward Morden.

I hope Galdin believes my message. He must control a spy here. How else did those men find out where we were?

CHAPTER 20

Mouse appeared subdued during the evening meal.

"What's eating you, Mouse?"

Mouse stared at her. "Eating me? I do not understand."

Kat sighed in exasperation. She covered her face with her hands and shook her head. "We may speak the same language, but my expressions confuse everyone. I become frustrated at times. What I should say is — what's troubling you?"

"Ah." He began to laugh. "Eating me. An amusing expression, and yet apt somehow." Still chuckling, he nodded his head. "Eating me." He leaned on the table with his elbows, supporting his chin with his clasped hands. "I am concerned. How did last evening's attackers discover we would be at the Cauldron?"

"Perhaps we can help each other."

Mouse straightened in his chair. "How?"

Kat pulled a piece of folded parchment from her pocket. "I received a message via pyrock from Deleth when I returned to my room after my midturn meal. My ability to translate pyrock writing is limited, and I don't understand everything she's telling me. Perhaps if you read the note to me, both of us will be better informed." She passed the message to Mouse.

He read over the dispatch.

Kat peered at him, eyebrows raised. "Can you read the note aloud, so I can understand what's happening?"

He glanced up at her. "Forgive me." He read from the note. "Deleth says our travel plans appear to be the subject of discussions at the Stronghold. Rhognor is incensed his plans are known by many before he had a chance to announce anything. However, he has no idea who spread the information. Deleth believes a spy is hiding at the Stronghold — one who does not have your best interests in mind. She is concerned you may be in danger. She says Rhognor is furious and insisted Hesginn discover the identity of the spy, and severely punish him, or her." He gave the parchment back to Kat. "This does explain how the attackers were apprised of our whereabouts."

"So what can I do about all this? I'm not Hesginn's favorite person."

"You mean, what can WE do about this?" He stared at her, a puzzled expression on his face. "Wait. What do you mean, not Hesginn's favorite person?"

"Nothing much. I made an assumption about his preferences and he took offense."

"If Rhognor requested Hesginn do something, it will be done, regardless of any disagreement between the two of you."

"If you say so."

"To answer your previous question. We need to be vigilant."

"Vigilant." Kat snorted. "This could be solved immediately if you sent me home."

Mouse sighed. "What little I am privy to, suggests neither Eduardo nor Rhognor possess sufficient power themselves. But you and I can change things in our favor to foil the spy."

"How?"

"I will revise our schedule. When I return to my room, I will consult the maps again, and plan a new route. You should retire early, and be ready to leave on the morrow. Order your morning meal in your room, but do this early, and only then, call an apprentice to deliver your bags to the stable. I will meet you with the horses as close to dawn as possible."

"Fine. I'll enlist Breen's help to wake me in time."

They both rose and headed for their rooms.

***

Kat brought her writing up to date, and packed everything except the clothes she planned to wear the following day. Her Rifellan outfit, cleaned and oiled, hung on the closet door.

She stroked Breen. *"Will you wake me in time for me to dress, eat a morning meal, and meet Mouse at the stables at dawn?"*

"I will. I shall request your pyrock refrain from making noise on the morrow, until we are an adequate distance from the inn."

"Thank you."

"Kat, Shade and I are here to be of assistance to you. There is no need to thank us for performing the tasks assigned us."

Kat sighed. *"Breen, so many people express annoyance when I miss performing what they consider courtesies, I prefer to attempt to be courteous whenever possible. So you and Shade must accept this."*

Breen uttered a series of what sounded like snuffling sneezes.

"Breen, have you got a cold? Oh no, what do I give a boradai for a cold?"

"Cold? From your mind I believe a cold is a sickness prevalent in your land. Relax, Kat. I expressed humor, similar to what people do when they find something amusing and make a loud noise to indicate the comical aspect."

Kat laughed.

"Yes, that is the noise."

Kat rolled her eyes and shaking her head, headed to the personal. *If I shower now, I can skip one in the morning.*

When she exited the personal, she gazed around the room. With everything packed, in the morning she only needed to pop Breen in the side pocket of her backpack, and carry Wink's travel cage.

She slipped beneath cool crisp sheets, and Shade jumped up beside her. "Don't hog all the bed tonight, okay?"

Shade purred and butted at Kat's hand. She massaged the cat's ears, and the purrs increased in intensity, lulling Kat to sleep.

***

The night, still dark when Shade's insistent head butts woke Kat from a sound, restful sleep, almost failed to stir her. "Rats, time to get up already?"

Shade's answer, another head butt to Kat's chin. Reluctant to rise, she threw off the covers and headed for the personal. *I need another quick shower, to wake me up.* She chose a final rinse of cold water, which succeeded in bringing her to full consciousness.

Tugging the cord for her morning meal, she dressed hastily, and was ready when a knock signaled the delivery of food. "Would you ask an apprentice to take my bag to the stable, please."

The young woman nodded. "Right away, Lady Kat." She exited the room

By the time Kat finished her meal, with her bag on its way to the stable, she opened the side pocket in her backpack. However, Breen jumped on Shade's back and sat preening herself. *"Suit yourself, Breen."*

Although not in physical contact with the boradai, Kat assumed the slight nod from the creature indicated her intention to travel atop Shade. Picking up Wink's travel cage, the group of them set out to meet Mouse.

The Finrase inn boasted a complicated arrangement of rooms and passageways, and twice, the panther steered Kat into a different corridor. She assumed, after hearing muted conversations from the avoided sections, Shade intended to lead her to her destination without the need to meet other people.

Exiting through the doors of the inn, Kat and her entourage, met Mouse holding the reins of two horses. He'd attached the pack animal to his horse this time.

"Excellent. Your timing is perfect. Did you meet anyone in the halls?"

"No. Shade steered me away from people in the passages."

"Ah yes. The cat." He glanced around obviously attempting to spy the black animal, and finally shrugged and mounted his horse.

Kat, with the freedom offered by her Rifellan leathers, placed her foot in the stirrup and hoisted herself aboard her own animal. They set off on the next part of their journey.

Once out of hearing of the inn, Mouse stopped in a small clearing. "I changed our route. Instead of heading for Glazenwyth, we will travel to the Kroakin woods and spend the night at Dizerth. Leaving this early will ensure we arrive well before dusk. We can spend at least two days, which I believe you will enjoy. The people of Dizerth are artists in wood."

"They sound interesting."

"I persuaded the kitchen at the inn to pack food for us, and we can stop for a rest near the entrance to the woods, and consume a midturn meal."

"Wonderful, because I didn't eat much at my morning meal — too early for me. If we are forced to wait until the evening to eat again, I'd probably need to snack on a horse."

Mouse grimaced. "Horses are too valuable to eat."

Kat sighed. "I'm joking." *This journey appears longer and longer every day. I hope I can last.*

CHAPTER 21

The path along which they rode, wound around trees and sharp outcroppings of the lower mountain. Easy underfoot for the horses, the motion hypnotized Kat, and she mused about what her life would be like when she returned home.

The weeks in Pridden mounted up. *Is anyone missing me? Does a job exist to go back to?*

The bark of the trees reminded her of heavily textured fabric, familiar somehow. *Cedar trees. They remind me of cedar trees.* Her horse brushed against some low-growing bushes, and released hundreds of pink and white butterflies. Shade with undignified haste chased the cloud of them. When she caught one in her mouth, she wrinkled her nose and sneezed. She attempted to spit out the little insect, and pawed at her mouth. At last, she spied a brackish pool of water, and with much sneezing and spitting, managed to drink from the pool. Muzzle dripping, she loped on with only an occasional sneeze, leaving the butterflies unmolested. Kat laughed aloud at her antics.

Mouse trotted up beside her. "Why are you laughing?"

Kat grinned at him. "Shade. She ate one of those flying insects and the thing must taste nasty. She's been pawing at her mouth and spitting"

"Interesting."

"What's interesting."

"If your invisible black cat hailed from Shendea, she would be acquainted with the foul tang of those flyers. Since she is not, she must be from some other land."

I wonder. Her eyes are the same color as my stone. Did Liandock… ?

Mouse trotted his horse to take the lead. "The spring in front of you is the head of Carrog Mannin. This river runs through Shendea to the Great Mannin Falls, which empty into the Gogleth Sea. Many who travel to the Thieves' Guild use this waterway — a more rapid route than the one we will use. However, the river is swift and turbulent, and travelers must end their journey at the Mannin bridge, or they will be swept over the falls to their deaths."

"If the river is so dangerous, why would anyone travel on it?"

"Those who wish to enlist the aid of the Thieves' Guild usually desire to solve what they consider untenable situations, as hastily as possible. The dangers of Carrog Mannin do not deter them." He grimaced. "Often, their challenges are solved by the deluge of the water."

"So they die."

"Yes." He shrugged. "If such a thing occurs, all believe Caleesh has deemed the outcome so."

Kat stared at him. *How fatalistic.* She stopped her horse, slid off the saddle, and began walking toward the spring. "Can I drink the water?"

"Do not get too close. There is much power in the stream. You may sample the river when we ride to the other side, where quieter pools form."

Kat stopped. The waters of the spring burst from the earth, a veritable jet of water feeding a series of waterfalls, and gathering momentum as the river surged down the mountain. She glanced back at Mouse, still astride his horse. "You're right. This river is treacherous." She remounted her horse. "Can we go to the pools to drink?"

Mouse nodded and led the two of them around the rocks from where Carrog Mannin gushed, and stopped when they reached a number of quieter pools. Both dismounted and drank, and the three horses dipped their noses in the water. Kat caught Shade lapping at the edge, at which point, Breen leaped off Shade's back and sprang in the pool, splashing and cavorting like a child.

Mouse laughed. "I am aware boradais enjoy water, but I never witnessed such actions before."

Breen continued to splash about, showering Kat, and batting at Shade's head. Kat, eager to take part in the fun, removed her boots, rolled her leathers up to her knees, and splattered both the animals. Shade growled and backed away from the pool, sneezing. She withdrew about four feet and sprang at Breen, creating a barrage of water, which covered Mouse, who, unaware of Shade's intentions, had been watching Kat and the boradai with a puzzled expression.

He sprang back, soaked. "What?"

Kat, desperately attempting to hide her amusement, could not respond. She shook with silent laughter.

Mouse's eyes shot daggers at her.

Powerless to hold in the laughter, Kat snorted. "Sorry." She had trouble speaking and laughing at the same time. "Shade jumped on Breen in the water." She doubled over in laughter once more.

Mouse's mouth twitched at the corners, and Shade and Breen exited the pool and shook themselves vigorously. Another shower of water and his scowl returned.

"We will take a short ride to the edge of the Kroakin woods and can stop for our midturn meal." He glared at Kat and the boradai. "By then we will be dry, provided of course, you are all finished playing like young offspring."

"Mouse. Lighten up. You must admit we enjoyed ourselves at the pools."

His mouth twitched at the corners again. "Amusing." He laughed. "Most amusing. However, I am experiencing hunger, and since you generally eat more than I do, I suspect you may be ravenous."

Kat's stomach complained. "Yes to food. Let's go."

***

The two of them ate and drank their fill, seated on a soft blanket in the middle of a miniature meadow at the entrance to the woods. Kat, tummy now happy, mounted her horse eagerly, anxious to meet the people of Dizerth.

They rode through the woods into a town seemingly out of an illustrated children's book, with neat red-roofed houses set side by side in a row, and streets laid out in a perfect square. The people they encountered stood two heads shorter than the majority of Shendeans, with happy rosy-cheeked faces, and colorful clothes, sporting shirts and pants for the men, and crisp blouses and skirts for the women. A portly individual approached them, wearing what appeared to be a chain of office, and accompanied them to a building to stable their horses.

"My name is Farnon, and I am the head for the village. We do not possess an inn in our town, but two or three families are more than amenable to welcoming guests in their homes. Bring your bags and I will take you to the Mazon family now."

"I am Lady Kat, Farnon, and this is my friend, Mouse." She gazed around her. "Your village is so well laid out and everything is neat. How did this come about?"

"I will give you our history as we walk to the Mazon family."

"Perfect."

The three of them walked on, Farnon carrying Kat's bag. "Many paths ago, we lived in villages in every part of Shendea. We never discovered why we did not grow as high as the average Shendean, and we failed to perform in many of the professions within our land. Over the seasons and paths we found others like ourselves, and most of us congregated in the Kroakin woods. We came to understand our differences, but living with others who are similar, we received the opportunity to create artworks and a life which suited us."

He paused at a display of toys and villages built of wood and painted in bright colors of red and green and blue. "This is an example of our work." Pride shone in his eyes.

Kat examined the largest of the miniature villages closely. The houses were carved with beautifully crafted patterns on doorways and windows, and trees and bushes were created from curls of wood, painted green. "These are exquisite, Mazon. I see each house bears a plaque with a carved name. What do they represent.?"

"Those are the names of the individuals who carved the piece, and are perfect replicas of their own homes."

Kat peered closer. "There are also tiny people. I wish I'd had a village like this to play with when I was a child."

"These are more than toys. Many people all over Pridden possess a model of their own homes, which they eventually pass on to their offspring. Our carvings became a history to many families in Shendea, and the popularity of keeping a family's history in a single carving works well for citizens who are not able to afford a tapestry."

"I assume as a result, any family could afford to possess a history of their life displayed as a work of art. Right?"

He smiled. "You understand what we created." He walked on. "We elected those most able to plan our village, and we built the houses we now live in from the models we created. One of our past leaders, Grand-master Dizerth became the first artist to make our models available as toys for children. He publicized them throughout Shendea. We are fortunate, a man in Finrase found our work to be so alluring, he created a pact with our village to travel about Shendea promoting our work to others. In his travels, he secured relations with people from other lands, who now sell our goods to markets throughout Pridden."

"What a wonderful story."

"We are indeed fortunate to live and work with our most passionate desires. None of us envision a life better than what we enjoy." He stopped outside a house larger than most. "Here we are at Mazon's home."

A man and woman stood at the door of their home, beaming welcome. After introductions by Farnon, Mazon himself insisted on carrying their bags to their assigned rooms. He smiled at the two of them. "You are invited to dine with our family, but we will give you time to relax and unpack before the evening meal."

Kat entered her room, and fed Wink. The little pyrock squeaked in appreciation and butted her furry head against her hand. Kat stroked the small creature before returning her to her cage. With a faint chirrup, Wink turned three times, curled in a ball, and promptly slept.

***

The two travelers spent the evening meal laughing and joking with the Mazon family. Mouse asked about more of their history and astonished Kat with his own knowledge about the people of Dizerth.

Darkness descended and Kat excused herself, desperate to gain the comfort of the welcoming bed. Once in her room, barely able to keep her eyes open, she dragged herself to bed, and spared little time considering their delightful hosts. *I wonder why they're so different from normal tall Shendeans? Sweet people… .*

CHAPTER 22

The foursome, although Mouse was still unable to see Shade, departed from Dizerth two star-turns later.

Mouse guided the group through the Kroakin woods. He called back to Kat. "These trees are a perfect hard wood for the people of Dizerth to use. While more difficult to carve, the wood does not flake or splinter, and maintains the integrity of the design. The wood takes paint without bleeding, and the carvings last many lifetimes."

His voice startled Kat who relished the silence as her horse ambled along the trail.

The floor of the woods, covered with yellow, green and brown needles muffled the horses' hooves. Only a shuffle and occasional crisp crunch of dry needles underfoot indicated their passing. Gentle breezes, despite being in the center of the forest, whispered among the trees. The woodland sighed and murmured, missing days long past, yet not forgotten.

When Kat failed to answer, Mouse glanced back at her, puzzlement on his face.

Kat, caught in the peaceful contemplation of the arboreal meditation, nodded to him, unwilling to disturb the tranquility with words aloud.

When they emerged from the woods, the clop of a hoof on a stone in the path woke Kat from her drifting meditation. She drew her horse up beside Mouse's. "I feel as if I woke from a deep nap. I'm rested and I'm able to ride for turns without needing sleep." She grinned at him. "But I'm hungry."

Mouse rolled his eyes. "Of course you are." He dismounted and led his horse to a bare patch of rock. "Mazon and his mate supplied us with food." He tied his mount to a spindly tree growing nearby, and when Kat dismounted, he attached hers to the same branch.

She removed the leather water flask from her saddle, and drank her fill. She lowered herself to a rocky seat, placed her water flask by her side, and reached for the food package Mouse extended to her. "I just realized the people of Dizerth don't eat meat, do they?"

"No. The fumes from Burning Rock Mountain and the Crimson Cauldron keep most animals at bay. But their land is rich in nutrients and their farm produce is lush and laden with excellent flavor."

"Mazon's mate is a fine cook, and I adore these cookies. They're crisp and full of nuts and fruit. Delicious."

The two completed their meal. Kat stood and brushed cookies crumbs from her clothing. "I know we must use the bridge to cross the Mannin River, but can we possibly grab a quick visit to the falls? You made them sound extraordinary."

"We can visit them. There is time."

Mounted once more, they headed across grassland dotted with bushes loaded with red berries, until the sound of water rushing downstream with throaty gargles reached them. The bridge loomed and Mouse guided his horse to the right, traveling a path beside Carrog Mannin. By the time he dismounted, the thundering and crashing of the river reached a crescendo, blotting out all other sounds. Mouse affixed his horse's guiding leathers to a tall rock thrusting up from the pebbled path. Kat slid from her saddle and he reached for the reins in her hand.

She pulled back. "I can do that."

Mouse sighed, and yelled above the roar of the falls. "I am aware you do not seek help, but this is a hazardous area. You are not familiar with the precarious conditions, but I am. Accepting my help is not a sign of weakness on your part, Kat."

She scowled and released her grip on the reins.

Mouse shook his head and secured her horse to the rock. "The cliff-side is reasonably safe, but tread carefully."

She nodded and cautiously stepped toward the cliff edge, and gasped. A torrent cascaded over the edge of the cliffs, spewing a smoke of mist, rising from the falls, and pounded and smashed to the bed of the river, a dizzying distance below.

Height, Kat's Achilles heel, forced her back from the edge. "What a long way down." She gulped.

Mouse walked to the edge and peered over. "The cliffs which surround Shendea are this high all along the coast, which is why the Shendeans possess no real port, but share the Mora Waters inlet with Rifella. The Mora Waters inlet boasts an excellent harbor, opposite Glowen. Carrog Pandy, flowing into the sea, creates the border between Shendea and Rifella."

"Shendea is land-locked. Yes?"

Mouse tipped his head as he appeared to consider her statement. "Land-locked. An excellent word to describe Shendea's borders. In effect, yes. The cliffs along the coast-line are remarkably high, and even if one could descend to the sea below, there are no natural harbors." He nodded. "So, as you said, Shendea is land-locked. On the Shendean side of the Mora Waters, there is a small village, whose sole food is sea swimmers, and the Southern Shendeans share the swimmers with the Rifellans." He shrugged. "They seem to be healthy, although I cannot imagine living on such a restricted offering."

Distracted by how close Mouse stood to the edge, Kat only half listened. "Do step back from the edge, you're making me uncomfortable."

Mouse, curiosity in his voice, regarded her with surprise on his face. "You are troubled by heights?"

Kat frowned. "Of course not. The wind is blowing fiercely, and if you fall over, I will not attempt to rescue you."

Mouse laughed. "If I fell over, Kat, you would not be able to rescue me."

"Well kindly step back. You still are required to guide me through Pridden."

"True." He retreated. "We should continue on our way to the bridge. We need to be at the Guild before night arrives."

On horseback again, the two followed a path to the Mannin crossing. A well-constructed bridge spanned the river, and Kat rode across and gazed at the water boiling and roiling over rocks and around midstream islands, on which grew bushes and stunted trees. Even this far from the falls, the din made conversation difficult. Not until they rode in among the trees on the other side, could she attempt questions of Mouse. "The waters are violent. How can anyone using the Mannin to travel to the Guild find a way to land?"

"When you looked upstream did you perceive how the river curved around a bend?"

"Yes."

"Prior to approaching the bend, at certain times of year, a calmer eddy allows travelers to bring their boats to shore."

"Only at certain times?"

"During the colder season, the water levels are lower, and the Mannin is less challenging. At this time of our path, we are entering the growing season, and the water is plentiful and traveling in a boat is particularly dangerous."

"I saw and traveled on many rough rivers in my experiences on my world, but anyone who uses this one is a fool."

"I tend to agree with you, but some people are so desperate, they will attempt anything."

Kat shook her head. *Unbelievable.*

***

When they arrived at the gates of the Thieves' Guild, Kat stopped, entranced by the approach of sundown. The Shendean star approached the horizon and stained the sky with glorious colors, from brilliant orange, fading to red, pink, mauve and then violet.

"Your sunsets are magnificent."

"I assume, Kat, you mean the time when our star descends behind our lands."

Kat nodded.

"Shendeans and most of Pridden refers to this time as Caleesh's celebration of our star's return to the land for rest. Your term sunset is what we name star-rest."

As Mouse finished his speech, the tall iron gates of the Guild swung open to allow them entry. Inside the gate, they dismounted the horses, which an apprentice led away to be bedded down. As he walked to the stable, he turned to them with a smile. "Welcome back, Sir Mouse. Guild-leader Derwynn has advised me to deliver your baggage to the rooms he has reserved for you."

"My thanks. Where may we find him?"

"In the dining hall. He awaits your arrival."

As Mouse headed for the hall, a tall, stately, white-haired man in an emerald green robe, emerged from behind a beautifully carved and polished door. "Mouse, welcome." He grasped both Mouse's shoulders, beaming at him, and then performed some complicated hand gesture. He faced Kat. "And you must be the Lady Kat. Welcome to the Thieves' Guild. We will be dining soon, but you both will need time to refresh yourselves in your rooms." He smiled again at Mouse. "You are familiar with our ways, and can escort Lady Kat to the feast."

Mouse bowed his head and nodded.

Feast? Terrific. As usual I'm hungry.

Derwynn returned to the hall, and Mouse led Kat through the Guild's corridors.

Mouse opened a door decorated with flowers, and motioned her inside. "You possess sufficient time to refresh yourself and feed your pyrock. May I suggest you don the clothes you wore to greet Lord Rhognor." He turned to leave and stopped. "Is your invisible cat here?"

"I haven't noticed her since the falls. I suspect she's exploring. Since no one else can catch sight of her, I wouldn't worry about her. She and Breen are probably familiarizing themselves with the lands surrounding the Guild."

"Since I cannot see her either, I find myself unable to worry about her." He shrugged. I will come for you when you are refreshed."

In her room, Kat unpacked the emerald green, gold-threaded dress, and shook out the creases. After feeding Wink, she hopped in the personal and took a brief but thorough shower. Not sure how long before Mouse would come for her, she dressed quickly and applied a minimum of makeup. She glanced at the mirror. *Presentable. You'll do.*

A knock indicated Mouse's arrival. She scanned the room. *Hmm, I wonder what Breen and Shade are up to?*

***

Two young apprentices opened the door to the dining hall and directed them to seats near Derwynn. A cacophony of voices greeted Kat's ears. Most of the males in the hall wore white robes as general members of the Guild, but the mates and female offspring were gowned in glorious color. Everywhere shone bright shiny blues, velvety reds and oranges, and silky dresses of burnished copper fabric. The hall, filled with happy smiling people reverberated with conversation. With the air festive, all in the dining chamber, happy and cheerful, chatted animatedly with each other. Derwynn waved them over and seated Mouse on his left hand side, with Kat beside him. "Welcome Lady Kat. Tonight's feast is a celebration prior to a time thievery for a new petitioner of ours."

"Mouse told me a little of the ceremony, but I'm not entirely clear on how the system works."

"The ritual is simple, and those who need us and are accepted to take part, reward us suitably for our services. Most of our petitioners are males. It appears our females make their decisions with greater care, so females are usually not petitioners."

"Really?"

"Indeed. A man will come to us to request time from his past erased and re-lived by him, to settle what he considers to be a poor initial choice. He will partake of the rite to make the choice anew. In this way he is given the opportunity to redo his once disadvantageous decision."

"Does this mean this option is only for the wealthy?"

"Not at all. Anyone can apply, and the fee is not always paid in the traditional way. Sometimes service to the Guild is exchanged for the ceremony." Derwynn waved over the apprentices to serve food. "Please eat, drink and enjoy yourself. On the morrow we will allow you the opportunity to view a time thievery so you may better understand the formalities."

"Many thanks."

Kat ate and drank with gusto. The scents and flavors of the meal enticed her to consume more than she was accustomed to. The spices, different from the meals in the Stronghold, tickled on her tongue, and the near ale, stronger than most she drank in the past, tasted sweeter. Throughout the hall, musicians offered tunes both exciting and stimulating. They played a variety of stringed instruments, plus glorious notes and sounds from what appeared to be flutes. Many couples rose from the tables and danced joyfully around the room. Mouse, grabbed by a woman in a silky gold dress, whirled around the dance floor and soon was lost to sight. Kat, tempted to join the dancers, felt disappointed no one requested her as a partner. *Well, I guess they don't know me.*

***

When she left the feast for her bed, Kat yawned broadly. *What a night. Fun people. How interesting. Everyone seems so fond of, and impressed by, Mouse. Who and what is he?*

CHAPTER 23

"Kat. Wake now."

"Nope. Wanna sleep some more."

"You must arise."

A cold wet nose on her own startled her and she reluctantly opened her eyes. *Breen. 'Where've you been?'* As she thought these words, Kat received a head butt from Shade. "And what have you been up to?"

Shade purred.

"You are invited to view the time thievery. You should ready yourself. Your guide will be here to collect you."

"Thanksfor the warning. I'm still so sleepy, I almost forgot."

Kat leaped out of bed and headed straight for the personal.

***

The knock at the door came after Kat completed her morning meal. "Come".

Mouse poked his head around the door. "Are you ready to attend a thievery?"

"I guess." She rubbed at her eyes. "I'm a bit fuzzy this morning. I ate too much, and drank more than I should. I don't understand why you're so awake."

"Did you not dance?"

"No. No one asked me, and I always manage to trip up on your customs, so I waited."

Mouse's eyes widened, and he entered the room. "You are the Lady Kat, and you resemble Rifellan royalty. The onus belonged to you to ask. Even Derwynn would not breach convention to request a dance from you."

"Way to tell me now." *Crap and double crap.*

Mouse closed his eyes and lowered his head. "My sincere apologies, Kat. I did not anticipate your ignorance in this matter."

"I'm not happy, Mouse."

"I regret I cannot repair my mistake last night." He strode to the tassel, and tugged four times. "An assistant will bring you a potion to help you regain your physical clarity."

Within minutes a young man appeared at the open door, holding a tray containing a mug of frothing misty liquid and one of clear water, which he deposited on the dresser.

"Drink this, Kat." Mouse handed her the fizzing cup.

She picked up the mug and took a huge gulp. "Arrgh. This is vile."

"I am aware of the flavor. Drink the entire mug. You will be better. To cleanse your mouth, drink the water."

Kat closed her eyes, held her nose and drained the mug. Shaking her head, she grimaced, grabbed the cup of water, and drank deeply. Kat moved her head around, and straightened her posture. "Oh. I am better, and my head is clear now. Much better."

Mouse eyed her. "You are welcome."

"Err… thank you Mouse." *I think he's got sarcasm aced.*

He nodded at her. "Shall we leave now?"

***

The hall of Time filled with members of the Thieves Guild, clad in white robes, buzzed with voices in conversation. Kat glanced at Mouse, clad in pale grey robes, with a long white scarf draped around his neck. All were seated on cushions around a central pit containing fire. Leading to the flames lay a stone path strewn with flower petals. Close to the fire rested a pallet, currently unoccupied.

The light in the chamber dimmed as apprentices removed every second light globe. Somewhere a gong sounded, and through a doorway draped with black velvet curtains, Derwynn appeared. Robed in emerald green, with an assistant two steps behind him robed in pale yellow, he slow-marched toward the fire. Both men wore white scarves draped over their robes.

Kate leaned toward Mouse and whispered. "Why the white scarves?"

"They indicate we are all members and are committed to this ceremony."

The black drapes parted again, and a tall bald man, clad only in a white loincloth, entered, supported by two assistants. Covered in oils he stepped to the foot of the pallet.

Mouse turned to Kat. "He is the applicant."

The man faced Derwynn and bowed.

Derwynn waved toward the fire and a flash of smoke appeared. "This male requested our Guild help him with a new life. He spent many star turns in our company and gave satisfactory answers to our questions. Two paths ago, he chose as his mate a female concerned only with worldly goods, of which he possesses many. He discovered to his dismay she does not love him, and thus his attraction for her did not last. He convinced our Guild his wish to reverse time to when he first met her, is legitimate."

He motioned to one of the assistants who accompanied the applicant to the chamber, and who now stepped forward and handed a cup of steaming liquid to Derwynn. "Today we grant this male's desire." He addressed the applicant. "Do you still agree to our help?"

The man nodded. "I do."

Derwynn handed the cup to him, and he slowly downed the beverage.

The two assistants moved forward and eased him on the pallet where he sank into a stupor.

Derwynn clapped his hands and other assistants entered the room, bearing cups of a different and foaming potion. The members of the Guild passed the draughts around, each taking two mouthfuls.

When a cup arrived at Kat, she glanced at Mouse. "Must I?"

"No. Nor will I. Pass the cup on. We are here as observers only."

"I thought you needed to be part of this?"

"Derwynn is aware I am on special assignment, and gave permission for me to simply be present." Mouse brought his finger to his lips. "Please be silent now."

The assistants all departed, leaving the members and the applicant alone in the chamber.

Derwynn raised his arms and began a chant in some unknown language.

The members joined in, including Mouse. Their voices filled the chamber with echoes, reminding Kat of Gregorian chants she experienced when researching monasteries for her games. The voices throbbed and resonated throughout the chamber, and all members swayed with the rhythm of sound.

From time to time, Derwynn would wave his hands and flashes would emanate from the fire along with plumes of smoke. The haze in the room increased, and Derwynn in slow sonorous tones, uttered commands to the now unconscious man. "Your error was minor, and the female deficient.

You can now perceive with clarity the more advantageous choice."

As the members continued to chant, Derwynn repeated these words over and over. Their chanting slowed, Derwynn ceased his words, and the fog began to dissipate. When the room quieted, a further gong sounded, and two helpers entered and carried the pallet from the hall.

The members rose and began to exit.

Kat stood, and groaned. "I'm stiff."

"The ceremony lasted an entire star turn."

Kat stared at Mouse. "Nightfall already?"

He nodded. "We should partake of a light evening meal, and retire early. You will need the rest. On the morrow we will view the result of the protocol."

"I'm not really hungry."

"Lack of hunger is not abnormal for this ceremony, but you will sleep better with a light meal."

***

Kat returned to her room after the meal, fed Wink, and indulged in a hot shower to ease the kinks in her muscles. In nightclothes, unable to stay awake, she slid into bed, and closed her eyes. Immediately, Breen crept beside her and touched a cold nose to her arm. *"A successful thievery, yes?"*

"Hmmm. *Night Breen. Tell Shade to stay off... .*"

J. M. Tibbott

CHAPTER 24

The following morning, Kat found her way to the dining hall, and joined Mouse at the table where he sat with Derwynn. "Good morrow to both of you." *Boy I'm getting just fine at this odd way of speaking.*

"And to you, Lady Kat." Derwynn regarded her with curiosity. "Did you learn much from the time thievery?"

"A lot. But please call me Kat. I find the other unnecessarily formal."

"As do I. But I appreciate receiving your permission to do so." He inclined his head to her. "I note you and Mouse are not formal with each other. He tells me you are both to spend much time together and agreed you would drop formalities during your journey."

Both she and Mouse nodded at Derwynn.

"The ritual for an applicant is a lengthy process, but I trust you are refreshed now and are ready to view the balance of the ceremony. Mouse, of course, is familiar with the process and is aware of what to expect. He prepares accordingly, but as a newcomer to the service I am not sure how you fared."

"My friend Mouse is a fine guide, and prepares me for most situations we encounter."

"Excellent." Derwynn rose from the table. "I must leave you now, I need more preparations for the final outcome of the applicant's request. You will be able to join us to view the conclusion." He smiled down at her. "Mouse will bring you to the ceremonial hall when we are ready to begin."

Kat thanked Derwynn and turned when an assistant asked if she wished food. She ordered journeyklim, and faced

Mouse. "They took the applicant from the hall when he lay unconscious. What happened next?"

"During the time of darkness, four guild members stayed with him and focused on helping him clear everything which occurred in his life from seconds before he met the women he wished to forget. With words, and potions and suggestions, they spoke with him throughout the period of darkness, and his mind is now clear of those memories. They anticipate, or at least they hope, his mind will now be free to accept a new beginning. At dawn, they provided him with a second potion to bring him to consciousness. They bathed him, clothed him, fed him and will bring him to the ceremonial hall to ensure all is well."

"Sounds like they brain-washed him."

"What an odd expression. But as I consider the entire ritual, your words do represent an accurate assumption."

Kat's meal arrived, and she ordered tea. "Do you want tea while I eat?"

Mouse nodded. "Indeed. Thank you."

As she ate, Mouse gave her snippets about previous applicants and how well or poorly they lived their lives after a thieving ceremony. "The process is complicated, and many are not as committed as they believe themselves to be. Thus their lives do not change in the way they originally expected."

"Do any applicants come back and request another ceremony?"

"Once or twice, but naturally we will not agree to a second ritual."

A number of people rose from their seats and headed out of the hall.

Mouse rose from his chair. "We are about to begin the conclusion. Are you ready?"

Kat swallowed the last of her Karri-san and stood. "Yes."

In the ceremonial hall, Mouse led her to seats near the front so she would be able to clearly view the finale. The guild members began chanting once more. They continued to chant and were joined by six additional female members, who added to the chant with a descant melody.

Kat discovered herself drifting in a type of meditation, and noticed she and the rest of the guild swayed to the rhythm of the voices in the hall.

Time passed, and unexpectedly a gong sounded, startling Kat into full consciousness.

Derwynn stepped up to the front of the room, and from outside the black drapes, two assistants escorted the applicant, this time dressed in a long white gown, similar in style to the djellaba worn by men in Morocco. As a small child, Kat's parents visited friends and family in various countries in the middle East, and they gave her a kid-sized flowered djellaba, which she adored.

The guild members ceased their chanting, and the assistants handed Derwynn a mug filled with a fizzing, bubbling liquid. He faced the applicant. "Are you ready to re-join your life?"

"I am Master Derwynn." He bowed his head.

"Now drink." Derwynn handed the cup to the applicant, who drained the contents.

Two new assistants entered, each one guiding a woman. They escorted the women to a position across the hall from the applicant.

Kat whispered to Mouse. "Who are they?"

"He first bonded with the woman on the left. The one on the right is the one he decided would be a better choice. She has always wished he had chosen her."

Derwynn guided the applicant toward them. "Choose your life."

The applicant contemplated the women. His body moved toward the woman on the left, but he stopped, a puzzled frown on his face. He gazed at the woman on the right. His face lit up in a smile of joy and he moved swiftly to her side. Her face wet with tears, she reached for him, moved into his arms, and embraced him. The entire hall remained silent, interrupted only by the sound of joyful murmurs from the applicant and his new mate.

At Derwynn's signal, four assistants escorted the pair from the hall. The other woman left quietly by a side entrance.

As the guild members exited the hall, Kat shook her head and grinned to herself. "Your guild didn't steal time at all."

Mouse appeared horrified by her words. "I told you before, our Guild does not steal, we change the memories of time." He sighed. "I believe you might manage to consume a midturn meal?"

"I am a bit hungry." She paused considering her need for food. "Actually I'm very hungry."

"Let us return to the dining hall, and we can discuss what you learned about the Guild today."

Once the two of them were seated with meals in front of them, Kat glanced about the dining hall and discovered very few others eating. "This place is almost empty, where is everyone else?"

"Most have returned to their homes, both here in Shendea and in other lands. We are a far-reaching Guild. We only gather in this hall once per path for our own celebrations, and, of course, when an applicant is chosen. We find no need for us to meet more often."

"Which is why you can live in Morden and only come to Shendea a few times a… a path?" *Now I remember — path is their term for a year.*

"Indeed."

Kat finished the dish in front of her and sipped tea. "Let's discuss what happened in the hall."

Mouse nodded at her to continue.

"As I said before, your guild didn't steal time. You messed with the man's mind so he forgot what happened, and might live as if he'd gained a new life."

"A reasonably accurate assessment, but I wish you would cease using the word steal We stole nothing. If you wish to be precise, we deleted the memories of a specific period of his life. We exchanged the details for a new option, so he could choose a new attitude and potentially live a life more desirable than the one before. In his mind, he experienced a shift in time."

"Let's be honest, Mouse. Calling yourselves thieves is a misnomer."

He folded his arms and sat back in the chair. "I believe I now understand what challenges you about our Guild."

Kat raised her eyebrows at him. "Really?"

"What precisely does the term thief mean on your world?"

"Well, a thief is someone who steals, who takes items from people without permission. They take for their own pleasure or for financial gain. They are criminals and are not tolerated in society. They can also be violent if they are thwarted in gaining what they desire." She stopped and thought. "The man who attempted to steal my bracelet in the passages of the Stronghold is what we would call a thief."

"I now posses true clarity why you find it strange I belong to a Thieves' Guild. The man who attempted to take your bracelet is what we call a brigand. Thieves by our standards are those who make exchanges for people. Brigands steal, thieves do not."

"No wonder you got so upset when I accused your Guild of stealing. I promise I won't associate the word with you and the other members again."

Mouse gave a relieved sigh. "Excellent."

"To change the subject, where are we off to next."

"On the morrow we travel to Roothlan on Lake Glenaddie. This will be a relaxing journey, and since many Rifellans visit the village, you will enjoy the admiration of the citizens, since you so closely resemble their royalty of the northern area."

"I like the idea of the relaxing bit, so I will finish up my writing today, and pack so we can leave after the morning meal."

They rose from the table and headed to their rooms.

Rifellans — yum. Must remember to stock up on Karri-san. What fun.

CHAPTER 25

The following day the two travelers set out for Rooth-lan. The path, wide and clearly marked through an ocean of grasses permitted them to travel side by side, the pack-horse attached again to Kat's saddle.

The tall grass stretched for miles on either side of them, and the wind caused the stalks to sway and swirl, creating patterns in the drifting reeds.

Kat stopped her horse. "Stop."

Mouse halted his. "Why?"

"Listen." She cocked her head. "What do you hear?"

"The wind in the grains. What else?"

"Close your eyes and listen. The sound reminds me of being at the sea, standing on a beach and hearing the waves whisper and hiss as they wash up the sand. To me this soothes and relaxes."

Mouse's eyes were closed, but he opened them and shook his head. "I understand what you speak about, but your suggestion holds little meaning for me, as I am not familiar with standing in sand beside a sea."

Kat's mouth dropped open. "Not?"

"I have viewed the sea. The challenge is, Pridden, is primarily ringed by high cliffs. Only Rifella possesses coastline at sea level, but most of the area is too rocky to enjoy. Although I did not visit Glowen, I understand the island does possess sand beaches."

"Since you've never been to Glowen, does this mean when we visit, you will be unable to guide me?"

"Somewhat. However, I maintain contacts within Glowen upon whom I can rely for information. I also doubt you will discover much friction in Glowen. The inhabitants only seek pleasure, and are unlikely to involve themselves in any strife."

Mouse clicked at his horse. "We should continue. We will reach Roothlan well in advance of star-set, unless we delay our progress."

"So tell me about Roothlan."

"The village is a substantial one. As I mentioned at our meal, many Rifellans attend the place on a regular basis, so the market specializes in products from our neighbors to the south. Rifellans offer leather clothing and long bows, and they are able to fashion leather armor for any who wish to turn their hand to guard duties. Rifellan metalwork is outstanding, and the swords they produce are the best in all Pridden, plus the shields they create are beautiful works of art. In their own land, they are also ship builders, because they boast a number of harbors on their coastline."

"You make them sound like a warrior-race."

"They are, and they offer their services to most of the Lords and Thanes of Pridden. They also offer themselves as trainers of warriors, and will help most villages to maintain their own protection."

"I like Rifellans. The ones I met are strong, uncompromising people. They're a most attractive race."

Mouse said nothing.

Kat lapsed into silence, remembering. *I wonder if I'll meet a clone of Liandock? It's been a while.*

***

Mouse stopped his horse. "The village you will view ahead is Roothlan. The town is haphazard, because the houses and shops grew without plan. Many from Shendea, particularly from the Stronghold, travel here in our primary growing season for the warmth and Lake Glenaddie. The waters are much appreciated for bathing, and bonded pairs bring their offspring with them as respite from the cold, fierce weather in the north. This is a place for enjoyment.”

“Sounds like a resort.”

Mouse glanced at her with a raised eyebrow.

Kat sighed. “I mean a place where people take leave from their work to relax and renew, so they return to their everyday lives refreshed.”

“Most true. Shendeans do utilize Roothlan and Lake Glenaddie in a similar way.” He shook the reins to continue toward the town. “We will pass through the town, and stay at an inn on the edge of the village near Glenaddie. This is the largest one, and does not enjoy as many visitors currently as will occupy the rooms in ten star turns.”

“As long as they serve excellent food and I get a comfortable room.” Kat heard a rustle in the grass, and Shade, with Breen on her back, appeared beside her. “Oh, and where have you two been?”

Mouse peered at her. “Are you speaking to your invisible cat?”

“Yes. She and Breen went exploring. I last saw them when we left the Guild.”

“Does your cat understand you?”

“I don’t know. I pretend she does. I also talk to Wink, my pyrock. I’m aware she doesn’t understand me, because Breen informed me. In my home, I often kept pets, and I always talked to them.”

“What is a pet?”

Kat squinted at him. “Pets? They’re animals you keep in your home. You take care of them.”

"You keep animals in captivity?"

"I guess. Sort of. They're company. We find enjoyment interacting with them. I guess this means you people do not keep pets."

"All animals on Pridden are free."

"So explain how you keep pontis, horses, and wullawerths. Are they free?"

"Indeed they are. Pontis and horses bond with someone, and during the day they are free to wander in the fields. At night we bring them into stables for protection from potential predators. As for wullawerths, they are not intelligent. We allow them freedom to wander in extensive fields, and they gather on their own in smaller paddocks at star-set. They are nervous creatures and dislike being exposed after dark falls. These animals receive our protection, and in return they work for us in their own way."

Mouse took the lead, and guided them through broad streets and winding alleys as he headed for the primary inn.

Kat knew she acted like a typical tourist, rubbernecking at the sights and sounds. Most of the shops appeared closed, but from the two or three inns they passed, she caught glimpses of laughing people. The entire town exuded a light happy air.

"Ahead of you is the inn where we shall stay, Kat. I will hand the horses over to the stable-master, and you can proceed into the inn. I suggest you head for the dining area."

Kat scowled at Mouse. "I'm perfectly capable of taking my own horse to the stable. Will you cease treating me as if I'm some helpless female. I supported myself, fought for myself and lived by myself for a long time."

Mouse blinked rapidly. "I did not mean to suggest you are powerless. I only meant you could secure rooms for us and a table for our evening meal. I made the suggestion to divide our responsibilities. As Lady Kat, you are far more likely to ensure we are provided with a well situated place in the hall and the best rooms available."

"Oh." Kat sheepishly handed the reins of her horse to him. "I'll arrange the rooms and the table."

As she strode to the inn, Kat glanced back. Mouse shook his head, glanced upward and sighed.

Kat entered the hall, filled with Rifellans, mostly male, blonde, strong and compelling. *Glad I drank lots of Karri-san.* All eyes turned to her. *Bet they think I'm Rifellan, 'cause I'm wearing my leather outfit.* The clamor of conversation ceased as the crowd stared at her.

A tall dark haired man hurried over. "Lady, are you dining with us?"

"Yes. I am Lady Kat."

The man bowed his head.

"My friend is stabling our horses. We wish two rooms, and will dine in your establishment this night." *Wow — don't I do formal speak well?* She chuckled to herself.

"We are pleased to welcome you, my Lady. I will seat you at our best table, and while you are both dining, will arrange excellent rooms for you."

He led her to a table near an indoor fountain, and snapped his fingers at two of his serving women. "My assistants will take your orders as soon as your friend joins you." He turned to the woman nearest him. "Near-ale for the Lady, and bring a second for her friend who will be joining her."

The woman scurried to follow his directions, and by the time Mouse entered, she returned with two brimming flagons of ale, condensation on the outside of the mugs, tempting taste buds. She deposited both on the table. "My Lady, Sire. We are fortunate to offer a favorite dish of sea swimmer cassolet for tonight. The swimmer villages caught the sea swimmers at midturn, so they are most fresh."

Mouse's eyes lit up. "Excellent. The cassolet will be perfect for both of us." He turned to Kat. "I did order for you, but I guarantee you will enjoy this dish. We are most fortunate to be offered this today." He leaned forward and whispered. "I told you being Lady Kat and dressed like a Rifellan warrior would bring us exemplary service."

When the food arrived, she and Mouse ate in silence. In the interim, conversation resumed in the dining hall, and Kat glanced around the room. Rifellan warriors made up the majority of people seated around the room. All but one sported blonde or platinum hair, and all were garbed in leather. Most wore pants and sleeveless tunics. The temptation to keep her eyes off chests and biceps, all well developed, all stirring delicious sensations within her, became difficult.

One man, whose hair blended red with darker blonde, wore a leather kilt-like garment similar to Liandock's attire in Kaylin. His tunic, opened almost to his waist, revealed reddish-blond chest hair. Kat forced herself to face her plate. *The last thing I want to do is drool. Whew he's hot.* She reached into her diplo bag and withdrew a small vial.

Irina had slipped the vial of Karri-san essence to her when she left Kaylin. She whispered to Kat as she pressed the container into her hand "You may sometimes need something stronger."

Surreptitiously, Kat uncorked the vial and placed a drop on her finger-tip and then under each nostril. Instantly the sensation of arousal lessened. *I can stare at him now without losing myself entirely.* She glanced up, and caught Mouse watching her closely. *I hope he didn't catch me using the vial.*

Hoping to cover her actions she broke the silence. "Mouse, you are correct. This dish is fantastic, and the spices are incredible. This is almost as delicious as Gornog meat."

"I agree. Even though, I, like most Morden's am more fond of Gornog than sea-swimmers."

I need to escape to my room. Too many Rifellan pheromones here. "I'm tired from the long journey we enjoyed today. I… I need to retire."

"I understand. I too will welcome my bed. On the morrow, we can explore Roothlan, unless you wish to view the town on your own. There is no need to fear any criminals here. With this many Rifellans, this is one of the safest villages in all Shendea."

"I'll meet you for the morning meal, and we can decide then."

Mouse nodded to her and they both rose and headed to their respective rooms.

I wonder if the red-blonde Rifellan is royalty?

⁂

In her room, Kat fed Wink, patted Shade asleep on the floor with Breen curled up beside her, and headed for the personal. Dusty from the journey, she anticipated a cleansing warm shower. She caught sight of the stone on her pendant in the mirror. *Is my stone a bit dull?*

Clean, she slipped into her bed, naked and remembered Liandock's words about charging the stone. "Pleasure yourself."

Once in her bed, she envisioned the reddish-blond haired Rifellan, and a wave of heat travelled up her body. Imagining the touch of the man, she stroked herself all over and reached between her legs. *Moist. Yes.*

After, limp and relaxed, she held up the stone. *Brilliant green again. Liandock was right.*

CHAPTER 26

Kat enjoying her favorite breakfast meal of nutty and substantial journeyklim, waved at Mouse as he entered the dining hall.

He approached her and sat down. "Have you decided what you would prefer to accomplish today?"

"I want to explore the town. I'm not a shopper, but everything here is unusual, so this is more like research. I spoke briefly to one of the serving women, and she mentioned Lake Glenaddie is perfect for bathing. The shore is without sand, but grass and earth allow you to wander right to the water's edge, without painful stones underfoot. One item I must locate in the village is clothing to bathe in. I'm hoping to find something less voluminous than the monstrosity they forced me to wear in Kaylin."

"Bathing in Glenaddie might be interesting. I shall accompany you and attempt to purchase something similar for myself."

***

A much bigger village, Kat discovered Roothlan boasted stalls and stores of all sorts. She and Mouse wandered down the streets and alleyways, nostrils assaulted by the odors of rich breads, roasted meats, the sweet smell of pastries, and floral and plant essences. Brilliant clothing, ranging from Shendean robes in blues and yellow, and in one window, a lone robe in an eye-dazzling emerald.

"The robe in this store must be meant for a master, or the head of a guild, right?"

Mouse pointed at the sign above the window. "The writing proclaims this store is for those who enjoy leadership roles, and only those."

Nearby, Kat spied a stall laden with Rifellan leather outfits. However, one section also contained clothing consisting of black leather pants, with tunics of rich fabrics in glorious reds and glimmering golds "Are those costumes also for Rifellans?"

"They are dress wear for female bond mates of guard unit leaders. These females are not guards themselves, even though many women do take part in such duty. They are only worn on formal occasions."

As they continued on, stalls offering long bows, spring bows, leather footwear, and leather armor, sat side by side with shops containing beautifully worked long and broad swords, and ornately designed shields. Further on, shops of wooden ship models, extraordinary jewelry and discreetly displayed underwear and bathing costumes.

"There's a store I need." Kat entered the shop.

Mouse joined her. "This provider also offers bathing attire for males. While you obtain what you need, I shall purchase something suitable for myself."

After trying on a number of costumes, Kat eventually settled on a pale blue creation, with loose leggings and a tunic, which ended at thigh level. The sleeves reached elbow length. *This is still a lot of fabric, but perhaps I won't be hampered like in Kaylin.*

She met Mouse outside the shop, carrying a package of his own. "Can we can eat a light meal around here?"

"Three alleys over, a small stall serves food."

"Let's go."

They wound their way through the alleyways of shops, and when they reached their destination, Kat secured a table, while Mouse approached the Shendean owner to order.

He walked over and sat across from Kat. "You spoke of your fondness for wullawerth meat, and fortunately the owner always keeps some on hand. I ordered for both of us."

"Yummy. I love the stuff."

Mouse appeared puzzled.

"Yummy is a word of delight in the taste of something."

A expression of comprehension lit up his face. "Your world possesses many different expressions.

I don't ever want to explain countries and languages. Ugh.

"The owner also mentioned he supplies a treat for visitors to Lake Glenaddie. Located in a building near the shore, is a set of rooms in which one can change into bathing wear. He and his assistants will arrange a seating area near the lake."

"Sounds wonderful."

"There is an additional option, Kat. Prior to star-set, they will return to build a fire for us, and bring food for our meal. Few others will be at the lake, so we will be able to relax in comfort."

"Mouse, what a terrific idea. Did you agree?"

He raised his hand to the owner and nodded. "I just did."

***

A small building, housing rooms for bathing wear changes, stood close to the lake, surrounded by apple-green grass. Between the pathway surrounding the building, and the town, lovely red flowers grew in taller grass. They nodded their brilliant scarlet heads in the breeze. The sun warmed them and the lake gleamed azure in the sun.

The lake's the same color as the water around Snake Island in Turkey. Kat hurried to the building, eager to swim.

She hastily changed, leaving her clothing in a type of locker, and turning her head as she exited the building, saw the stall owner beckoning her to a multi-colored covering on the shore, with cushions for seating. She intended to run over, but the sensation of the soft grass underfoot slowed her down. *It's like walking on fur.* She squished the soft green vegetation between her toes, and grinned to herself in pleasure. By the time she arrived at the carpeted area, Mouse appeared from the change rooms. He still wore his boots, which he shed before he stepped on the colorful blanket. *I wonder if naked feet are naughty?*

"I'll race you to the water, Mouse." Kat ran and plunged into the water. She leaped out almost instantaneously. *Arrggh, cold.* Gritting her teeth she jumped back in the water and swam away from the shore. Pausing she glanced back at Mouse. He gingerly made his way into the lake, wincing occasionally.

What a wuss. "You won't experience the cold if you jump in quickly."

He frowned at her.

She swam close to him and splashed water over him.

He growled and his frown turned to a glare. "You will regret that." He splashed her back.

Kat laughed. "I'm wet. You can't make me any wetter." She turned to swim further out in the lake.

Without warning, something grabbed her foot and pulled her under the water. She came up spluttering, and coughing. "You rat. Not fair. I didn't try to drown you."

Mouse's face displayed the picture of innocence. "Drown you? Had I tried, you would be underwater."

Kat eyed him speculatively. *He's got no idea how much I could hurt him. I'd like revenge, but I need him as a guide. I'll pay him back later, without too much damage.* "Really? You would be making a huge mistake."

Mouse eyed her, pursing his lips. He turned and swam away from her.

Kat swam in the opposite direction. *Hmm. Mouse appears to be gaining courage, or something.*

***

The stall owner, re-appeared as the Pridden's star began to drop below the horizon. The assistants placed upright torches around the carpeting, lit a fire between them and the lake, and served their evening meal. "We will clear everything once you return to your inn."

Her annoyance at Mouse, now melted, Kat thanked the men, and settled on a cushion to eat. "Delicious."

Mouse joined her, demonstrated heating the pieces of meat, by placing them on long sticks and roasting them in the flames. "This is a fine place. No challenging creatures live in the area, so we are safe from any harm."

By the time they consumed their meal, Kat yawned broadly. "The fresh air takes it out of me, and by the end of the day I'm pleasantly tired. Now I'd like to find my bed."

"Perhaps you would like to change first, and then return to the inn, while I gather any of our belongings. I will follow once I am wearing my robe."

"Thanks, Mouse."

***

Kat changed and headed to the inn. She passed closed stalls, and a small darkened tavern. A man wearing the clothes of a field worker stepped from the doorway. "Ah woman, in need of a near-ale. Pretty. I will rescue you."

185

She faced him. "I don't need rescuing. Let me pass."

"I musht help you get your drink."

Oh rats, a drunk. "I'm going home, and you need to do the same."

"No. You musht come with me." He walked up beside Kat, grabbed her around the neck with his arm across her chest. Leaning on her, he weighed a ton.

Uh oh. Problem. Kat made a fist, cupped it with her other hand and drove her elbow forcefully into his midsection.

He loosened his hold and Kat grabbed at his arm with both hands. She rammed her hip into him and using this leverage, propelled him across her back and slammed him into the ground. Something cracked as he collided with the stones of the walkway and he yelled in agony.

"I told you to let me pass, and you should never have touched me."

The man moaned and writhed in pain, but made no move to rise.

Kat regarded him scornfully. "Pig." She strode off to the inn.

What is going on with these men in Shendea? I thought this was a safe area?

CHAPTER 27

Mouse changed into his normal grey robe, and gathered the bags containing the bathing wear for both him and Kat. He glanced around. All else the stall owner would collect, although Mouse did pour water on the fire and extinguish the torches.

He stood at the shore of Lake Glenaddie, and breathed in the clean, clear scent of earth and water. He loved this time of star turn, enveloped in the ebony of night. He spent so much of his life living with the dark, and hiding in the shadows. This represented safe haven for him. The pools of faint radiance emanating from the pinpricks of light in the sky, and the silence, deep and dark, provided him with solace and concealed him from those who would harm him.

Another deep breath, and he turned and glided silently back to the inn, past darkened houses filled with people sleeping without worry or fear. He sighed. *One day.*

A cry of pain disturbed the night. Mouse paused. *Where did the noise come from?* He hurried through the alleyway following moans. The few globes in the streets provided only the occasional splash of brightness.

On the ground outside a shuttered tavern lay a man in distress, his leg bent at an unnatural angle.

"What happened? Can I obtain help for you?" As Mouse came closer he saw blood on the ground, and bone protruding from the man's leg. *He will not manage any distance with such an injury.*

The man's face contorted in pain and rage. "Keep the foul woman, the syeth kin, away from me. She is a stain in

Morden's black eye. Should I see her again I shall kill her."
In his anger, his words accompanied by flecks of spittle, the
unfortunate victim attempted to move and howled again in
pain.

He is apoplectic about… Kat? Did she do this to him?
"Do not attempt to move. I will go for help." *I must report
this to the guards.*

***

Mouse, pulling his hood well over his face, hurried
through the door of the guards' base. "I need your help. I
discovered a man severely injured outside the tavern on the
alley of Souls. He attacked a female and received punishment."

The leader questioned him. "Who are you Sire? How did
you determine he attacked a female?"

"I am named Mouse, and the man is conscious, and
uttered threats against a woman he claimed disabled him."

Three guards rose, and followed Mouse to where the
attacker lay, still moaning.

They questioned the man, who refused to give his name,
and screamed in agony when they lifted him on a cart to
transport him to the guardhouse. Once there, the leader of the
guards summoned a healer to treat his injuries.

"Mouse, this man is seriously mutilated. You do not
appear to be able to inflict this type of damage, but I must ask
if you wounded him."

Mouse stared at the Rifellan standing in front of him. "If
you will be aware, this man is much larger than me, nor am I
guard trained. You cannot possibly assume I managed to deal
with him in this manner."

The guard eyed him up and down. "You are correct I cannot imagine you accomplished this. Are you aware of the
identity of the female?"

"Yes, I believe so."

"Then bring her to me on the morrow, and we can determine what penalty should be inflicted upon the attacker." He glanced back at the cot where the assailant lay moaning. "I must confess, someone seems to have disciplined him appropriately, and further punishment may not be necessary."

"I will bring her to you on the morrow, after the morning meal."

"Excellent. I am named Ballinor. You can request to meet with me when you arrive."

***

Mouse knocked on Kat's door and waited.

A minute or two later, the door opened a crack, and Kat, with tousled hair and only one eye open peered at him. "What?"

"Forgive me for rousing you so late in the night." He passed her the package containing her bathing wear. "You left this at lakeside."

Kat took the package from him. "You could've waited 'til the morrow." She began to close the door.

"Wait. Something more. Were you attacked outside a tavern on your way here?"

"Yup. But I dealt with him."

"Kat, you left the man on road, and you did not report him to the guards."

She opened her other eye. "I wasn't aware I needed to, and the location of the guards isn't known to me." She scowled. "Plus I needed my bed. Tired."

"I understand, you are unaware of how to report this. We are summoned to appear at the guard unit on the morrow."

Kat mumbled an assent, and slammed the door.

Mouse reeled back, stunned. *She dealt with him? She shattered the man's leg?*

***

He joined Kat in the dining hall for a morning meal, and once complete, they set off for the guard unit.

"I wouldn't have found my way last evening."

"We will explain your actions."

"Explain? He attacked me."

The two of them arrived at the guard unit's building and entered.

Mouse spied the guard leader from the previous evening. "Ballinor, may I introduce the Lady Kat. The man you sequestered in badk room of your unit attacked her last evening."

The guard bowed his head. "Lady Kat, we are well met."

She nodded at him. "Ballinor."

Mouse caught a flash of recognition in Kat's eyes. *I recognize him too. He's the Rifellan with the reddish hair I caught her eyeing the previous evening.*

Ballinor cleared his throat. "Can you identify the man who attacked you?"

"Yes."

He led Kat to a back room, where she peered through a door slit at the attacker of the previous night.

"He's the one."

Ballinor escorted her back to the front office. "You could assist us, if you would advise me who subdued the attacker."

"I did."

Mouse examined Ballinor's face. *He does not believe she did it.*

Ballinor's eyes widened. "You did?"

"Yes."

"You inflicted all the damage on him?"

"Yes." Kat's mouth was drawn in a thin line.

Mouse eyed the two of them with delight. *This is becoming interesting. What will Kat do?*

Ballinor's mouth hung open. "Lady Kat. Many of our females are trained as warriors, but I never observed in them the ability to create such injuries."

"Simple enough. I studied a form of self-defense for many years."

"I find this difficult to believe you accomplished this on your own."

She is angry. Should I warn him?

Kat scowled at Ballinor. "I told you. I handled him without difficulty."

Ballinor grinned at her. "If you handled this man with such ease, perhaps you would be willing to demonstrate on me."

He is not reading the signs, and he laid his own trap. Mouse leaned forward relieved he was not the object of her anger.

"I don't want to hurt you." By now, Kat's nostrils flared.

At her words, Ballinor laughed aloud. "I do not believe I am in any danger. Please, demonstrate."

Big mistake. She will not back down from this. I should have warned him.

Kat stepped up to Ballinor. "He stood behind me, with his arm like so." She drew his arm across her chest.

Ballinor's grin grew so broad Mouse thought his face might split. *This will not be pleasant.*

Kat made a fist, which she cupped with her other hand, and drove her elbow into Ballinor's side. He expelled a gasp of air, and before he recovered, she grabbed his arm with both hands, thrust her hip into his stomach area, bent over and threw him over her back. Another gasp from Ballinor and he lay on the floor panting for breath.

Mouse, realizing Ballinor lay unharmed, only in need of air, fought to hide his laughter. *He made an error and seriously misjudged his opponent.*

Kat, a smug expression on her face, walked over to Ballinor and extended a hand to help him up from the floor. "I threw you as gently as I'm able. I hope you're not injured."

Ballinor took her hand and stood, staring open-mouthed at Kat. He began to laugh. "A fine lesson, Lady Kat. I deserved what you gave me. Perhaps you should demonstrate the move you achieved, step-by-step. I would appreciate the ability to teach this to our female warriors."

Kat smiled at him. "I would be delighted to do so."

This woman is a constant surprise. What other talents does she possess? This assignment is more challenging than I expected. Mouse rubbed his eyebrow. *And her attacker? Who is he? I cannot believe he is an unknown drunk. Roothlan is a safe village. I am convinced this was also deliberate.*

CHAPTER 28

A Rifellan guard approached Ballinor and supplied him with information about the upcoming day. He nodded at the guard and turned to Kat. "Lady Kat, a group of my people travel to Dizerth on the morrow. I would appreciate the chance to advise them about this new technique for dealing with the occasional criminal element, without the use of weapons. Would you agree to meet with me later to demonstrate your brilliant defensive move?"

"Yes, but please call me Kat. The Lady bit makes everything so annoyingly formal."

He laughed. "If you wish. After your effective example, I do not intend to annoy you in any way. If we meet here after the midturn, would you join me later for the evening meal?"

Kat beamed at him. "Thank you. I would like that."

Ballinor took her hand and touched his lips to her wrist. "I anticipate your arrival with pleasure."

Karri-san or not — whew. No guessing what he's got in mind.

She swiveled to Mouse. "Will we be able to visit Swimmers village?"

"Not this day. If you wish we can delay our departure from Roothlan by an extra day, and you would be able to visit the village."

Kat thought a minute. "No. I would rather continue on." *I'll never get home if we keep doing the tourist bit.*

"As you wish, Kat. In the eastern part of Roothlan I found a fine tavern where we can consume our midturn meal. Rifellans prefer to eat there, and I enjoy their company."

"You're the guide." *Fond of Rifellans? I wonder.*

***

The tavern they entered vibrated with laughter and song. A table of warriors at the far end raised their voices in a ditty about battle and drinking. At another, six men played some game with stones, painted with icons. Closer to the inn keeper sat a pair of female arm wrestlers. The men surrounding them yelled encouragement and exchanged chits to strengthen their support for their choice of the wrestlers. A few women sat at yet another table, conversing and laughing. With the exception of some Shendeans wearing their traditional robes, all in the room wore warrior leathers. The rich browns magnified the warmth of the colors in the room.

Kat, struck most by the palpable mantle of testosterone and Rifellan pheromones, swallowed nervously. The atmosphere surrounded and engulfed her. *Karri-san. I need Karri-san.*

"Mouse could I drink some Karri-san tea right away?" *Glad I'm wearing leathers. Otherwise they'd all notice the 'girls' standing at attention.*

"My apologies. I should have ordered some for you as soon as we entered. I forgot you experience a stronger reaction than the Kaylins do to Rifellans." He motioned to a table at the far end of the room. "Please wait at the table and I will bring your tea."

He returned and placed the mug in front of her. "I ordered a meal for us as well."

Kat drank the tea swiftly and shortly perceived the beneficial effect. "Thank you, I needed this." Waiting for her meal, she stared from one area to another. *What fun. I can use this in a game as a warrior celebration.*

One of the Rifellan women rose from her seat and approached Kat's table and dipped her head. "From what royal house are you, Lady? I do not recall meeting with you before. I am Keedin, and hail from the south of Rifella."

"Keedin, I am not Rifellan." *Gotta keep saying names so I'll actually remember them.* "I am Lady Kat, and I'm not from your world."

Keedin's mouth formed an O, and her eyes widened. "Yet you appear to be a royal Rifellan. You hair is red, and you wear leathers. Although I must admit, they are not the same as those we don."

Kat turned up the corners of her mouth. "Would you join us? We can discuss this further, if you wish."

"My thanks, but I must rejoin my friends, as we are on duty right after this meal." She dipped her head again. "I would appreciate another meeting Lady Kat." She returned to her own table, and from the animated discussion with the other three women, Kat assumed she passed on what she learned.

Kat shifted her attention back to Mouse, who gazed at her with a half smile on his face.

"I did tell you, Rifellans would take you for one of their own."

Kat shrugged. "I'm curious to meet some northern ones."

"You will find the opportunity when we travel to Rifella itself."

"Wonderful." Kat glanced back at the table of Rifellan women. "They're attractive people."

The meals arrived and Mouse requested near ale for himself, and a further cup of Karri-san for Kat. They ate in silence.

Gradually the tavern cleared of customers, and she assumed they were returning to their various duties.

Ballinor appeared at Kat's side. "Ah, Lady Kat. You are finished your meal?"

She nodded yes.

"Excellent. Remember, I would show my appreciation by inviting you to dine with me for your evening meal."

Kat raised an eyebrow. *I wonder what he's planning?* "Thank you for the invitation." She bobbed her head. "You mentioned this before."

Mouse rose from his seat. "Kat, since you will be occupied until later this evening, I need to congregate with some acquaintances, and gather more information about the rest of our journey in Shendea. After your morning meal on the morrow, I will meet with you at the stables. I will arrange with an apprentice to collect your baggage."

"Thank you. I'll come to the stables."

Mouse departed the tavern and as he cleared the door, Ballinor sat in the empty seat. "Kat, are you ready to teach my unit your tricks?"

"You lead, I'll follow."

Ballinor stood, and grinned down at her. "An interesting turn of phrase."

He led her back to the guard unit's building where six other Rifellans waited.

"Warriors. This is the Lady Kat, and she agreed to demonstrate a new defensive technique to allow us to stop a criminal with less use of weaponry."

Three of them grinned, but the others had seen what Kat accomplished in the morning and waited. She asked them to pair up, and demonstrated each move, step by step.

She turned to Ballinor. "Do you mind if I show the complete action?"

He grimaced slightly. "Please do."

She threw him again, and although winded, he seemed better prepared and did not gasp aloud. Kat addressed the rest of the guards. "I threw Ballinor gently. The faster and harder you perform this, the more damage you will cause. Perhaps you will each throw your partner, but slowly, to understand how the action feels."

The guards viewed Kat with what could only be interpreted as respect. They threw each other, and soon the room filled with laughter, as they gained proficiency. Cutting through their frivolity, Ballinor called them to attention, and they saluted Kat as they would an equal.

He grinned at her. "You won their admiration. No small task. These men would serve you in any situation. They will demonstrate this for our female warriors, so they too, are better prepared."

"Thank you."

"Thanks are not necessary. Your own capability persuaded them." He took her hand. "Now I think we need to consume a near-ale."

"Fine."

He led her from the building, down three alleys, across a broad street and behind a small white building.

"Where are you taking me?"

"To my quarters. My serving apprentice will bring our ales, and later our meal."

Hmmm, I suspect he's planning seduction. She grinned to herself. *Fabulous.*

Ballinor opened the door and Kat stepped through to a strongly masculine room. On one wall hung a beautiful stark white Cathnog hide, dotted with intermittent black tufts. Behind a black furry couch, hung a tapestry depicting a fierce battle. The furnishings, while sparse, were carved and polished by talented loving hands. Through a partially open door at the far end of the room, Kat caught sight of a huge bed, covered in a wooly comforter.

A home built for seduction. And he's obviously a wealthy man.

Ballinor tugged on a tassel near a table with four chairs, and when his apprentice appeared, gave a series of commands. The assistant bowed, left the room, but returned promptly with two frothy cold flagons of near-ale. He deposited both on a low table in front of the magnificent couch.

Ballinor led Kat to the couch, seated her and placed a flagon in her hand. He sat beside her and toasted her success with his men. They discussed Ballinor's plans to introduce the moves to other units of guards. "I believe we will find value to be in the position to halt a criminal without the need to use weapons." He cocked his head at her. "I am aware you are from another world. How did you come to be here? Why did you leave your world? Is your world so dangerous, women require strong defense abilities?"

Kat laughed at him. "Whoa. Too many questions at once." She told him about finding herself in Kaylin, and explained about her position as a person who designed games. The latter being the reason she researched so many items, including the art of self-defense.

Ballinor's assistant knocked at the door, and when invited, entered with their meals. He and a second assistant set linens and cutlery on the table and presented the food to them. They rose from the couch, Kat reluctantly, because of the comfort, and sat at the table.

The assistants presented an elegant table, with dishes of food, emitting tendrils of the most divine scents, and clear glassware filled with Orenberry wine. Off to one side, the assistants placed a vase of brilliant red flowers. From behind a door near the table, issued the sweet notes of some stringed instrument.

I think he's pulled out all the stops. Your lucky night, Kat.

Once they finished their meal, the assistants cleared the table, brought their glasses of wine to the stand in front of the couch, and departed silently from the room.

Ballinor guided Kat back to the couch, and raised his glass to her. "You did not consume much wine. Is the wine not to your liking?"

"I find Orenberry delicious, but exceedingly strong."

"Relax, Kat, you are in no danger here." He placed his glass on the table, picked up her hand, and kissed her palm, then her wrist. He moved up her arm, depositing kisses on the way. He arrived at her neck, and reached up and nibbled at the lobe of her ear.

Fire all over. Kat's nipples hardened and juices began to flow. Ballinor licked her lips and covered her mouth with his own. She tasted the wine on him. Her pendant glowed warm in the cleavage of her breasts. She moaned. He left her mouth and moved his lips downward. He unlaced the top of her leathers, and slipped it over her shoulder, exposing her rock hard nipple. He dropped his head and sucked on the stiff little nub.

"Oh Lian… ." She barely moaned his name, but the thought of Liandock became an ice-cold bucket of water, which drenched her. Kat pulled back, pushed Ballinor's head away, and covered her exposed breast.

Ballinor, eyes glazed, sat up startled. "What?"

Kat only stared at him, unable to speak.

"What happened? What stopped you?"

Kat closed her mouth with an audible snap. "I don't know."

A wave of disappointed emotion washed over Ballinor's face. "You thought of another. Am I right?"

"I… I don't think so. I'm not sure."

"I would never force you, Kat."

"I trust you wouldn't."

Ballinor gazed down at her. "I will return you to your room at the inn." He smiled at her. "I hope he is worth it."

Kat nodded. *We're from such different worlds. I dearly hope he is.*

CHAPTER 29

Mouse paced in front of the stable, waiting for Kat. *She made plans with Ballinor, and she is susceptible to Rifellans.* He growled to himself. *I hope she did not do anything foolish.*

Kat appeared around the corner of the building, yawning broadly. "I didn't sleep well. You better tie me on my saddle so I can nap all the way to the next town without falling off my horse."

"And what kept you awake?"

"I'm not sure. I did experience unpleasant dreams."

Mouse snorted to himself. *More likely she stayed awake because of a well-formed Rifellan. Has this woman no sense of wisdom? Momentary enjoyment will not serve her.*

Kat rubbed her eyes. "It didn't help when Shade snored so loudly."

This time Mouse snorted out loud.

"Why the snort?"

Mouse shook his head at her. "Perhaps Ballinor snored."

"Excuse me?"

Mouse glowered at her. "I said perhaps Ballinor kept you awake."

Kat's face turned red. "Ballinor? What makes you think I spent the night with Ballinor?" She spat the words at Mouse.

Oh, oh. Save me Caleesh. "You did make meal plans with him, and since you are sleepy I assumed you did so."

"Assumed? Assumed? What gives you the right, you arrogant mouse of a man, to assume anything about me?"

Oh, no. I seem to have fallen among a horde of cathnogs. "Er… I apologize if I made an error."

"Damn right you did." Kat swung herself into her saddle and cantered off, leaving Mouse to deal with the baggage animal.

He grabbed the reins of the pack horse, tied it to his saddle, mounted his own animal, which he clicked into a trot. "Kat, slow down. Our horses cannot keep this pace all the way to Magwin."

Kat refused to look back, but she slowed her horse to a brisk walk.

Mouse drew up beside her. *I shall not underestimate her temper again.* "We are headed for Magwin, but will pass through the edge of the Hafnod Forest. The innkeeper at Roothlan supplied us with a midturn meal for our stop in Hafnod."

She glared at him. "Fine."

They rode in silence on the path winding through tall grasses, and small oddly bent trees. The wind crept through the fronds, bending the heads of ripe grain, and sighing in the journey.

Mouse cocked his head at the wind's whispers. *I forgot how pleasant Shendea's grasslands are.*

Kat stopped. "The grass here sounds like the one near the Thieves Guild."

"Yes, you likened what you encountered to waves of water on a beach." *Excellent, she is over her temper.*

"I find the sound relaxing." She clicked at her horse, shook the reins, and proceeded on.

***

A line of taller, darker green trees appeared on the horizon, and as they drew closer, revealed themselves to be stately fir.

"At last. Time for food, right?"

Astonishing. Kat consumes food like a male and yet keeps the figure of a female. "A short way in the forest is a clearing, where we can light a fire and heat our meal." He glanced around. "I did not catch you conversing with your invisible cat. Is she in the vicinity."

"I can't see her. She and Breen are off exploring, I suspect."

Once among the trees, Mouse dismounted near a circle of stones and tied the three horses to a stake in the ground. "Many travelers stop at this location for meals, and each add to the comfort of the place. Kat, I shall build a fire with the kindling available, but if you would gather more, we may replace what we use."

"Don't you need some bigger pieces?"

"No. We would be wasteful to build a long-lasting blaze. We will only stop here for our midturn meal."

Kat nodded and set off to locate additional kindling.

By the time she returned with extra wood pieces, the meal bubbled perfectly in the small pot supplied by the inn. Mouse served their food, and they ate silently, but with enjoyment.

The meal over, brief but satisfying, Mouse began the cleanup.

Kat, finished with her drink, helped to tidy the small clearing.

"You do not need to do this, Kat."

"I understand. However, I realize you're my guide, not my slave. I should help."

I do not believe this. She is capable of consideration. "I appreciate the assistance."

***

Halfway to their final destination, Mouse observed a party of three Mordens approaching from another path. *Excellent — Southerners.*

He hailed them, introduced them to Kat, and invited them to join them on the journey to Magwin.

Kat turned to the leader. "You say you're from Morden, but you don't resemble the ones I met in the past. You're not as pale, and your clothing is more colorful. Are you sure you're from Morden?"

The leader, who introduced himself as Brigden, laughed out loud. "We are from the south. Those northern folks are so drab and dull, and they never do anything fun." His traveling companions chuckled at his description of his countrymen, but nodded their heads. "Perhaps the cold affects their humors."

Kat frowned at his answer. "Why would the cold affect them? The weather near Lord Rhognor's Stronghold is foul, but the Shendeans are fun and colorful."

"True. Often people are affected by their leaders."

"What do you mean, affected by their leaders?"

Brigden hesitated and appeared uncomfortable. "Nothing, only an expression. I am told Lord Rhognor displays a fine sense of humor." He changed the subject and asked about Kat's travels.

Mouse watched the exchange in silence. *Kat's curiosity is strong. I hope not too strong, to place her in danger.*

***

Shadows of the sparse trees growing in the grassland lengthened as the party approached the gates of Magwin.

"Mouse, this is the first town which is surrounded by a wall, with huge gates at the entrance. How come?"

"I understand you find their fortifications odd. The Magwins tend to be suspicious people. Being isolated creates a sense of unease when confronted by strangers. Do not expect them to be open and welcoming. Acceptance of those with whom they are not familiar, always takes time."

Brigden moved his horse beside Mouse. "We were apprised of the same rumors about the Magwins. I pray we will not encounter challenges here."

I suspect you will enjoy substantial challenges. "One cannot tell in advance how they will receive anyone. I suggest you be prepared."

All five approached the gate, guarded by four men.

Kat showed surprise. "They don't use Rifellans as guards? Why not?"

"Even Rifellans are not trusted by the Magwins."

The guards stepped forward to interrogate the five. Another portly but tall man appeared from inside the gate.

Mouse recognized a man of authority and introduced himself. "Sire, my Lady Kat is here with the blessings of Lord Rhognor to tour his land. I am her guide, Mouse."

The man from inside bobbed his head in welcome. "A delegation from Lord Rhognor is most welcome. I am Burgmaster Flank. You are here during a quiet time. Our inn is ready to serve you." He glanced at the other three. "What part do these men play in your journey?"

Brigden stepped forward. "I, Burgmaster, am Brigden from Morden and these are my two traveling associates. We come in hopes of establishing trade with your town."

Mouse caught a wave of horror on Flank's face. *This is not favorable.*

Flank faced Brigden. "Be off with you. We do not welcome your kind in Magwin."

Before Brigden could reply, Kat stepped in front of Flank.

"Burgmaster, you just informed us, did you not, you possess room at your inn?"

Oh no. Kat is doing her tactless bit again.

The man sputtered. "Not for the likes of them."

"Is your town wealthy?"

"We are not." Flank dropped his eyes and shuffled.

"So why would you turn away paying customers?"

Flank blustered. "Mordens cannot be trusted. They lie."

"You should be ashamed to listen to vile gossip. These men are from the south of Morden. They are cheerful, fine men. They come here hoping to trade with you. Why would you make assumptions without research? As to rumors, many say Magwins are rude, untrustworthy and suspicious. Is this true?"

Mouse stood like a statue off to the side. *She is a fool to speak like this to the Magwins.*

Flank, aghast at her words, choked. "Not true… not true at all."

"Well perhaps both of you should take time to find out the truth about each other. I personally will vouch for these men. After all, I am the Lady Kat."

Flank stood, mouth open, staring first at Kat and then the Mordens. His face red and his breathing rapid, he appeared unable to function. As his breath slowed, he closed his eyes, and his face returned to the normal color. "What you say makes sense." He turned to Brigden. "Welcome to our inn, we will prepare rooms for you as well as for Lady Kat and her guide."

Brigden beamed at him. "My thanks." He reached into a travel bag slung over his shoulder. "Please accept this small token. This is a most special carving from the white stones in the south of Morden. This stone brings luck and fortune to those who display the carving in their homes."

Mouse managed an inner chuckle. *At least Flank retains the grace to appear ashamed for his actions.*

***

Their horses stabled, a young assistant led them to their rooms. "Your baggage will be delivered shortly, Sire, Lady."

Mouse thanked him and followed Kat into her quarters. "You took a monstrous chance with Flank."

"Why? He was being extremely stupid."

"You are correct, but I still cannot believe you spoke the way you did. However, your words worked."

Kat peered at him. "Of course they did. Shendeans claim to be adherents of truth. I only told the truth."

"Indeed you did. But rather forcefully."

Kat shrugged at him.

Amazing. She has no idea what she accomplished.

J. M. Tibbott

CHAPTER 30

With the acceptance of the Mordens by Flank, the evening meal in the dining hall rang with merriment and laughter from all. The three Mordens told joke after joke, and most of the people in the hall roared with laughter. Mouse and Kat became virtually overlooked amid the hilarity.

"Your southern Mordens are quite different from those in the north."

Mouse glanced sideways at Kat. "I believe you met some Mordens from the north in Trigoran?"

"Yes, and I found them arrogant, humorless, and rude. You must admit the ones we encountered at the Ponti Inn were not social."

Mouse nodded at her words.

"And surely, Mouse, you didn't forget Drainin." Kat sat silent, remembering her capture by the assassins. "Why are the northern and southern Mordens so different?"

"Many ask the same question. The south is a generous land, filled with plenty of lush vegetation. The air is pleasant and warm and the people live well with the bounty produced by nature. They live beside the Baklai who are nervous folk, and pose no threat to anyone. Separating them from the northerners is the Donlan River, which is wild and fierce and possesses only two bridges over its length."

"The southern part almost seems like a separate land."

"Almost. But those in the south cannot escape the rule of the Thane."

"Would they want to, if they could?"

Mouse hesitated and avoided Kat's eyes. "Well… er… some think so. However, those in the north are steadfast in their support of the Thane."

Fascinating. Mouse is evading the question.

Before Kat said any more, he stood. "The night is upon us, and we must depart early for Glazenwyth. I suggest we retire."

He avoided discussion about the Thane. Why?

***

In the morning, Kat, loaded with backpack and diplo bag, headed for the stables. Wink slept soundly, tucked into her traveling cage. *I think I should send her on an errand. I'll bet she needs some exercise.* She reached down and stroked Breen and Shade, both of whom pilfered half the bed the previous night.

"Your pyrock sleeps to build up and preserve the energy she requires for transporting notes. Each endeavor requires much effort to complete. Sending her on an errand to create additional exercise is not necessary."

"Thanks Breen, I didn't know. I've not seen much of you and Shade for some time. What've the two of you been up to?"

"Satisfying curiosity and chasing possible prey."

"Doesn't sound fair. Prey can't perceive Shade creeping up on them."

"Not correct. Only people cannot detect Shade. All other creatures are aware of her existence. She has few she regards as prey, but most often chases for amusement. You must realize your horses possess no fear of her."

Mouse arrived with an assistant pushing a cart loaded with their baggage, which he set outside the stable. He disappeared through the doors and soon emerged, leading their horses. He and Mouse loaded the baggage, and Mouse handed him a chit for his service. The assistant thanked him and proceeded to aid Kat to mount her horse. She accepted his help and nodded her appreciation. *I'm kinda glad he helped me. I believe I'm eating too much and not exercising enough. The assistant bowed and returned to the stable.*

"Are your invisible cat and your boradai with us?"

Kat glanced at Mouse. "I don't think they're mine exactly. I believe they've decided they want to accompany us."

Mouse shrugged and took the lead.

***

They stopped in a clearing beneath a small copse of trees. Kat dismounted and sat on a flat rock.

"These trees are unusual." Kat gazed up at the foliage near the top. "The bark resembles scales on what you would call swimmers. But the huge leaves on the high branches are the best. They grow outwards and act like umbrellas."

"What is ummbrillas?"

"Um-bre-lla. They are items we carry, which open up to protect us from getting wet when the rains fall."

When Mouse still appeared puzzled, Kat picked up a stick and drew in the sandy soil. "Understand?"

"Your um-bre-lla does appear to provide protection. Would this also keep snow off a person?"

"No. Snow is too heavy, and they're not reliable in wind."

Kat rose from the rock she'd been using as a chair, and strolled over to some tall fleshy plants growing in rows extending from the path. "I saw plants like these at the Tapestry Masters hall. They're brynosh plants, aren't they?"

"Yes. Glazenwyth's people cultivate and reap the brynosh, which they sell to Master Godrith and others who need durable fibers. The Rifellans often purchase brynosh to mix with their leather to create the shields they use during battles."

"Amazing a plant can be soft and beautiful in Godrith's tapestries and also strong and hard enough for shields."

"The abilities for use of the brynosh fibers are what allow the Glazenwyths to make their living. You will enjoy them. They are straight forward people, without guile, and are open with all."

Kat's stomach rumbled. "Time for food, Mouse. Time for food."

Mouse grinned and extracted the packets of food supplied by the inn.

***

Kat stopped her horse, stood in the stirrups and pointed at the houses ahead. "I assume the village we're coming to is Glazenwyth?"

"Yes, we will stop until the morrow. We would not be able to make the Ponti Inn before dark."

"Fine with me. Once we meet with the people, I want a brisk walk. I need to move. Riding a horse for so long also stiffens the muscles."

"An excellent idea. However do not stray off the main paths."

"Oh, don't tell me there're criminals here too.?"

"Not at all. Glazenwyth is visited by few, except, of course, for those wishing to purchase the brynosh. The plants are taller than people, and you will find you can become lost within them, and also others will not be able to locate you."

"I'll be careful." *Children of the… er… brynosh? Creepy.*

A delegation appeared at the main street leading to the town, smiling and waving at the pair. A rangy, thin man stepped toward them. His face, browned by the sun, lined by years of toil and creases of laughter, possessed elegance in the same way Kat recalled the charm in the faces of Mayan descendants in South America. She liked him at once.

"Welcome to Glazenwyth, Sire, Lady. I am Ponsin, head of Glazenwyth. If you will allow us, we will bed your horses, and deliver your bags to rooms at our inn."

"On behalf of the Lady Kat and myself, I thank you."

***

Kat strode along the path through the brynosh plants, enjoying the clack and rustle of the stalks rubbing against each other. *This is way cool. I might be alone in a strange world.* She turned down a path leading off the primary one. *Love this.* She continued to take side paths.

She stopped in her tracks. Only the rattle of the stalks in the faint breeze reached her ears. *Time to go back.* She began to retrace her steps and stopped again. *Wait a minute. Did I only take paths to the right?* She shrugged and continued on. Constantly turning in the direction of where she anticipated the inn to be, Kat appeared to be walking longer on the return journey. *Oh, oh. I'm confused. Where's Shade when I need her?* Kat paused, listening for sounds of the town. Nothing. *Damn, I didn't pay attention.* She turned to her left, convinced the town lay in the direction she chose. The path stretched on, and now the sun began to dip lower in the sky. *Oh crap. I don't want to be out here all night. Mouse will get that I-told-you-so expression on his face.* She chose another side path. The light began to fade, and Kat detected an uncomfortable tickle of agitation in her spine.

She paused once more, but she had lost all sense of direction. *I'm lost and I don't like the feeling.* Something other than the wind moved among the brynosh. *What's that?* Footsteps approached, and Kat attempted to duck between some of the plants. She watched from her cover and caught sight of a man walking along the path, laden with bundles of brynosh. A wave of relief stilled her growing apprehension.

She stepped from her concealing plants. "Excuse me, I seem to be turned around. Can you tell me how to return to the inn?"

"My Lady, you startled me" He smiled at her, perfect white teeth showing in the dim light of evening. "I will gladly guide you back to the inn. You are close. Follow me."

Within minutes, they exited from the paths through the brynosh, and Kat hurried toward the inn, unsure if the growls in her stomach came from hunger or alleviation of the discomfort of being lost.

When she entered the inn, she spied Mouse, and hurried to join him.

He squinted at her. "You disappeared for a lengthy time."

"I needed the walk. I'm less stiff now."

"I see."

Kat ignored his quizzical expression. "Did you order?"

"I decided to wait for you. I will order from the serving assistant now."

Waiting for food, Kat surveyed the inn. Rifellans and Glazenwyths mixed with each other, exchanging stories and sharing laughter. Mugs of near-ale clinked each other as those in the hall toasted the fine harvest, sales of brynosh to the Rifellans, and a significant order to the Tapestry Master. The Glazenwyths, Mouse advised Kat, did not possess riches so a major sale demanded the entire village celebrate.

Studying the groups of men and women enjoying each other's company, Kat consumed her meal without registering the simplicity of the fare. The food filled her.

Without warning Kat yawned broadly. "My pardon. I'm for bed." She rose. "Meet you at the stable in the morning, Mouse."

He nodded, stood, and attempted to hide a similar yawn. "I will request the innkeeper prepare a midturn meal for us. We head for the Ponti Inn on the morrow."

Kat groaned inwardly. *Glad I walked today. After tomorrow, I'll have ponti butt.*

J. M. Tibbott

CHAPTER 31

The bed at the Glazenwyth inn, narrower than most she slept in usually, caused challenges for Kat. Shade and Breen attempted to gain most of the sleeping space, and after much pushing and prodding, Kat shoved them both to the rug on the floor. "The bed is mine. Use the mat, you pair of bed thieves."

Leaving Shade curled on the carpet, Breen leaped back to the bed and tucked into the crook of Kat's neck. *"The floor is hard. I prefer the bed."*

"Fine. Lie still so I can sleep."

***

A cold nose and warmth breath penetrated Kat's consciousness, and she reluctantly opened her eyes to a pair of emerald green orbs staring at her. "What now, Shade?"

"She is advising you to rise. Your guide is waiting."

"Rats. I'll get up."

Kat crawled from her bed, and headed to the personal. A cool shower woke her sufficiently so she managed to pack speedily, pausing only to feed Wink whose squawks indicated her acute hunger.

Packing complete, Kat called for an assistant to deliver her baggage to the stable. She grabbed her backpack with Wink's cage attached, slung her diplo bag over her shoulder, and made for the dining hall.

She spied Mouse at a table in the corner, and on her way over to join him, ordered food and Karri-san tea from one of the servers.

Mouse, his meal completed, studied a map in front of him. He pointed at the route they planned to take. "We will cross here at the Kennin bridge and make our way to the Ponti inn. We must be on guard after we cross the bridge, because we will pass through cathnog territory. We may be fortunate enough to encounter a hydodd. They are magnificent creatures."

"I would love to view a hydodd, but I can do without meeting a cathnog again."

Mouse peered at her. "When we last left the Ponti inn, I recall we did encounter a cathnog. The animal postured but ultimately backed away from us. You claimed responsibility on behalf of your invisible cat. If this cat is still with you, are we not safe from cathnogs?"

"I guess."

"Well, excellent." Mouse rose, rolled up his map, and headed for the door. He stopped a moment and glanced back at Kat. "Are you coming?"

She sighed, stood, and followed him.

***

The trail they travelled, broad enough to allow them to ride side by side, wound through the dry brynosh stalks. As they moved further from Glazenwyth, they passed through harvested plantings.

"This is much better, Mouse. We can see all around us. I felt claustrophobic in there."

"I often sense I cannot breathe if I spend much time in the brynosh fields. Is this what you mean with your words?"

"Yes."

"Would you say the word again?"

"Claus-tro-pho-bic."

"Interesting." He wrinkled his forehead. "Klos-tro-fo-bick. Am I correct?"

"You said the word correctly." Kat grinned to herself. *If this were Star Trek, I'd be breaking the prime directive.*

They travelled most of the morning, from fields to bushes tucked among budding trees, until Kat detected the sound of water. "A river."

"We are approaching the bridge over Carrog Kennin which is not a violent stream like Carrog Mannin, so we will stop for our midturn meal and allow our horses to drink. Across the bridge we enter cathnog area, so we are best to pause for our meal prior to crossing."

As they reached the water, they dismounted and Mouse led his horse and the animal with the baggage to drink at one of the pools at the edge. Kat followed suit with her horse, and when the animal drank its fill, tied the reins to a nearby tree.

She edged closer to the stream and plunked herself on a rock at the shoreline. She closed her eyes and listened to the river gargling in its throat. In the distance, raucous birds scolded each other, and a light breeze whispered in the branches of the trees closest to the water. *Almost musical.* She opened her eyes. Some of the trees clutched at the river-bank with their roots, soil worn away by the moving waters. A bird in flight flashed bright red wings from a coal black body. *This is magic.*

Mouse approached her with a plate of food in hand. "This is a plain meal, but should be filling."

"The Glazenwyths are plain people, aren't they?"

Mouse shrugged and sat on another rock.

They ate in silence, the orchestra of water, air and animals enough to keep them occupied. When they finished, Mouse buried the wrappings in the earth, leaving the area pristine.

He untied the horses, and handed Kat's reins to her. "Time to venture into cathnog terrain. Are you ready?"

Kat answered by accepting the reins and mounting her animal. She glanced around and caught sight of Shade and Breen coming through the trees. "I'm glad you're both here. Keep watch."

Mouse raised an eyebrow. "Your invisible cat?"

She nodded.

The horses' hooves clattered on the bridge and Kat eyed the placid waters below.

They barely cleared the bridge when Shade paused and roared at the path before them. Kat put her hands to her ears, but Mouse made no move. "You didn't hear the noise?"

Mouse glanced at her in surprise. "What noise?"

"Shade roared. Huge roar. I think she's telling cathnogs to stay away."

"Give my thanks to her. The journey is always more pleasant without those creatures."

They travelled for a short distance when Shade roared again. Mouse did not react. Then a bugle echoed from ahead. Mouse reined in his horse, and Kat followed suit. On the path appeared a monstrous elk-like creature, crowned with magnificent antlers, clad in lustrous hair the color of burnt sienna. The animal approached two steps, paused, bent one foreleg and dropped his head. *Is he bowing? Wow.* Shade moved toward the hydodd, touched her nose to his, and purred. Kat realized her mouth hung open. "I'll be… ." Both animals rose to their full height. The hydodd trumpeted again, turned, and sauntered off through the trees.

Mouse gaped at Kat. "What happened? Why did the hydodd act so oddly?"

Kat shook her head in wonderment. "Shade."

He gazed at her in astonishment. "What kind of animal is this cat of yours? I have never experienced any creature like this."

Kat shook her head again, unable to find words to describe how the encounter affected her.

***

They rested the horses at the Ponti inn and arranged to continue their journey the following star turn on pontis. Kat, still in awe over the contact between Shade and the hydodd, ate mechanically, unaware of the conversations among others in the dining hall. Anxious to speak to Breen about the situation, she excused herself early and went to her room. After feeding Wink, she indulged in a hot shower to assure a sound sleep.

Once in bed she called to Breen. *"We need to speak."*

The boradai leaped to the pillow, maintaining physical contact with Kat. *"You are curious about Shade?"*

"Of course. Why did the hydodd bow to her?"

"They deferred to each other, a sign of mutual respect. The creature called a hydodd recognized, despite the similarity to a cathnog, Shade owns dominion over them. They understood their duties do not conflict with each other. I like Shade, and I like hydodds too."

"So Shade can communicate with other animals?"

"Indeed, and all other animals understand she owes a significant duty to you."

"Why me?"

"I do not posses such information. Neither does she."

Despite all the thoughts whirling in her head, Kat expressed her thanks and drifted to sleep.

***

After a meal the following morning, Kat asked the stable master for a cushion and tied the protection to her saddle before mounting the ponti.

Mouse regarded her with raised eyebrows and a bemused smile. "If you spend less time thinking about your discomfort, and more blessing the fact you are able to ride most of the way to the Stronghold, you might not suffer as much."

Kat glared at him. *There's no harm in trying what he suggests, I suppose.* She closed her eyes. *I'm glad we can ride to Halfway Haven instead of walking.* She repeated the phrase over and over, matching her words to the rhythm of the gait of the odd little creatures.

So caught up in her personal mantra, she assumed they'd arrived at Halfway Haven far quicker than before. Fortunately no snow fell during their trip, so the weather appeared gentler. *Hmm, it did work a little.*

As they dismounted, Mouse took the reins from her. "Did that help?"

Kat glanced at him innocently. "Did what help?"

Mouse shook his head and sighed. "Nothing."

They entered the Haven, found a table and ate a substantial midturn meal.

Anwen, the woman who led them to the Stronghold when they first arrived, joined them. "Welcome again. When you complete your meal, I will gather assistants to carry your baggage, and we will head to the Lord Rhognor's Stronghold.

I remember, a challenging climb up the mountain. Well, I need the exercise. "Thank you Anwen. The weather appears to be better this star turn."

***

While finding the climb difficult, but without the blinding blizzards of their first trip, Kat fared much better. *My legs are stronger. I'll bet the riding's responsible.* Despite stronger legs, Kat spied the opening to the Stronghold with gratitude.

Here at last, and I'm ready for food. Anwen led them to their rooms. After settling Wink in her larger cage, Kat sank on her bed. As she did so, Breen appeared and jumped up beside her.

Kat surveyed the room, but Shade was absent. *"Where's Shade?"*

"She did not enter the Stronghold. She claims she dislikes living under rocks."

"Funny. Here I'm in the biggest bed of any inn, and I don't need to share this one."

"I am sharing the bed."

"Yes, but you don't take up as much room as Shade does."

A knock at the door and Kat called out "Come." She sat up.

Mouse entered. "Deleth sent me a message. Rhognor will meet with us on the morrow after the morning meal. So to enjoy our meal this evening, we will join the healers in the secondary hall."

"Fine by me. I plan to eat, and retire early. Although we had no snow or blinding winds, I still expended much energy climbing up here."

Mouse glanced around the room. "I see your boradai on your bed. Is your invisible cat here?"

"No. Breen says Shade prefers outdoors to rocks overhead."

"I understand. I prefer the same."

As they made for the dining hall, Kat eyed him thoughtfully. *One more thing I've learned. He doesn't like living inside a mountain.*

CHAPTER 32

Kat ambled through the halls of the Stronghold absent-mindedly studying the walls, when Liandock emerged from a side passageway. Kat ran toward him joy in her smile. "You're here. When did you arrive? Why did you come?"

He held up a hand. "Stop Kat. Time is short. You must be careful. Danger is surrounding you. Take the boradai with you."

"But… .

"I said take the boradai with you."

As she reached for him, he swept backwards, his form dissolving into a white vapor. The vapor transformed to a grey mist. Whispers surrounded her. The mist swirled and whirled, and evolved to an outline of a black robed man. He beckoned. Cold. Fear. Kat attempted to move, to call out. Frozen to the floor.

"Wake. Wake now. This is not real."

Kat's eyes snapped open, and she gasped for breath. *"Breen?"*

"You experienced a night dream. Not reality. You are safe."

"Something was real. My stone is cold."

"Your fear caused the cold. You are safe."

Kat threw back the covers and left the warm bed. *I thought Liandock real. Did he appear only to send me a warning?*

***

Showered, dressed and pyrock fed, Kat sat down to write in her journal when a knock at the door disturbed her. She raised her head. "Come."

A face appeared around the door. "Welcome back Kat." Kaydith giggled. "I remembered not to call you Lady Kat."

"I'm pleased to be back." She smiled. "And thanks for remembering."

"Before you order your morning meal, Sir Mouse sent me to request you join him in his quarters to eat."

"I will. Would you order me the lovely porridge-type stuff with the nuts?"

"You mean the journeyklim?"

"Yes. I can never remember the name. I keep wanting to call the stuff jerky."

"Our name is sensible. The nutty flavor comes from the pods of the klim plant, and many travelers use the mixture on their journeys. They add water and heat. Journeyklim keeps in all kinds of weather."

"I'll put my writing away and I'll join Mouse momentarily."

Kaydith nodded and backed out of the room.

On her way to Mouse's quarters, Kat encountered Deleth heading to the communal dining hall.

"Kat, welcome back. I know you will be leaving again soon, but before you do, come and say farewell."

"I will, I promise."

Kat arrived at the entrance to Mouse's rooms and knocked.

He opened the door, and ushered her in. "I am delighted you came so promptly."

"When you summon, Sir Mouse, I obey at once." She gave him a mock salute.

Mouse frowned, a bewildered expression on his face. "Am I to assume this is an attempt at some of your sarcasm?"

Kat sighed. "Yes, Mouse. You do need to lighten up."

He shook his head. "I will not ask what you mean by the phrase, lighten up. I am sure the meaning is not favorable."

Kat sighed again. "I meant you should relax more. You're always so tense around me."

"You are not an easy woman to guide."

Kat shrugged. "My food is here, so before you give me all the details of why you asked to meet in your quarters, can we at least eat first?"

"Of course. I merely wished to cover the journey from here to the Magicians Guild, and after, on to Rifella. We will present this to Rhognor when we meet him after the midturn meal."

They ate in silence.

Why did he want to meet here before we see Rhognor? I think I try his patience. Don't think he's used to independent women.

With the meal cleared from the table, Mouse opened the maps to explain the route to Kat. "As you are aware, we must return to the Ponti inn to obtain our own horses. We will head for Vendi's inn, cut through the Hafnod forest, and follow the trail along the foot of the Clog Nordad mountains. Eventually we arrive at the Magicians Guild, and when we leave them, we will use the bridge to cross the Carrog Pandy, and then journey to Rifella."

"I hope we won't run into any Cathnogs near Vendi's inn."

"If your invisible cat accompanies us, I cannot fathom a reason to fear cathnogs."

"I'm sure she will. Breen tells me she will meet with us once we leave the Stronghold."

"Which reminds me, Kat. You cannot take Breen with us. You are not allowed to remove a boradai from Shendea."

"But I must." *Liandock told me to.*

"Removing one from Shendea is forbidden."

"I can't choose to leave her behind. I received a vision to carry her with me."

"Kat, you are not listening. Boradai are most important to the Shendeans. If you take her, you will be breaking Shendean law. Punishment for such a transgression is… is death by fire."

Kat felt her eyes widen. She gulped. "Death by fire?"

"Yes. Do not take Breen with you."

I must. Liandock told me to. I'll pretend to obey Mouse, but Breen needs to come with me. I'll hide her. "Okay, you can stop drilling. You've struck oil."

Mouse's expression was more than puzzlement. He resembled someone confronted by a talking camel.

"I mean, you can stop the lecture. I understand what you are telling me."

"I hope you do. I am serious about this."

Crap, he's a worrywart. I'll conceal her well. And if they catch me with her, I'm convinced my part in this land is too important to set me on fire… I hope!

CHAPTER 33

Kat arrived at the entrance to Rhognor's quarters as Mouse appeared from a side passage.

Where did he come from? She stared at him "I stopped by your quarters on my way here and knocked, but got no reply. Where were you?"

Mouse shrugged. "Just completing some final arrangements."

"I packed most of my items, since I assume we will leave on the morrow."

"Excellent. You heeded my warning about your boradai?"

"Mouse. We've discussed this." *I hope he's not planning to search me as we leave.*

Mouse addressed the guard standing at attention. "Would you please advise Lord Rhognor, Lady Kat and I are here?"

The young man turned, knocked twice, and partially opened the door. "Lord Rhognor, Sir Mouse and Lady Kat are here for their meeting with you."

"Thank you, Beneth. Admit them at once."

Rhognor welcomed them with smiles and enquired after their well-being. A prodigious container of tea rested on a table in the corner of the room. He ushered them to three chairs and when seated, with tea in hand, he requested they fill him in on their travels.

Kat related her amazement at the sight of Burning Rock Mountain, and the pleasure of the Crimson Cauldron.

Rhognor appeared most concerned when Mouse mentioned the attackers at the Cauldron. "Where do you think they came from?"

Mouse shook his head. "I completed arrangements with an acquaintance to deal with the bodies, and even he possesses no knowledge of their origin."

"The lack of anything to indicate the identity of the men worries me." Rhognor scratched his chin. "I suspected unwelcome visitors to Shendea, but this instance appears deliberately aimed at the two of you."

"My suspicions as well." Mouse grimaced. "Kat experienced a second attack in Roothlan." He beamed at her. "However, she handled herself admirably. So much so, she provided an example of how she dealt with the man to Ballinor, the head of guards in the town."

Rhognor regarded Kat with raised eyebrows. "You appear to be fulfilling Eduardo's hopes."

"I'm not positive what I am supposed to be doing. I only defend myself when necessary. I suspect you are all expecting things from me I cannot give."

Mouse turned to Rhognor again. "She also intervened when the Magwins decided to turn away a group of Southern Mordens from their town." Mouse raised an eyebrow. "She used forceful words, and I feared she might be in danger. However the Magwins acted in the past, this time they showed signs of being mollified. A new trading partnership now exists with Mordens from the south."

"Mouse, I believe you're suggesting our journey was fraught with problems." Kat turned to Rhognor. "We met some amazing people over the past star turns, and the visit to the Thieves Guild I found most enlightening. I enjoyed myself." *Mouse and Rhognor just looked at each other as if I said something of significance. What's the undercurrent I'm not catching?*

"Regardless, Lady Kat, I am pleased with what you accomplished."

What? I appear to have achieved something important. "So how soon can I return home?"

Rhognor's face bore a grim expression. "I do not believe you possess agreements from sufficient people with power as yet." He held up his hand to forestall further comments from Kat. "I believe you completed what you needed to in Shendea, and I wish you safe journey in your travels to Rifella." He addressed Mouse. "I assume you will travel through the Hafnod Forest and via the Magicians Guild to cross Carrog Pandy into Rifella?"

"That is my plan."

"Excellent. My troops and I are planning my seasonal travels to meet with my people across Shendea. Since a substantial group moves slower than you will, would you consider allowing my Lady Halfin and her guards to travel with you to the Magician's Guild? I would trust few others to accompany Halfin in her journey."

Mouse dropped his head. "Lord Rhognor we would be honored to travel with your bond mate."

"My thanks. Kat, would you be willing to pause for an extra star turn at the Ponti inn, so Lady Halfin can join you there."

"I am, and I'm sure I speak for Mouse as well, Lord Rhognor." *Being on the road with Halfin should be amazing.* "Do you travel around Shendea often?"

"The Lady Halfin and I tour four times during a path, once each season. I can keep in touch with how my people are faring, and can supply aid to a community if necessary. Plus this allows my mate to commune with her beloved nature. I do believe our outings keep her balanced and able to deal with my peculiarities."

Well. There is more to Rhognor than I suspected. Deleth's right. He's a fine leader.

"As I said, Kat, we travel slowly. But at any point I might need to ask a guard to stay somewhere, and perform a service for me at a particular community. This is why I take so many with me." He smiled. "Halfin tends to be impatient to see everything. I am too slow for her. My problem is, I do not often find someone I can trust to travel with her."

"My thanks for your trust." Kat bowed her head to him. "Would you not prefer she travels with us from the Stronghold?"

"Thank you for your offer Kat, but the route to the Ponti inn is of necessity, slow, and I prefer to be with her during the portion of the mountain trip. It is important we travel carefully down to Halfway Haven. This section of the Clog Nordad can be treacherous at times."

Mouse stepped forward. "Lord Rhognor, Kat and I will begin our preparations, and we will depart in the morning."

Fine idea, and I'll talk to Breen about concealing herself. This is not the time for Mouse to grow into a sizable rat.

CHAPTER 34

Kat finalized her packing, including dismantling of her pyrock's permanent cage, and stowing her writings, cathnog pen and ink in her diplo bag. She ordered her morning meal brought to her room, and also consumed two cups of Karri-san. *Need to build up my immunity to the Rifellans.*

A sudden thought struck her as she spied Breen on the bed, watching her preparations. She strode over and stroked the boradai. *"Breen I received a vision which ordered me to take you with me on this journey, but Mouse warned me not to. What should I do?"*

"I must go with you, Kat."

"Are you sure? I don't want to face death by fire."

"You will not, and I am obliged to accompany you."

"I trust your judgment, and I'm grateful. Jump into the side pocket on my back pack, and stay out of sight."

Breen did so. Kat donned the pack, slung her diplo bag over her shoulder, and headed for the front gates of the Stronghold.

Mouse, plus two attendants carrying his baggage and those of Kat waited for her. They began their trek down the Clog Nordad to Half Way Haven. The weather was cold, but sunny and pleasant, so Kat wore a lighter overcoat. She left her warm fur-lined one with Kaydith, together with a request the parcel be delivered to Brith in Kaylin. Kat seemed unlikely to need anything as warm again. Brith would understand what to do with the garb.

They reached the approach to Half Way Haven, when Shade made her usual appearance. She yawned at Kat, curled her tongue and purred.

"Hi Shade."

Both attendants regarded Kat curiously, but Mouse shrugged.

As they entered the Haven, Mouse thanked both attendants and waved them on their way to return to the Stronghold.

The attendant at the Haven dining hall advised them their luggage was being loaded on the pontis they had brought before, and the other two would be waiting for them when they were ready.

Mouse thanked him. "Kat, we will pause for a meal, before heading for the Ponti inn."

"I'm not terribly hungry, but I could handle a light snack." *Wish I could send everything I eat to my butt when I am forced to ride a ponti.*

***

At the Ponti inn, Kat slid off the little beast with a groan, and turned the animal over to the stable master.

"On the morrow, Sire and Lady, we will prepare your own horses for travel and load them with your baggage."

"We will not be departing from your inn until a second star turn, stable master. You can wait to prepare our horses until then."

After thanking the stable master Kat set off for her room, leaving Mouse to take care of the inspection of their own horses.

Once in her quarters, Kat set Wink's cage on a small stand, and removed the sleepy fur-ball to feed her. "I'm going to send you to Brith, to advise her the fur lined coat is on it's way to her." She gave Wink an extra piece of food, and retrieving her pyrock word list and writing materials, proceeded to pen a note. "Are you ready, Wink?"

The little pyrock lifted a furry leg, and Kat attached the tube into which she placed her missive.

"Wink, go to Brith, please."

The animal squeaked, butted her head against Kat's finger, and flapping her wings lifted from the desk. Two more flaps and she disappeared with a pop.

Kat decided to enjoy a warm shower before dinner to ease the ponti aches from her limbs. When she returned to the room, she discovered Shade stretched out on the bed. Kat smiled and sat, and stroked the gleaming fur. The animal purred. "Where did you come from? Why are you here?" Shade closed her eyes, yawned, and slept.

***

The dining hall at the inn, filled with visitors bound for the Stronghold, and those leaving for other venues, throbbed with a hubbub of conversation and laughter.

Kat placed herself at a table and waited for Mouse to join her.

"My pardon, Lady, are you Rifellan from the north?" The woman standing beside her stood tall and boasted glorious blonde hair, streaked with light red strands.

Kat glanced up at the woman, startled. "No, I'm not. I'm not from Pridden at all." The woman appeared puzzled. "I'm Kat."

"Ah yes. You are the woman who visits us from another world. Your name is familiar to us. I am Kaleen. My male parent hales from the north, but my female parent is from the southern part of Rifella." She sat in the other chair at Kat's table. "You sit all alone, and we would welcome you to join us." She pointed at a table with five Rifellan women."

Kat glanced around. Mouse had still not arrived. *Why not?* "I'm honored to be asked, and I accept."

Both women rose and Kat brought her chair to the table, and sat. The women introduced themselves, and Kat soon discovered herself in a stimulating conversation about warfare. "You all are so well informed. I've a friend in Kaylin, Irina, who is mate to Bardu, the Praetor of Lord Eduardo's guards. She also passed on to me some information on the Rifellan understanding of warfare."

Kaleen stared at her. "You are dressed in Rifellan guard garb. We assumed you held a post with the guards."

"I don't. I disliked the constriction of the dresses most Kaylin women wear, so I persuaded the tailor to produce these leathers for me. Since I find this my most comfortable clothing, I would like to purchase similar outfits. Are any of you aware of where I might do so before I leave Shendea? I am headed for Rifella, but would appreciate some changes of clothing."

All the women replied at once. "Rantor's in Blain. He is the best at what he does."

"Where is Blain?"

"If you plan to stop at the Magicians Guild on your way to Rifella, you will no doubt stay one night in Blain, which is close to the Guild."

The women ordered food, and helped Kat to choose something unusual, which, despite the odd appearance, tasted delicious. They all chuckled when Kat ordered Karri-san. "Now we are entirely aware you are not Rifellan."

They continued to chat, until Kat attempted to hide a yawn. Three of the others yawned broadly.

Kat apologized. "I just arrived by ponti, and though they're surefooted animals, they're incredibly uncomfortable, and I must admit I'm tired."

"We agree with you about pontis. Rifellan women do not possess padded posteriors, and we too feel discomfort on their bony backs. We are headed for Finrase on the morrow, so Kat we may not meet again. We wish you a pleasant journey."

They parted with hugs all around, and Kat left the hall for her room.

She turned a corner and bumped into Mouse. "I ate dinner without you. I'm tired and off to my bed."

"My apologies, Kat. I needed to complete many preparations. Since we must stay this night and the next at the inn, the morrow will be leisure time for you. We should plan to meet for the evening meal, as Lady Halfin and her party should arrive by then."

"Fine." Kat yawned and staggered down the hall, visions of a plump mattress and cozy comforter beckoning. *I'm glad Mouse didn't make the meal. I met some terrific women I can relate to, strong, confident independent women. Super rad.*

***

Kat woke, ravenous, and hurried through her morning routine. The dining hall beckoned. *Mouse's comments were vague last night. Odd he didn't tell me he wouldn't be in the hall for the evening meal.*

She strode into the hall and stopped in surprise. "Deleth. I didn't expect to meet you here."

Deleth seated with three women wearing healer colors, stood and invited Kat to join them. "We are bound for the Dark Forest in Kaylin, part of our regular retreat."

"Does this mean no healers will be in Shendea while you're gone?"

"We would never leave our land without some healers in attendance. Most will be apprentices, but we also possess a number who are nearing the completion of their training."

Curiosity prompted Kat to ask for more information. "Can you tell me what sort of things you do in the Forest?"

"We spend most of our stay, meditating and requesting Caleesh impart us with new knowledge. This is a restful and regenerative experience for us."

The other two healers rose, and excused themselves from the table. "We will meet you at the stables, Deleth."

Deleth nodded at them.

"Deleth, since I will most likely not see you before I leave Shendea, may I ask you something?"

"Yes, of course."

"Eduardo told me I needed a number of people with power to help me return to my own home. I am aware you own the power of prediction. Will you agree to be one of the people who helps me when the time comes?"

Deleth smiled. "I would be honored. I assume you will request the same of Lord Rhognor?"

"I think I will. I learned he is a fine man, and an excellent leader. How much power he possesses, I don't know, but Breen assures me, he has more than I suspect even he realizes."

"Breen?" Deleth's eyebrows climbed skyward.

"Yes."

"Breen is with you?"

Oh, oh. "Um… yes."

"Kat, you cannot take Breen with you." An expression of horror crossed her face.

"But I must."

"Taking a boradai is against the law and is a serious offense."

"But Deleth, she insisted I take her."

"The boradai insisted?" Deleth's face now registered amazement.

Kat nodded.

"Such a thing is unheard of."

"I must take her Deleth. I also received a vision telling me to do so."

"A vision as well?" She put her hand to her mouth. "I do not believe this bodes well."

"Breen insists on coming. Even if I did not conceal her in my pack, she would follow on her own."

Deleth took both of Kat's hands in hers. "I can find nothing in my experience about this. Tell no one. Most Shendeans do not understand boradai retain their own agendas." She released Kat's hands. "I must go. The other healers are waiting. Be careful, Kat."

She nodded at Deleth, unable to say anything more. *Deleth didn't threaten to turn me over to the authorities. But I can tell she's frightened. What am I in for?*

CHAPTER 35

Mouse stood at the entrance to the dining hall, when Kat arrived for the evening meal.

"Has Halfin arrived yet, Mouse?"

"Her party is at the stable, they should be joining us momentarily. We will wait for her at the table for eight which I arranged with Vendi."

"Eight?"

"Four guards accompany her, plus her personal attendant."

"Makes sense. Rhognor wouldn't want her traveling without an escort."

"I must also tell you, when I spoke with Vendi he wished to give us the hide of the cathnog we encountered on our first visit here. The skin is rare and beautiful, but is not something with which we can afford to be burdened. I requested he either keep the pelt for the inn, or present the skin to Lady Halfin."

"Excellent idea, Mouse. You're correct we can't travel with a cathnog hide. What did he decide to do?"

"I understand he will present the skin to Lady Halfin."

Mouse led the way to a table, prepared for eight people, when conversation in the hall ceased, and the people rose to their feet and bobbed their heads in the direction of the entrance.

Kat pivoted, and smiled as she recognized Rhognor's bond mate. "Halfin."

Mouse's eyes widened at her words. "Kat, this is a time to practice formality. You are in the company of Lady Halfin's subjects, all who respect her as much as they do Lord Rhognor." He left Kat's side and greeted Halfin, escorting her to the reserved section.

He held out a chair at the head, and seated Halfin with due ceremony. He indicated Kat should sit at her right, and he positioned himself to her left. Halfin's attendant, whom she introduced as Fardith, settled herself beside Kat, and the guards filled the balance of the chairs.

Halfin's laugh tinkled amid the sounds of resumed conversations. "Mouse you outdo yourself. Such formality. My thanks."

A serving attendant, bearing a flagon of near ale, approached Halfin, and placed the mug on the table. "My Lady, may I be informed of your request for the evening meal?"

Halfin asked for a dish unknown to Kat.

Sounds exotic and I want to taste some. "I will try the... ." She stopped. Mouse subtly shook his head at her. *Perhaps I should order something else.* "I would enjoy wullawerth stew, if there is some available."

"We do have some, my Lady." The attendant move down the table and continued taking orders.

Halfin touched Kat on the arm. "Do advise me what adventures you and Mouse enjoyed during your journey though Shendea. Rhognor and I did not discuss what you accomplished during your travels. I feel sure we will speak of this at a later time."

Kat described her visit to Burning Rock Mountain and relaxing in the mud of the Crimson Cauldron. "I felt like the mud seeped into my bones, relaxing every muscle and piece of tissue in my body. The following star turn I found a shop in Finrase and received a total back manipulation."

"I too experienced the manipulation at Finrase. I relaxed so completely, I fell asleep, and the young shopkeeper allowed me to rest until the time of the midturn meal. I pleased my Lord Rhognor when I relayed how I reacted to the manipulation. He is always advising me I spend too much time helping others, and not enough time for myself." She smiled. "He is a most thoughtful mate."

They continued to exchange experiences, and Halfin expressed amazement at Kat's version of a time thievery. "Unfortunately I have not been a witness to such a ceremony. I hold the hope such a time will come."

They continued to chat throughout the meal, and ended with cups of tea, Kat with her usual Karri-san. All dishes and cutlery were cleared, when Vendi approached, carrying something white.

He cleared his throat. "My Lady Halfin. On their first stay at our inn, Sir Mouse and the Lady Kat encountered a cathnog on their journey. I believe the animal met its end during an encounter with a hydodd. Sir Mouse kindly donated the animal's remains to the inn. As hunting a cathnog is forbidden, unless during a rite of passage, the meat added welcome food to our inn. To give thanks for our beneficent life in Shendea, and especially to you and Lord Rhognor who govern us so wisely, we wish to present this magnificent hide to you both."

Vendi extended his arms, across which lay a glorious fur pelt, pristinely white, and dotted with small round tufts of black fur.

Kat held her breath. *This is the most gorgeous thing ever.*

Halfin reached out and stroked the magnificent skin. "Beautiful." She closed her eyes and continued to stroke. "This cathnog did indeed meet his end with a hydodd." She tilted her head. "How odd, a most unusual hydodd. Filled with power. Intelligent. I cannot quite sense everything." She opened her eyes and stared up at Vendi. "My sincere thanks for this magnificent gift. Lord Rhognor and I shall treasure this fine animal."

Mouse rose from his seat. "My Lady Halfin, please forgive me, but I deemed this turn to be overly long, and I need to prepare for the rest of our journey. May I request leave to depart your company?"

Halfin smiled at him, and then did a double take. "Of course." She stood and gazed at him intently. "I do believe, Mouse, you tend to overextend yourself."

Mouse lowered his eyes. "Thanks to you Lady Halfin." He turned and hastily departed the dining hall.

Kat scrutinized him, and turned to regard Halfin with curiosity. *What did I miss? What just occurred?*

Halfin remained standing. "I should take my sleep now. I suspect the rest of you would appreciate attending your beds."

Kat smiled at her. "Lady Halfin, my thanks. My bed does beckon. I assume Mouse and I will meet you at the stables in on the morrow?"

At Halfin's nod, Kat hastened to her room. She fed Wink, undressed, and contemplated the incident between Halfin and Mouse. *Something weird is going on between those two.*

Kat discovered Shade stretched out on a rug beside the bed, sleeping and snoring. She stuck out a toe and nudged the cat in the ribs. "Stop snoring. I need my sleep."

Shade shifted and her snores ceased.

Within minutes, Kat slid under the covers, cuddled in the warm comforter, and snuggled with Breen. She yawned so widely her jaw creaked. *"Night Breen... ."*

***

The morning dawned bright with fine weather, and the promise of a delightful day. Kat with backpack on, and diplo bag over her shoulder waited for Halfin and Mouse to appear. She had tucked Breen in the side pocket of the backpack, and attached Wink's travel cage the other side.

Halfin appeared from the inn, a spring in her step, and her voice cheerful. "Good morrow, Kat. What a wonderful day."

Kat nodded and drew in a deep breath of clean fresh air.

Halfin took a deep breath of her own. "I did not advise Mouse of my intention to travel without haste toward Garrin, but my men brought tents and equipment for the night at a perfect place the other side of the Nordad Pass. I prefer to travel through the Hafnod Forest during the brightest part of a star turn. Nature is at her best during the light."

A shriek from behind Kat startled her, and she jumped in alarm.

"She's taking a boradai from us." Fardith pointed at Kat's backpack. "She's taking a boradai."

Halfin gasped.

Kat peered over her shoulder at the edge of her backpack and caught Breen's nose poking from the side pocket.

Before anyone else reacted, Kat discovered herself surrounded by Halfin's guards, swords out, and the assistant expressing her shock. "Lady Kat, you commit a crime by removing a boradai from Shendea. We must take you to Lord Rhognor, where he will pronounce your punishment."

Halfin with a horrified expression on her face, stepped in front of her guards. "Kat, how could you? The penalty is death by fire. I cannot protect you." She faced her guards. "We must deal with this transgression now. Request a private room from Vendi, and we will assemble to handle this ourselves. Lord Rhognor need not be disturbed."

When the guard returned, the rest led Kat sputtering in protest, followed by Halfin and her assistant, into the room provided.

"I didn't steal Breen, Halfin." Kat's heart pounded in her chest. *Rats. I'm trapped.*

Halfin motioned at her to cease talking. She requested her guards set up chairs to resemble a type of court, with Halfin at the head. Kat sat in front, with a guard on each side preventing any chance of escape.

"Lady Kat. You are charged with attempting to remove a boradai from Shendea. How do you plead?"

"Halfin, please. I did not intend to remove Breen. Before we left the Stronghold, I received a vision telling me to take Breen with me on this part of the journey. When I spoke to Breen about the vision, she advised me it is vital she accompany me. I did attempt to leave her behind, but three times I discovered her hidden in my backpack. Again she insisted she must accompany me."

Halfin listened to Kat until she finished her explanation. "Lady Kat, please remove the boradai from the backpack."

Kat did so and placed Breen on the floor.

Halfin regarded the creature. "Boradai, approach." Breen loped across the floor and leapt in Halfin's lap, who placed both her hands on the animal's back. "This boradai confirms Lady Kat's version of what occurred. She insists she must accompany Kat on the journey to the Magician's Guild. She claims this is of critical importance."

Halfin shooed Breen from her lap and rose. "As Lady Kat holds no blame for the boradai being at this place, and the responsibility rests entirely with this creature, we can hardly punish her for this apparent transgression." She stared at Kat. "You are not at fault, and we apologize for assuming the blame rested on your shoulders. Please understand this law came directly from the boradai. We do not control them as they are governed by their own rules. We do not offer boradai to others. They are the only ones who decide with whom they shall bond."

She bent and picked up Breen and handed her to Kat, who shifted one strap of the backpack off her shoulder, and returned the animal to the side pocket.

"Wait, Kat. Before we leave this room, you must understand, you cannot remove Breen from Shendea. She will travel with you as is needed, but you may not attempt to remove her from the borders of our land. My conversation with this one is most unusual. No boradai ever requested what Breen demanded of me. But she did confirm she does not intend to leave Shendea. The bond you share with this one has never been encountered by any others."

"I'll not attempt to remove her from Shendea, and thank you, Lady Halfin for your understanding."

The party returned to the stable where their horses waited. The guards always protective of Halfin now regarded Kat with an expression of curiosity. Mouse appeared from the inn, and apologized for his late arrival.

"Lady Halfin, I received a pyrock message from Lord Rhognor. He confirms he will join our party at Blain."

A smile lit Halfin's face. "I anticipate his arrival with pleasure."

All mounted their respective animals and departed for the Hafnod Forest.

Kat's heartbeat slowed, and adrenaline dissipated.

Scary. I thought the fire thing was a joke. And how come these are boradai rules, not those of Shendeans?

CHAPTER 36

Kat rode beside Halfin as they approached a fork in road. The two guards at the head of the party, turned right.

"This appears familiar to me. The road to the left is the one Mouse and I took from Kaylin, via the Nordad Pass. Am I right?"

Halfin scrutinized the pass. "I believe you are correct, although I never visited Kaylin."

"Interesting. The leaders of lands in Pridden don't appear to meet each other. Why?"

"Kat, you should understand each of our lands are very different in their practices and customs. The individuals within each land expect their leaders to remain in their own lands to solve the problems of their own people. Only beings with beneficial abilities or traders, tend to travel and remain in other lands."

"When you talk about beneficial abilities, who do you mean?"

"The two best examples of them are our healers, who are much sought after, and are revered in all lands, and the Rifellans. The latter are in demand by the rulers of most of the lands to provide security. They are almost always those who deal with challenges of crime or violence within each land. The sole exception is Morden. Thane Galdin does not welcome those of other lands."

"Weird. Doesn't he also need people to provide security?"

"Naturally. However he has the Assassins' Guild to call upon."

"I met some of them." Kat shuddered, remembering her brush with the assassins in Kaylin. "So the leaders never meet each other in person?"

"They do on rare occasions. When a situation arises and causes challenges for all Pridden inhabitants, they will gather together." Halfin raised her hand to her mouth to hide a half smile. "Often the problem which follows, determines in which land they will meet." Halfin snorted delicately. "The last time they met, Rhognor shared the messages with me. I could not help but be greatly amused at the discussions."

"I can imagine. When men vie for superiority over one another, the result is often hilarious."

"You forget, Lord Murwenna of Rifella is female. Her antics are often more intense."

Mouse rode up beside the two. "Thane Galdin never attends a meeting outside of Morden."

Kat turned to him. "Is he ever at any meetings?"

"I remember only one, many star turns ago. The Thane from Glowen said or did something to annoy Galdin. The following star-turn, we discovered Glowen's Thane dead in his room. No one uncovered the cause. However, all suspected Galdin to be at fault." He frowned. "Without announcing their intention aloud, the rest of the leaders decided never to meet again in Morden."

Kat clicked her horse on, and rode ahead of Halfin and Mouse. *I suspect this Galdin guy is one person I will not seek to help me return home. But perhaps some other person from Morden will be blessed with enough power.*

The guards leading the group halted and one rode back to confer with Halfin.

Kat unable to hear what they said, watched Halfin nod and all four guards dismounted and began erecting a series of tents.

Soon a small encampment rose, with a tent in the middle for Halfin and her assistant, and which she invited Kat to share. A tent sat on either side of Halfin's, one of which belonged to Mouse and the other for two of the guards. At the rear of Halfin's, another tent contained the other two guards. One of the guards constructed an excellent fire, and they all would share watch duty beside the fire during the night.

The entire party gathered for a meal prepared by the inn who also supplied them with the snacks they consumed during the day. This substantial repast contained a variety of foods. Kat stared at the plate prepared for Halfin. "You don't eat meat?"

Halfin smiled at her. "No. Members of the Enchanters' Guild never consumed the flesh of animals. I do believe if I did so now, I might become ill."

"Many friends in my home world eat as you do. I tried to follow their ways, but I cannot sustain such a way of eating. I suppose something exists in meat, my body requires."

Halfin nodded. "Every one should follow the dictates of their own bodies. What works for one, does not necessarily work for another."

Kat followed her meal with a huge cup of Karri-san. *Just as well I drank this now. Some of the guards are beginning to appear too delicious to me.*

A small tent off to the side, provided some of the amenities of a personal, and Kat followed Halfin's use and headed for her bed. Within minutes, Breen joined her, and sleep overtook them all.

***

The sun, bright in the morning sky, shone on the travelers as they entered the first trees of Hafnod Forest. The newborn leaves reminded Kat of spring growth back home. The forest vibrated with sound — birds calling to their young, rustlings of animals in the undergrowth, leaves rattling against each other and the soft gurgling of diminutive creeks.

Traveling through the cheerful Hafnod Forest affected the entire party. Even the horses lifted their hooves a little higher. Halfin burst into lighthearted song, a bright melody about beginnings and renewed growth. Her ebullience influenced her assistant to add her crisp contralto. But the addition of the gorgeous baritones of the guards, created the final symphony of jubilant harmonics.

Kat hummed softly in accompaniment. *Happy — this is what happy sounds like.* She glanced at Mouse. He smiled as he rode, but kept silent.

Almost as if a curtain lifted from a stage, the trees thinned and the village of Garrin lay before them. The houses, painted in different colors, resembled a newly completed tapestry. Small, but neat, with slate roofs, every house sported colorful walls, with contrasting window shutters. To Kat's right, a sizable building covered in blushing salmon pink, and decorated with apple green doors and windows attracted her immediate attention. Mouse riding beside her pointed at the edifice. "What you glimpse is the inn we will rest at this night."

"How beautiful." *Happy is also bright and full of color.*

The innkeeper and a number of others exited from the inn and welcomed Halfin, with joy stamped on their faces. The citizens of Garrin showed their delight in welcoming her to their town. *Halfin is much loved by these people.*

Halfin slid from her horse and immediately the Garrins surrounded her, laughing and chattering with their Lord's bond mate. Her guards, familiar with this village, appeared resigned and kept as close as they could to Rhognor's Lady. The crowd grew as news of Halfin's arrival spread through the town, and like a relentless tidal wave, they swept her indoors.

Mouse did his best to keep up with her. "Kat, the innkeeper advised me he will take our baggage to our rooms, and he has reserved a table for the evening meal for us."

"Thanks." She headed for her room, and using the personal washed her face and hands.

When she re-entered the dining hall, Kat caught Halfin's eye who beckoned her over. When Kat reached her, she motioned to a table for two. "I asked our hosts to allow us some space from the others. I suspect you wish questions answered."

Kat raised an eyebrow at her.

Halfin shook her head. "No, I am not able to read minds. The boradai, who claimed you as belonging to her, informed me you are curious about Lord Rhognor and me."

They moved to the table, sat and ordered their meals.

Kat cleared her throat. "I must admit I am. Lord Rhognor lives at ease inside a mountain. But to me you're like a product of sunshine, air and light. How did the two of you ever become mates?"

"We do indeed form an unusual bond. My female parent, also part of the Enchanter's Guild, birthed me here in Garrin. So few of us existed, our Guild assumed we would be replaced by those in the Healer's Guild, which sounded sensible. We enchanters disliked travel to other lands, but Healers embraced the opportunity to do so, and those in the other lands, welcomed their abilities. We in Shendea know Caleesh orchestrated this. We need no reason to fight this change. All is moving the way life is meant to be."

"But how did you and Rhognor meet?"

"The entire thing was most fortuitous. No longer under pressure to marry within my Guild, I had an entire world to choose from." She smiled. "Lord Rhognor, young and only recently raised to the position of Lordship, began the habit of visiting with the people of Shendea in the first year when he ascended to his position. He traveled to Garrin and we met. He found me to be the perfect foil for him. He claims I brought light and laughter into his life. He provides me with stability, safety, strong abiding love and a sincerity of character unmatched by any other. The mutual attraction struck us simultaneously. The joy I possess with Rhognor outweighs living within a mountain."

"Thank you for telling me."

A young woman brought their meals to the table and poured near-ale in a flagon for Halfin, but set a pot of Karri-san tea beside Kat.

"Halfin, may I ask you some things about the magicians, since we are headed for their guild?"

"What do you wish to ask?"

"You showed me where the light globes come from, but truly, I understand those lights existed before the magicians claimed responsibility for creating them. I do admit they possess an enormous amount of knowledge about your stars and the various heavenly bodies. They impressed me with their knowledge of these things when Walden brought me to their stall in the marketplace at the Stronghold. I also viewed a couple of mild illusions. However, I don't believe I saw any true magic. Why the reverence surrounding these people?"

Halfin chuckled. "The magicians themselves fostered this belief in their abilities. Two types of magicians exist — the grey magicians who indulge in strong and mysterious practices, and the white magicians, who pursue the mysteries of our skies. The latter also perform small magical feats, which may or may not be illusions." Halfin shrugged. "When we reach the Guild, you will be given the opportunity to judge for yourself."

"I understand why Rhognor values you. I enjoyed our discussion tonight more than you realize. Thank you."

Halfin rose from her seat. "You are most welcome, Kat. If you will excuse me, I possess greater weariness than I anticipated. I require my bed."

Kat stood as well. "I too would appreciate my bed. I will meet you on the morrow when we travel to Blain."

They smiled at each other and each headed toward their own room.

Hmm. She's an amazing woman. Imagine giving up Garrin for the Stronghold. Kat entered her room, still thinking. *So Hesginn comes across as a darker magician than Walden. I wonder what the difference really means?*

CHAPTER 37

Galdin paced his interview room. *The man is a viper in my side. No other would dare keep me waiting.*

A knock disturbed him. "Enter." He barked the command.

A guard clad in heavy armor, opened the door. "Thane Galdin, your visitor arrived at the front portal. Do you wish him allowed entrance at once?"

Galdin hesitated. *I would be most satisfied for him to be subjected to my displeasure, but… .* "Yes." *Syeth kin.* "I need speak with him with haste." Galdin turned his back to the door and moved to his throne.

Another knock and the guard ushered Ssarff into the Thane's presence. Clad in a white robe, his head bereft of any hair, the man glided toward Galdin. The overall appearance reminded him of the blind-worms in the caves of Clog Blue, totally without color. The exception, Ssarff's eyes, black as charcoal, held no sheen of normal life.

The leader of the Assassins' Guild dropped his bald-head only enough to avoid a blatant affront. "Galdin, you summoned me?"

Galdin gritted his teeth. "You were no doubt occupied, since you stalled your coming."

Ssarff's smile held a hint of insult. "My delay fell beyond my control."

The Thane waved toward a table with chairs in the corner of the room. "No doubt." He frowned. "I require your services."

The two men moved to the table and sat in chairs opposite each other.

"What do you need, Thane?"

"I still wish the woman brought to me."

"Our guild suffered heavy losses in the last attempt. Your intelligence was faulty."

"On the contrary, Ssarff, the abilities of the men you entrusted with the task discovered themselves ill prepared. I cannot afford a similar outcome."

"With adequate foreknowledge, we will succeed in delivering the woman to you."

"I possess a contact within Rhognor's inner circle who will be your connection when you arrive in Shendea."

"How do you manage to incorporate so many Mordens in the inner workings of the other lands of Pridden?"

"This man is not from Morden, he is Shendean."

"How can you be sure of his loyalty to you?"

"Loyalty is not what binds him to me." Galdin stretched his neck with a pop. "He is ambitious. He desires to supplant Rhognor and become Thane of Shendea." He grinned. "He also desires Rhognor's mate for his own."

"Where is the woman you seek currently?"

"Within two or three star turns, she will be at the Magicians' Guild."

Ssarff sat back in his chair. "This will be a more serious undertaking. The journey will be long and tedious. We will use the Morden Pass into Kaylin, and avoid all others to travel to the Nordad Pass. From Nordad we will wend our way to the Magicians Guild. As I said, a lengthy journey."

"You will not need such a tedious route. My contact in Shendea has advised me a tunnel exists through Clog Arth at the only point where Shendea and Morden share a short border."

"A tunnel? I am not aware of the existence of any tunnel."

Galdin smiled in satisfaction. *Something this viper is not privy to.* "Until my contact advised me of the passageway, the only ones cognizant of the underpass, are a few in the Magician's Guild."

Ssarff leaned forward again. "We will help capture the woman on the same terms as before. The usual amount of credit, and your guarantee the Assassins' Guild will be recognized as a Guild of importance, and will be legitimized."

"I do understand, and I agree."

"Rather than only your word, Galdin, I wish a blood document."

Galdin raised his eyebrows, and glared at him. "A blood document? Tread carefully Ssarff. I owe you nothing from the last endeavor. You did not fulfill your part of the contract."

"Nor did you. We never received the payment which you promised, regardless of the outcome."

"I owe you nothing. The entire undertaking became a fiasco from beginning to end. I will not sign a blood document. I will, however, give you one half of the agreed upon fee in advance. The balance will be paid only when the outcome is successful."

Ssarff nodded his head. "I agree to this contract."

The two rose from their seats.

"Thane, who will be my contact in Shendea? I assume, based on what you imparted, he is a member of the Magicians Guild?"

"He is. Only the few grey magicians are apprised of the existence of the tunnel. His name is Hesginn. Contact him and meet with him to finalize the details in the town of Blain."

"I will advise him via pyrock, and the passage to Shendea will enable us to keep our party together and prevent any interference from Rhognor or his guards."

Galdin extended his hand with reluctance to seal the agreement. "I anticipate an effective conclusion."

Ssarff took Galdin's hand and nodded his acceptance.

Galdin released the other man's hand as soon as he could. *And when you return with the woman, and I achieve what I want, I will deal with you, my slithery adversary.*

CHAPTER 38

A shaft of red light in her eyes woke Kat from a sound sleep. *Crap. Hell... . Fire!* She leapt from the bed and ran to the open window. The curtains fluttered in a breeze and Kat assumed they moved because of the heat of flames. As she parted the drapes, she gasped at the sunrise. *Fabulous. Not fire. What colors — pink, blue, purple and brilliant red.* She stood at length, marveling in the flow of streaks of brilliant orange and mauve as the sun rose. *They call their sun a star. When I encounter a sunrise like this, I believe their term may be more accurate.* She breathed the clean air scented with the perfume of blooms in the garden below her window. The leaves of trees close to the inn, rattled like miniature casta-nets.

A high-pitched squeak from the pyrock calling for food drew her attention. "Oops, sorry, Wink." Kat reached into the cage and withdrew the furry little creature and placed her on the desk, grabbing treats from a dish. Wink demolished three pieces before her eyes began to close, and she rolled into a ball. Kat picked her up delicately, and returned her to the soft bedding in the cage.

After a shower and donning her clothes, she headed for the dining hall. She entered and caught Halfin beckoning Kat to a seat beside her assistant, Fardith. On her way over to the table she caught a glimpse of Mouse, eating with Halfin's guards who laughed uproariously at some shared anecdote.

Kat sat beside Halfin. "Good morrow." She gazed around the room. "Everyone appears to be bright and happy."

"Garrin is a happy village. Blain, where we are headed is also a pleasant and joyful place. I adore visiting the merchants in Blain. I discover articles from all Pridden when I am there, many of which I never understood existed."

"You remind me, I must visit Rantor's to purchase another set of Rifellan leathers."

"You did not visit Blain before, so how are you aware of Rantor's?"

"I met a party of Rifellan women at the Ponti inn. We spent an evening together, and I enjoyed my conversation with strong confident women."

Halfin smiled. "They are indeed. However, Kat you will discover most women in Pridden possess strength and confidence in their own way." She hesitated. "Perhaps not so much in Morden. However few males or females display much confidence or strength in Morden."

"Why?"

Halfin sighed. "I never met him, but their Thane appears to rule harshly, without compassion."

"The southern Mordens we met are happy people."

"They are fortunate enough to be separated from their Thane by the vast expanse of Carrog Donlan, which allows them much leeway. However, they tread carefully within their own land."

"They did seem reluctant to discuss their ruler."

"Kat, all the other lands make use of Rifellans as the warriors and peace keepers. These males and females are strong yet possess consideration and empathy for those they protect. Thane Galdin uses the Assassins' Guild as his guards. Only males are assassins, and they are generally considered savage and brutal in their duties."

"The more I am told about Morden, the less I wish to visit."

"I understand, but I believe your journey is pre-destined."

Kat humphed. "I so dislike being unable to control my actions."

Halfin laughed. "You retain full control over your actions. Since the results of those actions lead you in a certain direction, the assumption about lack of control over your future, is false."

Kat glared at her. "Your logic is most annoying."

Halfin laughed again, and patted Kat on the shoulder. "You should relax and ask for more help. Life works well for those with staunch hearts. Despite your irritations and your tendency to intimidate those around you, you are blessed with a staunch heart."

Kat scowled. *I don't try to intimidate others.*

Halfin patted her on the shoulder again. "I can observe you disagree with me, but now we must leave for Blain. Mouse and my guards are headed for the stables." She turned and conveyed instructions to Fardith, rose along with Kat, and set off to join her guards.

As they exited the inn, Kat's ears were assaulted by seeming chaos. The guards readied the animals, using voice commands to convince the creatures to stand still as they loaded baggage on the three pack-horses. Everything became a symphony of sound and movement, accompanied by the clank of bits and bridles, hooves which clopped on the paving stones, and the creak of leather armor as they mounted their steeds. *It's like an old western movie, where all the wagons are readied for a journey across the mountains.*

Finally the party set off for Blain, Halfin tucked in the center of the group, with guards at both front and back. Kat rode on one side of Halfin, with Mouse on her other.

Shade trotted up to Kat, Breen ensconced on her back. "There you two are. Did you enjoy yourselves?"

Breen nodded, but Halfin gasped. "Stop."

The entire party halted.

"Who and what is this creature?"

Startled, Kat turned to Halfin. "You can see Shade?"

"I cannot recall encountering her like before. She resembles a cathnog, but bigger and dark as night. What sort of animal is she and where did she come from?"

"I never found out. She appeared when we first left the Stronghold, and has been with us ever since."

Halfin gazed at Shade. "Come."

The black cat strolled over to Halfin's horse, and brushed her jaw against Halfin's leg, who reached down and patted the huge black head.

Shade purred.

The two remained in this position for some time, and at last, Shade walked on.

Kat called to Breen. *"Breen what happened?"*

Breen jumped from Shades back, to the saddle in front of Kat, who placed her hand on the boradai.

"The Lady communicated with Shade. I do not understand how, or what they imparted to each other, but something Shade conveyed saddened your friend."

"What made her sad?"

"I could not understand, but I believe Shade warned her of a calamity."

Breen returned to Shade's back with a prodigious hop.

Halfin motioned her guards to carry on.

Mouse moved his horse from beside Halfin and trotted up next to Kat. "What just went on?"

"From what I gather, Shade is visible to Halfin, and she conversed with her. Breen doesn't understand what they spoke of. Whatever they discussed saddened Halfin."

Mouse appeared thoughtful. "Interesting. We may need some assistance in Blain." He scratched his chin. "We stop for a midturn meal soon, and I will take the direct path to the Magician's Guild. I believe I need to converse with Hesginn."

"If you think this is necessary, Mouse, by all means go. We are surrounded by sufficient guards to protect us on our route to Blain."

***

Kat enjoyed Halfin's midturn meal formality. She never experienced such luxury before on her journey.

Mouse excused himself. "Lady Halfin, I will head for the Magician's Guild, to make sure they are expecting us."

"I understand, Mouse. Please remind them my Lord will be accompanying me and is anticipating his visit with pleasure."

Mouse nodded. "I will." He mounted his horse, wheeled the animal in the direction of the Guild and set off at a brisk trot down the shortcut to the Guildhall.

Kat watched him leave. *Odd. What did he discern about Shade's discussion with Halfin. And what made her sad?*

J. M. Tibbott

CHAPTER 39

In the special room within the Magicians' Guild Hall, Hesginn sat at the head of a highly polished table in the private conference room for grey magicians. The floor, comprised of black and white squares of material resembling marble, shone in the light of the globes set in sconces around the circumference of the room. Six of the other seats were occupied by the balance of magicians who enjoyed grey status.

Hesginn cleared his throat. "Friends, changes are coming to Shendea. The time is come when we will be recognized as the true power in this land."

All six pairs of eyes fixed on Hesginn in rapt attention to his words, and they murmured agreement.

"Master Hesginn you are no doubt in possession of information regarding this change. Would you share with us the way in which we will achieve this power?"

"I will indeed, Kraklin. I am awaiting a message via pyrock to supply details as to when our allies will arrive with help in our quest for greater ability to control the administration of Shendean affairs."

"Are we able to trust these allies?"

"I would not form an alliance with them if I judged otherwise." He gazed at each of them. "We labored long and hard for this moment. We made requests of Rhognor again and again with no indication he considered our inquiries valid." He sighed and stood. "As soon as I receive the message I will contact you to accompany me to the meeting. Meanwhile, prepare to travel."

All rose, and cleared the hall, heading for their individual rooms.

* * *

Just prior to the midturn meal, a pyrock popped into existence over Hesginn's desk and squeaked at him. He reached out and gently removed the tube from the leg, avoiding touching the body of the animal. "Wait for a reply."

The pyrock stayed where the small animal first settled.

Hesginn read the note from Ssarff, written in a code only Hesginn recognized. He spent a few minutes translating the missive.

'You will meet with my primary assistant, Saglit, in Blain, at the small inn closest to the Clog Arth tunnel. The two of you will arrange how to bring the woman into the tunnel, where I and your magicians will be waiting to help subdue her. Once the border is crossed beneath Clog Arth, my members will take charge of her and bring her directly to Morden's Thane. As discussed we will eliminate Rhognor, and you will possess Lady Halfin as your mate. How you handle Halfin is your concern, not ours.'

Hesginn, well versed in the code, needed only to translate a few words, which he wrote beside those he had not memorized. He folded the note and tucked it under a book on his desk.

He grabbed a second piece of parchment, and penned the words 'understood and agreed'. He rolled his note into the tube, which he reattached to Ssarff's pyrock. "You may return to Ssarff."

The small animal flapped leathery wings, rose into the air, and popped out of existence.

Hesginn sat back in his chair, smiling as he envisioned a new life with Halfin. *She is an extraordinary woman, and*

I can no longer live without her as part of my life… as my bonded mate. Rhognor could never be right for her. I will not condemn her to dwell in a mountain, but in the greens of nature, where she should always reside.

He rose and rang for his midturn meal to be delivered.

Soon a knock indicated a young apprentice standing at the door.

"Come."

The apprentice delivered his usual meal, but Hesginn stopped him before he exited the room. "Would you please advise each of the grey magicians to join me in my quarters once they complete their meals."

"Yes Master." The young man exited the rooms and headed to complete the assignment.

***

The grey magicians trickled into Hesginn's quarters, one by one. He invited them to seat themselves around a table, which contained flagons of near-ale.

"I received word from our allies, and we are to meet with them in Blain. We are requested to capture the woman from the other world, since she works against us to create disharmony in our land. We will turn her over to our allies and they will ensure she is not allowed to practice her wiles on any other person in Pridden."

"Does not Lord Rhognor respect her?"

"He does, but I am hoping once we reveal her perfidy to him, he will approve our actions this star turn."

"Master, if she practices deceit as you advise us, we will certainly agree to aid you in removing her from Shendea."

"I appreciate your support, Kraklin." He scrutinized the room. "Are you packed and ready to depart the guild?"

They all nodded.

"One more item. Many brought to my attention how starved for nature and the outdoors is our Lady Halfin. I learned Lord Rhognor is frustrated by her evident dissatisfaction with her life imprisoned in a mountain. I sent word to him I will relive him of the burden, and take the Lady Halfin as my bonded mate. Thus he will be free to seek another who fits with his life in the mountain."

The magicians glanced at each other, eyebrows raised with surprise, and conversation buzzed in the room.

Hesginn scanned their curious faces. "This will work well for all of us." He rose and motioned the others to do likewise. "I must depart now. Follow me as quickly as possible so we may all arrive in Blain before the dark descends."

He swept out his door and headed for the stables.

I handled the meeting well. None suspect I plan a rebellion. Before this night is over, Halfin will be mine and Rhognor will be deceased.

CHAPTER 40

Mouse rode up to the Magician's Guild entrance at the time when the sky colored its intention of turning day into night, and the young apprentice waiting at the entrance, took the reins of his horse as he dismounted.

"I believe Master Hesginn is here. Where is he located?"

"Forgive me Sire, but Master Hesginn is not at the Magicians Guild at the moment."

"Which of the grey magicians is his second?"

"Forgive me again, Sire. Neither Hesginn nor any of the grey magicians are present."

Mouse frowned in puzzlement. "Is Walden at the Guild?"

The young apprenticed appeared relieved. "Yes he is. If you would seat yourself in the dining hall, I will stable your horse and then fetch Sir Walden and bring him to you."

"Thank you." *Where is Hesginn? And, where are the grey magicians? Their absence seems most odd. I am discomforted.*

Mouse sat in the hall, and one of the serving women brought him a tea. He sipped in silence, waiting patiently for Walden to appear.

Finally the man himself walked through the door. "Sir Mouse. I hope you did not wait too long."

"Not long, Walden, but I appear to have stumbled on a mystery. Neither your silbling Hesginn, nor any of the grey magicians appear to be at the guild. The circumstances must be most unusual for them all to be away from the Guild at the same time."

"I remained unaware of the absence of our grey magicians as well. I watched Hesginn prepare to depart after the midturn meal. However, I headed to a meeting, and did not observe the balance of the grey magicians departing."

"Do you possess any knowledge in which direction Hesginn headed?"

Walden peered at Mouse. "You give the impression of being concerned by this. Perhaps we should check his room for some indication of where he may be."

"I would find the idea acceptable."

Mouse rose and the two departed for the interior of the guild. On their way, Walden haled a senior apprentice. "Do you carry the keys to the rooms?"

When the man indicated his positive answer, Walden took his arm and pulled him along the corridors. They stopped at a wooden door, decorated with iron bands. "Open Hesginn's door."

The apprentice gasped and his eyes widened. "Surely not Master Hesginn's room?"

"Yes, Hesginn's room. We possess no reason to believe he has disappeared, but we need to discover where he might be at this moment." Walden appeared worried about Mouse's expressed concern over his sibling's absence from the guild.

After the apprentice unlocked the door, Mouse and Walden entered the room and began a search. Nothing unusual caught their attention.

"Logically we should assume my sibling deemed protocol demanded the necessity to escort Lord Rhognor and Lady Halfin to the Magicians' Guild. He is most assiduous where protocol is concerned."

"I am not well acquainted with Hesginn, I assume he would consider the well-being of Lord Rhognor and his mate of importance." Mouse frowned. "Did he perform this service at any of Lord Rhognor's previous journeys?"

Walden screwed up his face. "I cannot remember. I am certain he would always contemplate doing so, but I cannot recall previous journeys."

Mouse turned toward the door. "I find nothing here to indicate his destination." *Odd. Odd. Walden claims this is logical, yet I am unsettled. Why?*

Mouse left the room followed by Walden and the apprentice. He glanced back at the young man. "Re-lock the door to Hesginn's quarters. We may require you to admit us again later."

The apprentice did so and left to perform other duties.

"Walden, I believe we should request information from the magicians who are still here. One of them may be aware of Hesginn's whereabouts."

"Most of them will be in the dining hall. We may request information from them during the meal."

The interrogation of the white magicians proved fruitless. Hesginn apprised no other of his intentions. *I can understand Hesginn is under no obligation to inform the white magicians of his plans, but to clearly leave with no other aware of his destination or length of his leaving is disquieting.*

Walden suggested he and Mouse enjoy an evening meal, while they considered other options, which might account for Hesginn's absence.

Within minutes sizable bowls of vegetable stew sat in front of them. *Enjoyable, but I do prefer meat in stew.* Mouse said little during the meal, involved in thoughts about Hesginn's location. He glanced over at Walden and understood his table-mate was also gripped by worried thoughts.

"You are concerned about Hesginn. Understandable. The food helped clear my concentration, and I suggest we attempt one more examination of his quarters."

Walden nodded his agreement and they rose from the table. On the way to Hesginn's room, they encountered the apprentice and persuaded him to open the room once more.

This time Mouse and Walden went through the items in the room, one by one. When Mouse reached the desk and lifted a book, he revealed the note tucked underneath. "What is this?"

Neither Mouse nor Walden could interpret the code, but Hesginn had completed the translation of a few words — Rhognor, Halfin, tunnel, Saglit. Without the balance of the note translated, these few words made no sense, but Mouse found the signature familiar.

"I do not understand this code, but I am sure Hesginn believes in the importance of this report." He sighed in frustration. "Walden, I suggest you should request your magicians ready themselves to travel, and we may be required to aid our Lord and Lady. I am troubled by the words on this parchment."

Walden swallowed. "I will speak to the magicians and instruct they be prepared to travel… and possibly fight."

Mouse rubbed his forehead. *If Rhognor and Halfin are in danger, I suspect Kat is too. What is going on?"*

CHAPTER 41

Hesginn stood waiting beside the copse of trees just outside the town of Blain. He anticipated the arrival of the first of his Guild members, and scanned the area for them. *This is an enormous undertaking we plan this day. Rhognor's time to leave is here. How my beautiful Halfin ever bonded with him is beyond belief.*

At the sound of horses' hooves, Hesginn ducked behind the bushes surrounding the inn. *My men are here.* He stepped out and greeted his members. "Follow me to my quarters. Privacy is necessary."

The six slid off their mounts and led the horses to the stable beside the inn. Grabbing their bags from the animals, they left the rest to the stable hand. Each man passed a chit to the young apprentice, and proceeded toward the inn, following Hesginn.

Once in the room, Hesginn rang for refreshments. The men milled about until they heard a knock at the door. Hesginn furiously indicated they should conceal themselves, and strode to the door to admit the serving female. She deposited a laden tray on a round table of substantial proportions, and glanced curiously around the seemingly empty room.

Hesginn walked her to the door. "Thank you. When you notice my friends arrive, perhaps you would send them to me."

She smiled and nodded.

As soon as she departed, Hesginn closed the door and turned the lock firmly. "You may come out now. I did not wish anyone to be aware you are with me. We must be care-ful to remain in the shadows, until the time is right."

The men sat at the table and consumed the refreshments provided.

Hesginn waited until the chatter about their journey died down. "We need to achieve much. I met with one of our al-lies, and he advised me of the problems the female known as Kat, created during her journey through Shendea. She is re-sponsible for disharmony between the southern and northern Mordens, and even now works to turn the Rifellans against us. One of our helpers in the Stronghold overheard her deni-grating our Guild. She said we possess no ability with magic and what we do is only illusion, with no tangible results."

Kraklin gaped. His face flushed red and contorted in rage. "Heresy. The woman cannot be allowed to continue such foul lies."

"You are correct. These falsehoods will destroy our standing in Shendea, and Lord Rhognor will be less likely to endow us with the place of honor our Guild deserves."

"What can we do?"

The other grey magicians murmured and nodded their heads.

"Kraklin. Magicians. We need to act. We will capture the woman and deliver her via the Clog Arth tunnel to our allies. They will deal with her." He sighed. "I hope her words did not poison all Rhognor's thoughts about our Guild."

"If she did, Master, what must happen?"

"If Rhognor is biased against the Guild because of her, we may be forced to discover a way to persuade to him to step down from leadership of our land. However, I am sure he will realize what a problem the woman has created and will ban her from Shendea"

All six of them gasped, eyes wide.

Not one spoke.

Hesginn waited.

Kraklin cleared his throat. "You are right, Master Hesginn. If Lord Rhognor will not remove the woman from our land, requesting he step down may be our only hope. If such a thing happens, you must assume leadership of Shendea."

Fools. They are manipulated with such ease. "I never considered who would replace Rhognor. I could contemplate doing so, but we would need to examine all possible candidates."

"Of course we would, Master, but all here will agree you are the best possible replacement."

The rest nodded their heads in agreement.

Fools indeed. They are so readily influenced. This is easier than I anticipated. "You should go to your rooms, and I will advise when we will meet to capture Kat." He spat the name out.

The men rose and exited Hesginn's room.

✸✸✸

Hesginn completed an early evening meal, and seated at his desk viewed the map of the Clog Arth tunnel, when an unexpected pop startled him. He recognized Ssarff's pyrock because of the ring of white fur around one eye. The pyrock extended a foreleg, and Hesginn removed the message tube. Ssarff did not encode the note this time, and advised Hesginn of his arrival, instead of Saglit. He further requested he meet him at the tunnel opening as soon he could.

Hesginn added the word yes to the message, and after clamping the tube to the pyrock advised the animal to return to Ssarff.

He summoned Kraklin and advised him to ready the other grey magicians. "I am meeting with our ally at the base of the tunnel through Clog Arth and request you all gather near the inn where the woman is lodging." Hesginn grabbed his cloak and set off toward the base of Clog Arth.

Despite the glow of the light he carried, Hesginn almost missed the opening, because of the many trees and bushes obscuring the entrance.

Fortunately, Ssarff slipped from the shadows and hissed at him. "Hesginn, over here."

The man in front of him, stood out in the faint glimmer of light, totally devoid of color. His robe, the stark white of bleached bone, and his skin so pale reminded Hesginn of tales of spirits and ghostly manifests. His black fathomless eyes, and the blood red of the interior of his mouth, when he spoke, provided the only color about him.

Hesginn resisted the urge to shudder. *He is the most repulsive male ever. I will not trust this one.* "You are Ssarff?"

Ssarff ignored the question and motioned Hesginn to walk in the tunnel a few steps. "We share a mission." His sibilant whisper, only faintly audible, pierced the still of the dark night.

Hesginn followed him in, but experienced a tremor of revulsion. "I readied my men, and the woman is in Blain at the tavern." *Forget trust. I shall never turn my back on this fowl creature.*

"Excellent."

"I am advised she plans a walk through the town before returning to the inn for the evening. Numerous alleys exist which we can use as a surprise trap."

"Fine. We should plan to meet with your men a small distance from the tavern so we are able to deal with her quickly and quietly."

"I arranged for them to meet us near the inn."

"Perfect. I possess here the perfect weapon for her." He picked up a small basket from the ground beside him, and allowed Hesginn to peek in.

Hesginn recoiled. *A syeth.* "I assumed you wish to capture, not kill her."

"Not a problem. Once she is bitten by the syeth, I will have sufficient time to inject a partial antidote and bear her to the tunnel. Once she is in the tunnel, we will administer an additional injection, which will ensure her survival."

I hate snakes, and syeths are almost as vile as this snake of a man. Hesginn swallowed. "You appear, Master Ssarff, to be well prepared."

"Preparation is what guarantees success." Ssarff grinned, exposing his red mouth and red-tinged, sharpened teeth.

Hesginn again resisted the urge to shudder.

Ssarff stopped and held up his hand, listening.

The two men waited in silence.

Ssarff dropped his hand. "A noise. Did you hear it?"

"I heard nothing."

Ssarff gazed around. "All is quiet now. Perhaps just an animal in the brush." He bent down and picked up a voluminous grey robe, with which he covered himself and exited the tunnel,

Hesginn joined the assassin outside. "One more thing, Ssarff. If we attempt to capture the woman without first dealing with Rhognor, he would be in a position to unleash his guards against us."

"Interesting. We did not anticipate removing Rhognor from this life so soon, however, you are fortunate. My little concealed weapon is potent enough to deal with and obliterate Rhognor before we require the creature next."

"You guarantee this will destroy Rhognor? He will be dead by the morrow?"

"Quicker than the morrow, Hesginn. He will die within a few heartbeats."

Hesginn smiled to himself. *My plan comes together. By the morrow I will lead Shendea with Halfin as my mate. And the annoying woman will be gone.*

CHAPTER 42

Kat and Halfin rode up to the stable in Blain, and dismounted. The guards stayed and negotiated with the stable master for the comfort and care of the eight horses, plus the three transport animals. Kat knew her baggage would be sent to her room, and although she always enjoyed unsaddling her mounts in the past, suspected this would not serve her to insist on performing her own work. *I still don't understand why we can't take care of our own animals. Halfin does give the impression of being delicate, but I'll bet she's a lot stronger than she appears.*

The three women entered the inn and Halfin's assistant arranged rooms for them all.

Kat decided to change into a comfortable pair of wide loose pants, which she purchased in Roothlan and combined them with a casual top Brith created for her in Kaylin. The top was one she designed to match the capri-like skirt. She grabbed a jacket because she intended to take a walk after the evening meal. Wink curled in her cage and uttered a satisfied squeak. *I think I overfed her again.*

Kat hung up her leathers and brushed the dust from them. *I need to clean these leathers again. Perhaps Rantor's can handle the cleaning.* Before leaving the room she walked over to the bed and stroked Breen, lying curled up next to Shade.

"I expect before I come back from my walk, you'll persuade Shade to sleep on the rug? The bed is much too narrow for all three of us."

"You will walk after your meal?"

"Yes."

"I shall come with you."

"You're highly visible."

"You may place me in the sizable outside pocket of your jacket, which should conceal me."

"OK, if you insist."

"I do."

Kat shook her head. *Boradais. Odd creatures.* She tucked Breen in the outside pocket and folded the jacket over her arm.

She headed to the small dining hall of the inn, and met Fardith waiting outside the room.

"Lady Kat, Lord Rhognor arrived with his party of guards, and the inn does not possess enough room for all our group for the evening meal. Lady Halfin requested you come with me to the tavern we passed on our way through the town."

"Perfect, I brought a jacket with me."

***

The two women walked briskly to the tavern, Kat because her stomach began rumbling, and Fardith, Kat noted, because she always hurried. The sound of voices and music and laughter heralded their arrival at their destination.

A symphony of scents curled around Kat's nose as she entered.

Halfin, seated next to Rhognor, waved at Kat to join them, which she did. Four guards and Fardith completed the table for eight, while the balance of Rhognor's entourage sat at a series of tables throughout the tavern. Rhognor beaming held Halfin's hand. *He's glad she's here.* Kat smiled at the two of them, both much in love. She hung her jacket over the back of her chair with care. *Hope Breen is comfy in there.*

The near-ale flowed, food appeared on steaming plates, and a trio of musicians played in the corner. The eating establishment, filled with laughter and pleasant company, swelled with the noise of animated conversation.

Kat ate sparsely, despite her hunger, and when completed, rose and apologized to Rhognor and Halfin. "Do excuse me, but I'm stiff after being seated on a horse all day, without any other movement. While you finish your meals, I'll take a walk toward Clog Arth. I'll return here, but if you are already departed, I'll meet you at the inn."

"We understand, Kat. Enjoy your walk." Halfin turned to Rhognor. "We will walk back to the inn as well. All our exercise for the day."

Rhognor grinned. "Perhaps not all."

Halfin blushed.

Kat retrieved her jacket and hurried from the room. *Wow. I believe Rhognor just made an innuendo.* She slid her hand into the outer pocket of her jacket and touched Breen.

"Are you comfortable Breen?"

"Yes, and you are correct about Lord Rhognor. He and Halfin enjoy a fine physical relationship."

"Breen. Please. Their relationship is their own business.

"This is excellent information to possess."

"TMI, Breen, TMI."

Breen uttered the small sneezing sounds, which Kat came to associate with boradai laughter. *"Your people possess such odd expressions."*

Kat withdrew her hand. *How fascinating Breen understands my expressions. I guess it's because we talk mentally.* She walked with purpose past the darkened houses and merchant stalls. A village at night lacked life. Nothing moved, no sound crossed the roadway. She stopped. *A snore.* She chuckled to herself. *Such a small sound, yet life returns to the town.*

Kat approached the inn, which still boasted light, although the conversation from the dining hall hinted most travelers sought an early bed. She walked on toward the dark mountain and the trees at the foot of Clog Arth.

Kat, certain she caught the murmur of male voices, moved closer to the darkest patch of trees. A dry leaf crunched underfoot. Kat froze. The voices stopped. *Don't breath. Keep still.*

She waited and the voices continued and the bushes off to the side rustled. The noise the men created supplied Kat with an opportunity to move back and conceal herself. She peered from behind her bush, as two men emerged from the rock wall of the mountain. *Where did they come from?* She held her breath and listened. *Hesginn. Who is the other?* She allowed herself a tiny breath, and attempted to catch their words. *Difficult, they're speaking so quietly.*

And then she overheard… "you guarantee this will destroy Rhognor? He will be dead by the morrow?"

"Quicker than the morrow, Hesginn. He will die within a few heartbeats."

The men said no more, but walked toward Blain.

Kat stood for a few moments in horror. *They're plotting to kill Rhognor. I must warn him, and I must send word to Mouse.* She extricated herself from the concealing bush and hurried toward the inn. She kept a close scrutiny for Hesginn and his companion.

Kat rushed to her room, grabbed a piece of parchment and wrote the one word in the Pridden writing she always remembered. Help! Reaching over to Wink's cage she brought her to the desk, inserted the note in a tube, which she attached to the little creature's leg. "Hurry Wink, find Mouse." Wink instantly popped out of existence.

Kat ran from the inn and headed for the tavern. *I'm glad I paid attention to the layout of the town every time we passed through.* Up ahead, she caught sight of Rhognor and Halfin walking toward her. As she glanced to the side, she saw Hesginn, and the other man, now in company with a number of men clad in grey heading in the same direction. *Oh no, they're after Rhognor.*

She ran faster. "Rhognor, watch out, Hesginn is going to kill you."

At her words the strange man in the billowing grey robe threw a black wriggling creature at Rhognor.

Halfin, hearing Kat's words, stared in horror at the creature, and without any delay threw herself in front of her mate. The black animal revealed itself as a snake, and as it struck Halfin, dug its fangs viciously in her neck. Halfin dropped to the ground, and the snake wriggled swiftly back toward the man in grey.

Rhognor momentarily paralyzed in shock, dropped down to Halfin and screamed her name.

Simultaneously, Hesginn howled in anguish. "No, not Halfin." He grabbed at Ssarff. "Give me the antidote for Halfin. Hurry."

"It is too late, the Syeth caught her in the throat. There is no cure for her."

Hesginn howled again, turned to Ssarff and pointed at Kat. "This is her fault. Ssarff, kill her. Kill her now."

I don't believe it. Hesginn loved her. Kat ceased all other thoughts, caught between horror at Halfin's death, and the realization that the man in the grey robe aimed the black snake at her. Unable to duck aside in time, she raised her arm to protect herself and the creature landed on her right wrist. An excruciating pain. She tried to shake off the snake, but as her world faded to black Kat had only time for one last thought. *Ssarff the assassin, and a syeth bit me… .*

***

Rhognor cradled Halfin's head in his arms tears streaming down his face. *My beloved Halfin is gone.* He glanced at Hesginn standing and staring at Halfin, agony written over his face. Rhognor felt a red tide rising in his blood. His face flamed with fury, and the ligaments in his neck stiffened like ropes. *Revenge!*

Hesginn stared at Rhognor, and white with fear, turned and ran with the rest of the grey magicians toward Clog Arth.

Rhognor rose. "Follow them." He screamed the order. "Bring Hesginn back to me. Dead or alive." He stopped one of the guards. "Take my Lady to our room at the inn and request Fardith stay with her until I return. Once you convey the message, gather all my other guards and we will capture these vile assassins and deal with them appropriately."

He steeled himself. *I must be cold now and be a leader.* He breathed in, calming his raging emotions.

Hoof-beats. Is Mouse returning? He rubbed his forehead. *Of course. In my rage and loss, I almost forgot about Lady Kat.*

He called to his guards. "Bring the horses." *Eduardo needs her, and Halfin, were she alive, would insist I help.*

CHAPTER 43

Mouse and Walden sat in the Guildhall and discussed the unusual situation. The Guild, empty of grey magicians, resonated with questions.

"Walden, I cannot help but be disturbed by the disappearance of Hesginn and the grey magicians. Where are they, and why did they all leave the Guild?"

"Hesginn always kept his own council. This is more unexpected than usual. I do not believe Shendea is in danger. If danger did exist, Rhognor's guards would be present, and any difficult situations would be obvious." He held out his hands and shrugged. "Remember, Rhognor himself is due to visit our Guild in three or four star turns. I am unable to formulate a guess as to why Hesginn abandoned our hall, but I suspect he may wish to meet with Rhognor ahead of time so the Guild is prepared for the visit from our leader."

"I am still concerned Hesginn has taken his grey magicians with him."

Walden sighed. "Truly not so surprising." He sighed again. "White magicians hold little sway in this Guild. All command rests with those who wear the grey robes. Hesginn has been most plain spoken. We study the sky and nature. Hesginn and his men indulge in darker matters. We learned not to interfere."

"I think I now understand the working of the Magicians Guild."

Without warning a pyrock snapped into existence, and squeaked at Mouse, rapidly beating her wings.

"Wink." He faced Walden. "This is Kat's pyrock. This is worrisome." He removed the tube from Wink, which he opened and read the note tucked inside. The word 'help' hit him in the chest like a blow. He leapt up from his seat and grabbed Walden's arm. "Kat is in trouble. She once mentioned Hesginn took issue with her. We must go. Now." He returned the tube to Wink. "Return home. We come."

He issued orders to all. "Magicians, ready your horses. We ride to Blain to aid Lady Kat. Lord Rhognor and Halfin may also require our help. Gather what you need and head for Blain. We will meet there." He turned to Walden once more. "I made a mistake sending Wink back. Do you own a pyrock?"

"Yes." He called to another magician and told him to send the Guild pyrock on behalf of Mouse.

Already on the move, Mouse shouted to the man as he left the room. "Send your pyrock to the Thieves Guild and tell them Mouse needs their help in Blain to save the Lady Kat. Ask them to hasten."

He and Walden raced for their steeds, and mounting them, rode with all speed toward the village of Blain.

The journey to Blain although brief, found both their horses foaming in sweat, when they arrived close to the inn.

They approached a group of men, and directly in front of them, Rhognor sat astride his horse and called to Mouse to join them. "The Assassins' Guild poisoned my beautiful Halfin. She has passed from this world." He gulped.

Mouse's eyes widened in horror. *Not Lady Halfin. I judged her the gentlest of souls.* His throat clogged and he needed to swallow to control his voice. "We are here to give aid, Lord Rhognor."

"Hesginn and his men are involved in a plot to murder me, and they captured Kat, and she could be dead by now. They head toward Clog Arth. We caught one of the grey magicians, and under interrogation, he blundered and spilled information about a tunnel through Clog Arth leading to Morden."

"Lord Rhognor, the white magicians, more Rifellans and Thieves Guild members are on their way to increase our ranks. Between all who will gather, we can stop them. What would you ask of us?"

Rhognor's face contorted in an ugly grimace. "Find Hesginn. Capture him. Bring him to me. Alive or dead, the outcome is irrelevant."

Mouse horrified by his words, comprehended how urgently Rhognor needed to seek retribution against Hesginn. "My Lord we must find Kat. We cannot afford to lose her to Morden."

Rhognor opened his mouth to object.

Mouse held up his hand. "I promise you no matter what happens, I will bring Hesginn to you. But we must rescue Kat first." *He needs to understand Kat's importance in this.*

Rhognor sighed, but nodded. "You are correct. We should head for the tunnel. I am convinced Ssarff and his assassins, with help from the rest of the grey magicians, plan to take Kat through to Morden." He inhaled deeply and breathed out slowly. "I must calm myself. I lust for revenge, but I cannot think clearly when consumed by this."

"I understand both your grief and your desire for revenge, Lord Rhognor. I ride beside you with the same challenges. But we will prevail."

The entire troupe wheeled their horses in the direction of the tunnel to Morden, Rhognor in the lead. As they reached their destination, all dismounted, grabbed long swords and daggers and other weaponry from their saddles and headed toward the black opening. The grey magicians and assassins at the rear of the fleeing group, swiveled to meet Rhognor's guards. The fighting, swift and bloody, cut down the few miscreants in short order. The tunnel proved so narrow, only two guards at a time managed to chase after the abductors and Kat. Walden, Mouse and the guards, fired with desire for retaliation, more than matched the fighting skills of even Morden's Assassins.

"Hurry, Rhognor, we must intercept them before they reach the midpoint between Shendea and Morden."

Rhognor snarled. "As long as they do not exit the tunnel in Morden, who will witness where the midpoint rests?"

I did not understand until now, the depth of emotion in Rhognor.

CHAPTER 44

Kat opened her eyes, her arm wracked by pain. She lay on a type of gurney, carried by two strange men, who bumped along a dark passageway, lanterns providing only a dim amount of light. She put her hand on her right arm and touched Breen.

"Forgive me Kat, but I knew I needed to bite your arm. These men did not apply any antidote, so I am not confident they wish you to live. Luckily, the syeth expelled some of its poison before using its fangs on you."

"What do you mean bite me?"

"As I explained, you were fortunate the bulk of the poison had been expelled before the syeth bit you. However what remains in your bloodstream could still kill you, and the only way to remove the poison from you is for me to insert my fangs into the wound and apply suction."

"But Breen, then the poison will be in your body?"

"I possess means of ridding the syeth venom from my system."

"I hope you are telling me the truth, Breen."

"Lady Kat you realize lying is not possible during think-speech. Now you must rest. When you relax completely you make withdrawing the venom from your system more simple."

Kat allowed herself to sink into the stretcher, but she strained to gain enough breath. She glanced beside her and caught sight of Shade, who kept attacking the abductors, but since they could neither see nor feel her attempts to stop them, her efforts were futile.

Kat sank back in a stupor, but roused when she heard the sounds of men in pursuit, and clanking of blades involved in fights. Occasionally a scream of pain reached her, and she understood her rescue loomed closer. She stroked Breen again, but the boradai shivered and her thoughts became labored.

"Breen stop. The poison is killing you."

"I am not yet ready to cease saving your life."

Hesginn found his way back to the stretcher to check on Kat. He noticed Breen extracting the venom from her. "Stop, you weird animal. This woman must die." He pulled at Breen to take her from Kat, when the boradai with a sudden surge of energy whipped around and sank her fangs deep into Hesginn's forearm. He howled in rage and pain. "No, stop this."

Kat stared in astonishment. *I'm sure she's putting the poison into him. She is less grey looking.*

As Hesginn yelled at Breen, Mouse and Walden caught up with the stretcher and dispatched the men at each end. The litter banged to the ground, and Kat groaned. Walden leapt over the gurney and plunged his sword into Hesginn's abdomen.

Kat caught Breen as she fell toward the ground, and Hesginn grabbed at his guts, blood pouring between his fingers.

Kat called to them. "Don't touch his blood, Walden, he is filled with syeth venom."

Kat cradled Breen in her arms. *"Breen, you're so cold. Please don't die."*

"We are too late. If the man had lived longer, a possibility existed to rid myself of all the venom. The little creature shuddered. *"Forgive me Kat. I understood the outcome, which is why I insisted you take me with you."*

Kat swallowed, but a huge lump filled her throat. *"Please don't die. Please."*

"May the rest of your journey be met with ease. Farewell Kat."

Salty hot tears gushed from her eyes. Kat brought Breen up to her face, nuzzled her and sobbed.

"Come Kat." Mouse lifted her up in his arms and carried her back to the tunnel entrance. He sat her on a horse blanket, and left Breen on her lap.

Soon the various members of Rhognor's troupes emerged from the tunnel, covered in blood and dirt, some wounded, and some carrying the dead. The stench of blood and death covered them all.

Walden arrived with the body of Hesginn slung over his shoulder, protecting himself from Hesginn's blood with a blanket under the body. He headed to Rhognor, speaking with his guards, stood before him, and lowered Hesginn to the ground. "Your wish is fulfilled, my Lord."

Rhognor placed his hand on Walden's shoulder. "You are siblings. Do you wish to conduct a specific ceremony for him?"

Walden gazed down at his brother, his lip curled in disgust. "He is no family of mine. Deal with him as you will the other assassins."

Rhognor patted Walden's shoulder again and moved to address his guards. "Place this one and all the rest of the dead in the clearing near the rocky outcrop. We will conduct the death pyre tonight." He glanced around at his men. "I thank each of you for your loyalty to me and to Shendea. How fortunate we lost no fighters of our own this night. Once the pyre is set, return to the inn. We retained two apprentice healers to help you with any injuries. You will also receive food and drink to nourish you. My regret is the leader of the Assassins, Ssarff, was not among those we captured."

Kat studied Rhognor in awe. *He's watched his own wife die yet he makes time to think of his men.*

Mouse approached Kat. "I suspect you are still weak from the venom, and if I may help you on my horse, we will return to the inn. A dose of antidote will be waiting, supplied by the Thieves' Guild."

Kat, tears still on her cheeks, sniffed. "I must take care of Breen first." She searched around but Breen had disappeared. "Where is she? She lay in my lap only a moment ago."

"I am not well conversed in the customs of the boradai, Kat, but I do believe they will arrange their own way of dealing with Breen. They are an unusual species. The healers suspect the intelligence of the boradai is more advanced than man. Having seen what men often do in my life so far, I cannot disagree with the notion."

He helped Kat to her feet, and walked her over to his horse. He then led her up three stones piled together to create steps, so she managed to mount the animal without falling.

"Thank you. I'll be glad to return to the inn."

Mouse guided the horse back to the inn and he and another guard helped her down. The guard took the horse to the stable, and Mouse led Kat through the doors.

The innkeeper hurried over carrying a small package for Mouse.

He opened the package and withdrew a vial, which he handed to Kat. "This is the antidote for syeth venom, and you should consume the contents right away. Are you able to reach your room on your own?"

Kat nodded and downed the liquid from the vial.

"Fine. I will ask the innkeeper to send a light meal with Karri-san tea to your room. Take to your bed as soon as you are able, and by the morrow you will feel much better."

"Thank you, Mouse. Thank you for responding to my pyrock message."

Mouse shrugged and dropped his head. "I am your guide, after all."

Kat limped slowly along the corridor and entered her room. Wink sat crouched on her desk, with the tube still attached, which Kat removed. She stroked the little head as she fed her. "Wink you performed an important task today." She kissed the top of the furry head, picked the little creature up and deposited her in the cage. Wink yawned sleepily, circled three times, and curled in a ball.

The innkeeper delivered her meal and once Kat ate, she indulged in a quick warm shower and stumbled to her bed. *Wait a minute. Did I imagine it, or did Mouse carry me from the tunnel. Where did he find the strength? What are you Mouse?*

CHAPTER 45

Kat woke lying beside the warm body of Shade. The cat faced her, brilliant green eyes meeting hers. She reached out and rubbed her ears, but Shade did not purr. The animal stretched over and licked Kat's cheek. She drew back. "Ouch, Shade, your tongue's rough." The cat rolled over and landed on the floor and shook her head. Kat pushed the blankets aside, and sat on the edge watching Shade wander around the room, nosing at the furniture, and items on the floor.

"I'm sorry Shade, but she's gone and won't be coming back." Tears welled up and ran freely down her face. Shade loped over to Kat and licked the salty tears from her cheeks. "Thank you, but your tongue's still rough." *How can the death of such a little creature be so devastating? She was my guide in Shendea, and I miss her.* Fat tears rolled down her face. *I've just realized, I can't even go to Halfin to receive clarity.* She sobbed out loud, completely bereft. Finally her sobs subsided, and Kat wiped her hands across her eyes and breathed. Drained. *Enough. I'll talk to them, both of them, but later.*

She arose from the bed, walked past Shade stretched out on the rug, her head lying on her paws, and moved toward the personal. Kat stopped and listened. She strode over to the curtains and drew them apart. Outside the world dawned grey, overcast, and rain beat against the window, drumming death. *All Shendea is mourning the loss of Halfin.* This thought eased the ache in Kat's chest. She did not stand alone in her grief. *Halfin became my friend. When all this is over, the sun will rise again, flowers will bloom again, and birds will sing again. The love she showed all Shendea shall never be forgotten.*

Leaving the window, Kat spent a lengthy time in the shower, allowing hot water to drown pain, stiffness and sorrow.

***

She headed for the dining lounge, and met Mouse at the entrance.

"How are you today?"

"Better. You anticipated correctly. The antidote worked."

"I believed the antidote would remove any remaining venom. Shall we obtain a table, or would you like to join some of the others?"

"I want a table for the two of us. I've grieved for Halfin and for Breen. I understand how your Caleesh suggests death is not the end. I've done so much grieving this morning, I feel empty. I'm not sure where the others are about what happened, but if they speak too much about grief, I may lose it again. I don't want to move backwards."

Mouse tilted his head at her. "As you wish."

They sat and ordered their meal.

Kat knew Mouse watched her closely. "I'm sure you suspect I released my grief about Breen and Halfin too quickly, but my belief system provides me with the comfort of knowing all life is eternal. I know Halfin and Breen both are now somewhere else, in a better place."

"On the contrary, Kat, while I've not heard you express yourself this way before, your belief system is no different from those of us on Pridden. Death is not some monster. She is really Caleesh, leading us to new lives and experiences. She teaches us not to dwell on the loss of friends or companions, but instead rejoice in what we learned from those who leave this plain."

"How odd."

"Our beliefs are not odd to us, Kat."

"No, I meant how odd I took so long to find something in your world with which I agree."

Mouse only smiled at her words.

They completed their meal and Kat drank her usual Karri-san, when a young apprentice approached their table. "Are you Mouse, sir?"

Mouse glanced up, a surprised expression on his face. "Yes."

"Lord Rhognor requested I give this note to you and said I should wait for a reply."

Mouse took the parchment. "Thank you." He opened the letter and read the contents aloud. "My friend, would you and Lady Kat meet with me at the Magicians' Guild for an evening meal. We need to discuss much, and I would appreciate your input regarding what occurred the previous evening. Rhognor of Shendea." He glanced at Kat and raised his eyebrows in query.

She nodded yes.

Mouse asked the apprentice for writing instruments, and when he received them, added at the bottom of the note, *'We will be honored to meet with you at the Guild this evening.'* He refolded the piece of parchment, which he handed to the young man. "My reply is added."

The apprentice left the room, hurrying to deliver the missive to Rhognor.

Mouse faced Kat. "This means you should pack all you need for the trip to Rifella, because we will not be returning to Blain. Rifella is hotter than either Shendea or Kaylin, and you will require clothing which allows air to circulate, and is comfortable for the next three lands we visit. If portions of your clothing in your luggage are too warm, you may wish to dispose of them in some way before we travel to the Guild."

"When should I be prepared to leave for the Guild?"

"As soon as we complete our midturn meal."

"Perfect. There'll be enough time for me to pick up my new leathers at Rantor's, and get my current outfit cleaned. Perhaps he can deal with my other warm coat. Footwear is located in the stall next to his shop, and I can buy some comfortable shoes and boots. Can I assume the inn is able to provide me with a substantial supply of pyrock treats?"

"They are." Mouse regarded her with respect on his face. "You are well organized. This is a trait which is beneficial for smooth travel." He paused. "Do you still possess your spring bow and arrows."

"Yes, and I keep them well maintained."

"Excellent. Except for cathnogs, Shendea has few aggressive creatures, but Rifella is a different matter. Many animals will test your spring bow skills in their land."

Kat screwed up her face and lifted one eyebrow toward the ceiling. "Oh. Sounds like such fun."

Mouse appeared appalled. "Fighting dangerous creatures is not fun, Kat… ." His voice trailed off. "I assume by your expression you are practicing sarcasm."

"Yup." She rose. "I shall leave now. I'm going to do my second favorite thing after fighting a dangerous animal… shopping." She growled the last word so he'd get the point.

Mouse rolled his eyes.

Kat snorted and left the room. *Poor Mouse, I do believe I try his patience.*

***

In town, carrying her leathers and her cold weather jacket in a bag, Kat first located the shoemaker's shop. Unlike shoe stores back home, the shelves did not contain hundreds of shoes, but a few completed ones and a series of illustrations on the walls depicting the various styles.

The shoemaker hurried up to her. "Good morrow my Lady. How may I serve you today?"

"I need footwear. I would like a pair of comfortable shoes for walking and I also want a pair of boots for riding. I own Rifellan leathers, and they should work with those types of outfits."

"As for the boots, my Lady. I suggest the ones pictured here." The boots in question rose above the ankle, with straps across both sides for support and protection. A medium heel attached to the sole, would keep the stirrup safely in position. "On these boots, we turn the leather inside out, so the outer wear is soft to the touch. To make sure they are comfortable we line them with a thin layer of wullawerth wool, which also allows air to circulate so your feet will never experience too much heat."

"They're perfect."

"Let me check the size of your foot." He measured and scribbled notes on a scrap of parchment. "We generally require a day to make the boots, but you are fortunate, your exact size is in our storeroom. Now for the walking shoes — one pair?"

Kat nodded at him.

"I would suggest these." He pointed at an illustration showing a soft ivory shoe with a hint of a heel.

"Fine."

"These are most popular, and we always keep a number of pairs in our stock room. I know your size will be among them."

The stall owner obtained the shoes and boots from his storeroom, wrapped them for her and Kat, happy with her purchases departed for Rantor's.

She'd previously called on Rantor when they first entered Blain, and now he passed her the parcel of her clothes, prepared and packed for travel. When she asked about cleaning her current leathers, he kindly took them to the back room where some efficient apprentice shook, dusted, washed them, and applied polish to the worn areas.

Kat's final request of him referred to her cold weather coat. He affirmed his delight. "We often meet those traveling to the Stronghold who are unprepared for our cold season. The person who receives this coat will be most grateful, Lady Kat."

Shopping complete, Kat dragged her purchases back to her room at the inn, where she repacked her baggage to accommodate her new clothes and shoes. She hung the clothes she intended to wear for her travels in her closet. She stuffed a last few items in the pack she wore on her back, and her writings she deposited in the diplo bag. She made sure of Wink's comfort in her traveling cage, which she then attached to the backpack.

Clad in underwear she sank into the folds of the bed. *I need a nap.* She patted the bed beside her, motioning to Shade to join her. The black cat leaped up and curled along her back, warm and comfortable. *Can't keep my eyes open. I'm knackered from the last couple of days. I'm so glad you're here Shade.*

CHAPTER 46

Kat sprang to her feet. *Banging? What the… ?*

Someone knocked at her door.

"Who's knocking?"

"My Lady, Sir Mouse wished to remind you to meet him for the midturn meal."

Kat blinked her eyes, and swallowed. "My thanks. Please advise him I'll be with him momentarily. Oh, and can you ask someone to take my luggage to the stable and load the bag on our pack horse?"

"Yes my Lady, I will do as you request."

Kat eyeballed Shade who tumbled on the rug when Kat leapt out of bed. "Sorry about disturbing you, but I fell asleep. We need to leave Shendea. Will you come to the dining hall, or meet us at the horses?"

Shade without comprehension of her words, blew a breath at Kat.

"Whatever." She laughed at the black cat. "I must dress in a hurry."

She threw on her clothes, stuck her arm through one strap of her backpack and hung the diplo bag from the other shoulder. Her movements elicited a small squeak from the plush bag holding Wink's cage. "Oops, sorry Wink."

She glanced quickly around the room in case she'd forgotten something. *All clear.* Gathering her thoughts, she walked briskly down the corridor to the hall. She grinned to herself when she caught sight of Shade loping along with her.

When she arrived at the hall, she detected Mouse gesturing her toward a table.

"I took the liberty of ordering what you refer to as your 'nutty cereal', and Kari-san, as we will be traveling with a number of the Rifellan guards."

Kat glared at him. "Under the circumstances, I'm not about to attempt to seduce anyone. Sometimes Mouse, you can be so annoying."

Mouse sighed. "I am aware of your fatigue. I assumed you fell asleep."

Kat yawned, nullifying the objection she considered making. "I am tired, and weary of this whole journey thing. I want to go home. To my world." She rubbed her forehead. "I may not have encountered loads of ferocious animals in Shendea, but the events I witnessed here are enough. I'm not overjoyed I'll need to battle a bunch of unpleasant creatures in Rifella. So now I'm grumpy. So what."

Mouse held up his hands to ward off her anger. "I did not intend to appear to find fault with you. I am aware of how you feel. I, too, am weary."

"I guess you are." *If he's expecting an apology, He'll be waiting a long time. I don't do apologies well."*

"Tired or not, Kat, we must complete our meal and leave to meet Lord Rhognor at the Guild."

***

Riding at a leisurely pace, soon cleared Kat's head, and the weariness lifted. Seated on horseback always raised her spirits, despite the events from the day before. The smell and sound of her horse trotting through grasses interspersed with fragrant blossoms on small trees buoyed her frame of mind. Kat, filled with the appreciation of life, even in the aftermath of death, rode with lightness regained in her heart.

"We do not need to hasten, and perhaps we are better served to allow our horses to set their own pace. They are fine animals, but we drained their stamina during the past few star turns. The journey to the Guild is short, and slowing them to a walk will still enable us to reach our destination well before dark descends."

"O.K. Mouse. I don't need to rush." *Wonderful, he's over his weariness too.*

***

They arrived at the Magicians' Guild to discover Rhognor had arranged a hall for both their evening meal, and for him to make his various announcements.

Walden met them and asked his assistant, Neerin, to escort them to their rooms. "Lady Kat, you will be given sufficient time to refresh yourself, and we will send a messenger to call you to the hall for the meeting with Lord Rhognor."

"Thank you." *They've all become so formal since the challenges of yesterday. The atmosphere is no longer relaxed.*

At her room, Neerin unlocked Kat's door and handed her the key. "I will return for you when Rhognor is ready, my Lady." He faced Mouse. "If you will follow me Sire, you room is in the next corridor." As Mouse and Neerin disappeared down the passageway, Kat caught sight of Shade beside her.

In her room, she set Wink's cage on a side table, and reaching in her backpack, withdrew the sack of pyrock treats, which elicited immediate squeaks from the furry beast. "Cool it Wink, I'm coming." She brought the pyrock from her cage, no longer curled up in a ball, but jumping up and down eagerly, with mouth open to receive her treats. Kat popped three pieces into her open maw, and Wink chewed slightly and swallowed. "If you gobble like you're starving, you'll develop a tummy ache." *I'm losing it. I'm chastising a small dragon-like fur-ball, whose only delight in life is to eat and sleep. I need a cold shower to wake me up.* She glanced down at Shade stretched out on the thickest rug in the room. *She must be tired too.*

After the shower, which did indeed waken her, she dressed in the split skirt and blouse Brith prepared for her in Kaylin. Cool and comfortable, she wondered what she should take with her to the gathering and the meal, when a knock at the door caught her attention. "Come."

Neerin stuck his head in the doorway. "Lord Rhognor awaits you, Lady Kat."

"Should I bring anything?"

"I would consider such a necessity unlikely. I shall escort you, as you may not remember which way we came."

She followed him, and entered an immense and beautifully furnished hall, set with a long table in the center. The furnishings, well polished and the four tapestries on the walls spoke of a long tradition of gatherings in this place.

Rhognor seated at the head of the table, appeared tired and drawn. Although a chair rested at the other end, no one occupied the seat. A garland of flowers sat on the table in front of the empty chair.

Walden walked over to Kat and took her hand, escorting her to the right side of Rhognor. "This room, long designated as the primary gathering area for the grey magicians is the most striking hall for my Lord's meeting. They required much less space than this, but since they no longer exist… ." He shrugged and moved to the left of Rhognor and seated himself.

Kat gazed around the table. Mouse was seated next to her, with Fardith on his other side. The balance of the chairs, nearly thirty of them Kat estimated, contained a mixture of Rifellan guards and white magicians.

Rhognor stood. "I need to announce much to you all. We are unable to fit the entire Guild in the hall, nor all my guards, so I ask each of you to advise your friends of the words I will impart to you."

Everyone nodded in agreement.

"Today we experienced a sad turn for Shendea. Today, my beloved mate Halfin passed from this world. Without her, the Enchanters' Guild departed from our land. As the last of her kind, all Shendea will miss her wisdom, her laughter, and her kindness. But we will never forget her."

Rhognor swallowed visibly. "On the morrow, my guards and I will be escorting her body to the village of Garrin, which is where Halfin came to life, and lived as the offspring of another wise enchanter. Garrin, as the place of Halfin's birth, will be permitted to say their farewells before we commit her to Caleesh's pyre. The ashes which remain will be scattered in the forests where she roamed before she attained her maturity."

Rhognor gazed down at Kat. "You became a friend to my dear Halfin, and I would invite you to travel with us to Garrin, but your mission must continue and you cannot afford to be delayed. I thank you for the friendship you bestowed on her."

Rhognor picked up a glass of orenberry wine beside him. "Raise your glasses, please, to Lady Halfin.

The entire hall stood, raised their glasses and all their voices declared. "To Lady Halfin."

Kat, who'd said her own goodbyes to Halfin, experienced a sudden lump in her throat. She swallowed two or three times, and blinked rapidly to prevent the rush of emotion from converting to tears.

Rhognor sat, and all followed his lead. "As you are aware, the Magicians' Guild is empty of all grey magicians. I discovered these men adhered to practices not advantageous to Shendea. I am therefore declaring, never again will grey magicians be recognized or allowed in our land. Furthermore, because of his loyalty and proven leadership, Walden will become Leader Walden, the new head of the Magicians' Guild.

The entire room applauded this announcement.

Walden stood and thanked them all. "I am pleased to accept this post my Lord. I am aware of how many fine males and females are part of the white magicians in this guild. I am convinced I can count on their loyalty to Shendea and to you. Unfortunately my sibling, Hesginn, did not allow females to be raised to the rank of a grey magician." He cleared his throat. "I am embarrassed by the fact I never suspected him of harboring such destructive desires. As his brother, I am horrified I missed this."

Interesting Walden used the Rifellan term of brother.

Rhognor picked up his glass. "Walden you should not be embarrassed. I also did not deduce the thoughts he held." He raised his glass and motioned toward Walden. "To Walden."

The rest of the room raised their glasses to their new Magicians' Guild leader.

The central doors of the hall opened and a number of serving women and assistants entered with food for the evening meal. Soon the buzz of conversation and sounds of laughter echoed around the room.

Kat leaned over to Rhognor. "My Lord, would you allow me to address this group just for a moment?"

"Of course, Kat. Wait until the dishes are removed, and once the clearing is complete, I will obtain the attention of those in the hall."

Rhognor waited while the serving people cleared the tables and stood and clanked his flagon of near-ale. "Thank you for your attention. If you will allow her a moment, Lady Kat wishes to address you."

A number of surprised faces turned her way, and Kat stood. "I wanted to thank everyone in this room. I am known as an independent woman and never understood the reason one would need to ask for help. I since discovered how important requesting help is for anyone, and is something I learned to do over the past few star turns. If you found me rude for refusing your offers of aid in the past, please forgive me. Sometimes we need to be thrust in an untenable situation before understanding how valuable assistance becomes, particularly when given without an expectation of credit."

Kat raised her glass. "To each and everyone of you, my thanks."

She sat down to stunned silence.

Mouse reached over to her and whispered in her ear. "Well done, Kat. Well done."

Rhognor stood again and addressed the room. "We all experienced a demanding turn, and many are weary. Please you are welcome to address your beds, and those of you who wish to keep company with your compatriots, you are free to do so. I regret I am more weary than anticipated. My bed calls to me."

Many in the hall rose and filed out after Rhognor, including Kat.

Walden approached her and Mouse. "We will see you on the morrow. I believe Lord Rhognor wishes one more request of you."

Mouse nodded at him. "On the morrow, Walden. On the morrow."

Shade nudged Kat. "You tired too?" She leaned over and scratched the black cat's ears.

Walden regarded her curiously.

Kat shrugged her shoulders at him. "I must be tired, I'm talking to myself."

Mouse rolled his eyes at her, which she ignored, turned her back on him, and walked away.

CHAPTER 47

Kat slept deeply, disturbed only by a dream of Halfin's coffin resting on her chest, which made breathing difficult, but she never roused. Light from Pridden's star shining in her eyes eventually awakened her and she discovered no coffin, but Shade lying across her upper body.

Kat pushed at the animal who rolled off, twisted in mid air and landed on all fours on the floor. Kate peered over the edge of the bed at Shade who yawned at her, displaying a mouth crammed with enormous teeth. "I'm familiar with the sensation. I didn't sleep well, thanks to you."

Kat rose from her bed, scratched an itch, yawned and dragged herself toward the personal.

The shower refreshed, and once Kat dressed, she fed Wink and set out for the eating hall.

When she appeared at the entrance, a serving woman approached her and led her to a table. Mouse could not be seen, so she ordered her usual morning cereal. When the bowl of nutty oatmeal arrived, pieces of a sweet orange fruit decorated the top, and a tiny jug of creamy condiment nestled beside the bowl. She poured the creamy liquid over the bowl of cereal and fruit, and jumped when Mouse addressed her.

"Ah, bonbrie fruit, my favorite Shendean delicacy. I shall duplicate your order." He signaled the serving woman, and his hand gesture indicated he wished to order the same meal.

"You startled me."

"You appeared so engrossed with your meal, you did not witness me waving at you. Lack of awareness on your part is unusual." He sat in the chair opposite her, hanging a document bag on the back.

"I'm still lacking energy. I assume the remnants of the venom are still in my system."

Mouse frowned. "Odd. I would wager the opposite."

"Perhaps because I'm not from your world, the effects are different."

He shrugged. "Perhaps. I will check with the apprentice healer to determine if they can supply some additional antidote."

"Thanks for the help. I appreciate it."

Mouse presented her a Mona Lisa style grin.

"OK, Mouse, so you're amused I used the word help. I meant what I said last evening."

"I smiled, Lady Kat, because I now understand your intention to be genuine."

Mouse's meal arrived and the two ate in silence.

Kat ate the last from her bowl and sipped at her cup of Karri-san. "Can I ask a question."

Mouse raised both eyebrows in query.

"Do you think I can obtain a significant supply of Karri-san from the Guild? We are, after all, on our way to Rifella."

He rose. "While the apprentices clear our table, I will make the request for the tea. I am positive no challenge exists." He left the hall and Kat lost sight of him.

The table cleared and Kat sipped from a fresh cup of Karri-san, when Mouse appeared carrying an ample bag of tea.

He sat beside her and placed the bag on the table. "Here is sufficient tea to last a minimum of two seasons." He reached for his document bag, which hung on the back of the chair, and extracted a map. "This is Rifella, and here is the route I intend us to take through their land. Our initial stop, once we cross the border, will be to visit Lord Murwenna's keep. Making contact first with the leader of Rifella is vital for keeping relationships in excellent standing."

"A woman leader. This should prove interesting."

"I believe what will be most interesting, is when she views you with your hair and skin coloring, and wearing Rifellan leathers. Although perhaps the most unique aspect of you is your eye color. I am aware of no other with eyes of two different colors."

"All I care about, Mouse, is I move at least one step closer to going home." She stood. "We are informed Rhognor wishes to meet with us. Can we go now? I would like to return to my room to write in my journal, and I need a nap."

"I will check, and I suspect he will wish to see us without delay. He needs to leave for Garrin before the midturn meal." Mouse folded his maps into the document bag, and moved to the entrance of the hall. He stopped one of the apprentices. "Would you tell Lord Rhognor, Lady Kat is ready, and may we meet with him now. We will wait here until you return."

"Of course, Sir Mouse." The man scurried off.

***

The apprentice appeared, out of breath. "Lord Rhognor wishes you to attend him now. I will lead you to him."

"My thanks. You were exceedingly quick."

The man smiled, obviously grateful for the acknowledgement. He did an about face, and guided them to a door further toward the interior of the Guild. A knock at the portal, answered from within, and the apprentice pushed the door and peered around the opening. "Sir Mouse and the Lady

Kat are without, Lord Rhognor." He pushed at the door, and stood aside to allow them entry.

Kat strode ahead, and Rhognor rose from a comfortable chair and with two long strides, clasped her hand, led her to a conference table, and seated her. "I thank you both for coming. Mouse, will you sit?"

Rhognor cleared his throat. "Kat, we in Shendea owe you much. You more than fulfilled Eduardo's wishes for our land. Your efforts and results will serve all Shendea in paths to come."

What's he talking about? I didn't do anything

"You give the impression of puzzlement, Kat. What did I say to cause this?"

"Rhognor, I didn't do anything."

"You do not understand how well you served us?"

Kat shook her head.

"You are, as Eduardo promised, an extraordinary woman. Perhaps I may refresh your memory. You thoroughly endeared yourself to those in Dizerth, and because of the relationship you established, they and Master Godrith, the Tapestry Master, formed an alliance. Godrith agreed to promote their beautiful carvings to those who cannot afford a tapestry as a visual remembrance of their familial history. The Dizerths, in return, are producing a complete history of Shendea in carvings, from which Godrith's assistants and helpers will produce a tapestry for our major hall. This is much help for the coffers of the Dizerths."

I can't believe he thinks this is important.

"In Magwin, a village often accused of extreme prejudice, you helped create a bond with the southern Mordens. This in itself brings an enormous benefit for all Shendea. I state again, how much I appreciated the friendship you bestowed on my beloved Halfin. The most important item is your help in discovering the foul treacheries Hesginn and the grey magicians created. This last act eradicated what in retrospect might be considered a nest of vipers. For all this, we thank you." He smiled at her. "Lady Kat."

Face hot, Kat blushed.

Is this what Eduardo wanted? The whole thing is so amorphous.

She brightened. *What a marvelous word. I should add amorphous to my word list.*

"I didn't understand what Eduardo wanted me to accomplish, and most of these seem so trivial."

"Perhaps individually they might be. Together, however, they add up to things of importance. Now I would ask another request of you and Mouse."

Kat regarded him expectantly. "Of course."

Rhognor snapped his fingers and one of his guards approached with something white in his arms, which he handed to Rhognor. "This is the cathnog hide Vendi kindly presented to Halfin. The hide is, I believe, of the cathnog you both encountered on your first visit to the Stronghold."

Mouse nodded agreement at him.

"A most generous gesture, but I find owning this beautiful creature's skin gives me sorrow, because of the reminder of the last days of my beautiful soul-mate. To return this to Vendi would be most inappropriate, since the hide is incredibly valuable. He might view a return as a slight." He sighed and gazed at the skin across his lap. "What I would ask you to do, is to present this to Lord Murwenna of Rifella as a token of my appreciation of her leadership in her land." He held the skin toward the two of them. "Are you willing to do so?"

Mouse reached over and took the hide from Rhognor's hands. "We are willing my Lord. Thank you for your trust in us." He stood and prepared to leave. "We are aware you leave for Garrin, and we will refrain from creating delays for you. We found much pleasure touring your land, and we wish you peace in the future."

Rhognor smiled wanly at him. "And you as well."

Kat leaned toward him. "Lord Rhognor, may I speak a private word with you?"

"Of course." He addressed the rest of those still in the hall. "We should prepare for our journey. I need a brief word with Lady Kat and I shall join you after our discussion."

The hall cleared.

"Rhognor, Eduardo advised me I would require a number of people of power to help me return to my own world. I am asking you, as one of those with power. When the time comes, will you agree to aid me in my quest?"

"I am flattered you consider me with power. However maybe you will be better served by Walden."

"No. You enjoy far more power than I realized when I first met with you. Not Walden, as capable as he may be. You are the one. I am sure."

"If this is your desire, I will agree."

They both stood. Rhognor reached out to Kat and patted her hand. "Travel safely Kat. You are fortunate to be guided by Mouse." He turned and left the room.

Wow. Amazing man. I understand why Halfin continued to be content to live at the Stronghold.

***

Kat entered her room and sat at her desk. She pulled her writings and pen and ink toward her. *What word did I want to add?* She screwed up her face. *Ah yes amorphous. I must think of more, 'cause the list is limping.*

She added the happenings of the last few days to her journal. At peace with the loss of Halfin and Breen she managed to face recording all the experiences. *I'm not sure how I will add any of this to my games, but I need to account for everything.*

She still carried the returned note with the word 'Help' on it, which she screwed up and tossed on the floor. Shade pounced, batted the paper around the room, which she picked up and dropped at Kat's feet. "You wanna play?" She tossed the note across to the bed. Shade jumped for the bed, knocked the parchment to the floor and chased her new toy until she again dropped the crushed parchment at Kat's side. They played back and forth until Shade dropped to the rug, tongue hanging out her mouth, panting slightly.

She misses Breen

Kat pulled the tassel in her room and ordered a midturn meal. The meal was pleasant, but she ate mechanically, and yawned throughout.

She finished her food and walked to the bed. *I'm so tired. I'm sure the venom is at fault. I must ask Mouse again for more of the antidote.*

She lay down with a light covering, and Shade, warm and purring beside her. Within minutes, consciousness faded.

***

The knocker on the outside of the door, banging, woke Kat from deep slumber. She threw off the cover and staggered to the door and opened it. "Mouse. Am I late for something?"

"No particular reason, except I wished to discover if you planned on joining me for the evening meal."

"Time already? I slept ever since my own midturn meal." She rubbed her eyes. "Go ahead. Can you order me something like a soup? I'm not terribly hungry. I'll be with you soon, but I need to throw cold water on my face."

***

She joined Mouse at his table, and sniffed appreciatively at the steaming bowl of some unknown soup dish. She tasted the concoction and sighed with pleasure. "Delicious."

Mouse regarded her with a furrowed brow. "I am concerned about you sleeping so much."

"I mentioned I think it's the remnants of the venom."

"I believe you may be correct. The Thieves Guild have sent some more antidote, which will arrive by our morning meal. You will be able to consume the liquid before we set out for Rifella."

"Fantastic. I really want my energy back. At this moment, I feel lower than a snake's hips."

Mouse regarded her in astonishment. "Snakes do not posses hips, Kat."

She dropped her head in her hands. "Just another silly expression. I told you I'm tired, and I'm not thinking clearly."

"I understand. I will attempt to pay less attention to your 'silly expressions'."

Kat jumped from her chair. "Well I'm going to bed before I confuse you more. I'll be packed and ready to leave when I meet you here for the meal on the morrow. OK?"

Mouse, seemingly taken aback, nodded. "OK."

She exited the hall and strode directly to her room. The soup appeared to be responsible for some restored energy. Setting aside her Rifellan leathers for traveling, and the old boots, she packed all else into her baggage. She fed Wink and set her cage on the desk beside her backpack and the diplo bag. All she would need in the morning would be to shower and dress before meeting Mouse.

She sank into bed, wondering about the extent of her weariness. Her stone felt cold, so she withdrew the necklace from under her clothing. The crystal held almost no luster, and the green, faded and weak, inspired no admiration. *I remember what Liandock said I should do, but I can't summon the energy, despite the fact I might find this as something delightful.*

She lay on the bed attempting to summon up energy for pleasure, but the pleasure parts of her slept.

Shade leaped on the bed beside her, placed her paw over the stone and gazed into Kat's eyes. The glorious ebony face filled her view, and the emerald eyes bored into her own. Shade purred so loudly, Kat experienced a comforting rhythm in her chest.

Under Shades paw, the stone began to heat.

As she stared at Shade the animal began to fade before her, but Kat experienced a growing energy. Mesmerized by the fading of the huge black cat, and unable to turn away, Kat watched Shade disappear. The weight of the animal on her now gone, no time existed to experience abandonment, because when she held her stone, warm to the touch, in front of her, she discovered the luster and brilliant green restored to the former glory.

Liandock, did you create Shade?
Are you always watching me?
Where are you?

J. M. Tibbott

DRAMATIS PERSONAE

NAME	DESCRIPTION	FROM	RELATION
Anwen	Apprentice Healer & Guide for Mouse & Kat	Shendea	
Argelwyd	Original Lord of Pridden	Morden	
Bardu	Praetor of Eduardo's guards	Rifella	Bond Mate of Irina
Ballinor	Leader of Guards in Roothlan	Rifella	
Bannon	Caretaker of Pontis	Kaylin	
Brigden	Leader of Morden travelers	Morden	
Brith	Seamstress	Kaylin	
Bronwyth	Head of functions for Eduardo	Shendea	
Caleesh	Spirit Goddess for Pridden (except in Morden)	Pridden	
Carlo	Designer/coder for games	Our world	
Colwin	Apprentice serving Kat	Shendea	
Clune	Financial clerk for Eduardo	Kaylin	
Dafid	Door guard for Eduardo	Kaylin	
Deleth	Healer to Lord Rhognor	Shendea	Wynneth
Derwynn	Head of Thieves Guild	Shendea	
Drainin	Counselor to Eduardo	Morden	
Eduardo	Lord of Kaylin	Morden	Mouse
Fardith	Assistant to Halfin	Shendea	
Farnon	Headmaster for Dizerth	Shendea	
Flank	Burgmaster of Magwin	Shendea	
Galdin	Thane of Morden	Morden	

NAME	DESCRIPTION	FROM	RELATION
Godrith	Tapestry Master for Shendea	Shendea	
Halfin	Lady of Shendea	Shendea	Rhognor's bond mate
Haydar	Horse-Master in Kaylin	Baklai	Mayda's father
Hesginn	Grey Magician head of Magicians Guild	Shendea	Brother to Walden
Illian	Apprentice builder (mother from Glowen)	Kaylin	Penrow's daughter
Irina	Member of keep guards Bond mate of Bardu	Rifella	Sister to Liandock
Istra	Serving woman at Vendi's Inn	Shendea	
Kadnu	Bardu's Second in command	Rifella	
Kaleen	Met Kat at the Ponti Inn	Rifella	
Karen	Friend to Kat - Nick's Wife	Our world	
Keedin	Rifellan warrior stationed at Roothlan in Shendea	Rifella	
Kat Karim	Katherine Karim, Mother a Scot, Father Arabic	Our world	
Kaydith	Serving woman for Kat	Shendea	
Kraklin	Grey Magician	Shendea	
Laylin	Serving woman for Kat	Kaylin	
Liandock	Master Metal-Smith in Kaylin	Rifella	Brother t o Irina
Lanerch	Lord of Kaylin prior to Eduardo- Adopted Eduardo	Kaylin	
Makinti	Praetor for Thane Cathked	Rifella	Bardu's friend
Mayda	Serving woman & apprentice to Wynneth	Baklai	Daughter to Haydar

NAME	DESCRIPTION	FROM	RELATION
Mayrin	Wife of Haydar	Baklai	Mayda's mother
Mazon	Family who welcome guests	Shendea	
Morshag	Legendary horse thief of Baklai	Baklai	Now a curse word
Mouse	Serves Galdin Guide for Kat in Pridden	Morden	Eduardo
Murwenna	Lord of Rifella	Rifella	
Neerin	Assistant to Walden	Shendea	
Nick	Kat's supervisor	Our world	Karen
Penrow	Master Builderof Kaylin	Kaylin	Father to Illian
Ponsin	Head of Glazenwyth	Shendea	
Rantor	Store Owner in Blain	Rifella	
Rhognor	Lord of Shendea Titular Head of all Guilds	Shendea	Bond mate to Halfin
Saglit	Ssarff's second-in command	Morden	
Salssin	Agent of Assassin's Guild	Morden	
Sherwyn	Head of Housekeeping for Eduardo's keep	Kaylin	
Souris	Waiter at hotel in Tortola	Our world	
Ssarff	Leader of Assassin's Guild	Morden	
Ssayleese	Snake Goddess in Morden	Morden	
Thontook	Master Weaver of Kaylin	Kaylin	
Walden	White Magician	Shendea	Brother to Hesginn
Wynneth	Healer to Lord Eduardo	Shendea	Deleth

J. M. Tibbott

FLORA AND FAUNA OF PRIDDEN

NAME	DESCRIPTION	FROM
Bonbrie	Delicious fruit similar to peach	Shendea
Boradai	Furred creature size of a kitten who can read minds	Shendea
Brantor	Small, short-legged, carnivores who hunt in packs, with massive claws, two small horns and black teeth.	Rifella
Brynosh	Tall plants which are used for tapestries and by Rifellans	Shendea
Cathnog	Large ferocious cat-like creature with four huge canines resembling a saber-toothed tiger.	Shendea
Drag	Largest snake in Morden, similar to python in that is crushes it's prey	Morden
Gondal	Two foot long lizards with black tongues, and which are excellent for eating.	Baklai
Gornog	Pig-like animal, size of a jaguar, grey & black, covered in stiff bristles two set of tufted ears, six clawed feet, 12 inch tusks in a warted mouth. Meat is tender, sweet and delicious, although causes gas in those who consume it.	Kaylin
Gwindle	A health tea for mind & body focus	Shendea

NAME	DESCRIPTION	FROM
Hissar	Rodent-like creature 1.5 feet, with the temper of a Tasmanian devil, three rows of barbed teeth, and the strength of a creature 10 times its size.	Baklai
Horse	Almost the same as in our world, except much larger in size.	Baklai
Hydodd	Large elk-like animal with huge horns, cantankerous and a match for the ferocity of the Cathnogs.	Shendea
Kithra	Dog-sized rodent with black eyes, needle sharp teeth and brown hair travel and attack in packs.	Kaylin
Klim	Plant which produces nut-like seeds and is cooked into journeyklim, a porridge-like meal.	Shendea
Ponti	Resembles a horse, but with very large head for it's body size, large splayed feet, short legs, wide girth very sure footed in mountainous regions. Pontis grow to about ten or eleven hands high.	Shendea
Pyrock	Tiny, furry animal, with long tail and leathery wings can transport instantly, and locate any person anywhere on Pridden. Answers only to one person during lifetime. When rolled n a ball, fits in one hand.	Kaylin
Red Rash	A dangerous virus, which emerges every seven years, and unless treated may cause excruciating pain and death	Pridden

NAME	DESCRIPTION	FROM
Sea Swimmers	Fish from the Bay at the Mora Waters usually either roasted over coals or presented in a stew called cassolet	Shendea/ Rifella
Shade	A huge black panther-like animal with brilliant emerald eyes that becomes Kat's protector in Shendea	Shendea
Syeth	Small but deadly poisonous snake venom causes almost instant death but is used by Shendean Healers to produce potion to combat Red Rash	Morden
Wullawerth	Sheep-like animal with masses of fine soft hair, excellent for clothing. Prized for eating.	Kaylin

J. M. Tibbott

ABOUT THE AUTHOR

J. M. Tibbott has been writing since childhood. The Arrival was her first published novel. As a writer of magazine and newspaper articles, being an editor for an online newsletter, and a writing instructor, J.M. belongs to a community of local writers, all of whom are dedicated to the upgrading their own skills.

While the initial intention was to publish a myth/fantasy novel, as J.M delved further into the creation of a new world in which The Arrival takes place, it became obvious that the complete story required multiple books. Thus Book 2, The Healers is now complete.

J. M. is currently hard at work on the third book in the series.

SNEAK PEAK

We hope you enjoyed this second book in the Pridden Saga, and just to entice you, we've included a peek into the next novel in the series, The Warriors.

CHAPTER 1 OF THE WARRIORS

The trip from the Magicians Guild in Shendea moved slowly, tediously and silent. The two travelers clopped across the Carrog Pandy Bridge, and passed from Shendea to Rifella, and Kat stopped her horse midway. At her back the winds were cool and gentle, yet dispassionate. She glanced behind her.

Mouse walked his animal beside her. "Shendea is done."

Kat nodded. Although she found her peace over the death of Halfin, she still missed Breen so much. The loss of the ability to speak with a creature with the intelligence of the boradai left her with a hollow feeling. She came to rely on Breen for information and guidance about social customs and people's agendas while traveling through the land of the healers. Unfortunately, her little pyrock could not fill the space left by Breen. Wink, a sweet and cuddly ball of fur, boasted little intelligence, which appeared limited to delivering messages, eating and sleeping.

Shade left a different vacuum within Kat. Her panther protected her from dangers, but when the challenges of Shendea no longer occupied them, Shade, it seemed, was no longer needed. *I think Liandock somehow tied her to my ston*e. Positive the gorgeous Rifellan held responsibility for the huge black animal, it belied her initial conclusion he possessed only limited power. Clearly, he controlled something more arcane than she had encountered with any other.

She breathed the air blowing toward her. The wind from in front of her was warm, fecund, beckoning, filled with strength. To Kat, the wind smelled of Africa.

Mouse was still paused beside her. "What?"

"Can you feel it? Rifella?"

Mouse closed his eyes, breathed in and out, turned to her, his eyes now open, and nodded.

As they left the bridge and set hoof on Rifella, the landscape changed. Ahead and to the right, the terrain lay flat before them, covered in knee-high grasses, stunted trees, and bushy undergrowth, which stretched for miles. Not far to the left, however, loomed the crags of Clog Arth, on the Rifellan side.

Kat stopped her horse again. "Does Murwenna live in the mountain like Rhognor?"

Mouse stopped beside her. "No. She has her own keep, which is home to many of Rifellan royalty. Please remember Kat, when we are in her company, use Lord Murwenna's title."

"You've told me about titles often enough. There is no necessity to keep reminding me. It's like teaching a pig to sing. First, pigs can't sing, and second, you annoy the hell out of them."

Mouse blinked rapidly at her. "What are you talking about? Pig cannot sing?"

"You are correct, pigs can't sing. What I should have said is you are annoying me so much with your constant reminders about protocol, I'm beginning to ignore your words. I suggest you allow me to be myself, and only correct me when I make a mistake."

Mouse hesitated. "Kat, such an action would seem appropriate, except when you make errors, they are quite substantial."

"So? Explain to them I am not of this world and I'm still learning about the customs. Surely most will accept your words. You people need to learn to accept me instead of trying to fit me in a box."

Mouse sighed and rolled his eyes.

Without warning half a dozen creatures, each the size of a fox sprang from the undergrowth and headed for them grunting and growling.

"Move, Kat. Fast." He swatted the pack horse on its flank, and spurring his own animal forward headed for the less bushy areas at the foothills of Clog Arth.

"What are they?" Kat called to him as they galloped toward the mountains.

Mouse yelled back at her. "Brantors. And they run in packs and can bring down a full-grown horse, if the animal is slow enough. Keep riding."

Kat rode and the grunting noises became fainter as the three horses galloped for their lives.

Silence reined. "Did we outrun them?" She slowed her mount.

"Um, I think so." Mouse began. "Oh, oh." He rode over to the pack horse, where clinging by its teeth to a sack on the luggage frame on the horse's back, hung an animal with tufts of black fur on its head, surrounding two small horns. Each foot sported two massive claws, perfect for disemboweling its prey.

Kat gasped at the size of the claws. *No wonder Mouse urged me to move fast.*

Mouse raised his dagger and plunged the point into the throat of the brantor. Blood gushed from the wound and the foul animal tumbled to the ground. "This one got caught in the sacking, and could not free itself. As you can see by the teeth, they are formidable creatures. Luckily their legs are so short they experience difficulty keeping up with animals who can run faster. But what they lose in speed they make up for in stamina. Their quarry usually collapse from exhaustion, and then fall victim to the nasty creatures."

Kat peered closer and shuddered. The animal, covered in a leathery skin similar to an elephant, possessed a repulsive face. Bulbous blood-shot eyes, surrounded by black hair and the horns Kat had seen as it hung from the saddle, gave the appearance of a nearsighted miniature Satan. All this sat atop a yellow snout from which dripped a viscous green fluid. The teeth, which Mouse so kindly pointed out as formidable, shone midnight black, and contrasted vividly with the yellow interior of the mouth. "Is this one of the creatures I should have shot with my spring bow?"

"Indeed. Please ready your bow, because while we evaded one pack, more may be waiting ahead. We will leave this one here, as any who follow us, will make a meal of the dead one before pursuing us further."

Kat pulled her bow from the sheath on the saddle, lifted her foot from the stirrup and set the spring. Her arrows in their quiver were slung over her back. She hung the set bow from her saddle and the three of them trotted toward Clog Arth. *Am I getting used to gross animals? I'm hardly out of breath. Damn. I gotta get home. Horror and tragedy are becoming too normal.*

They passed out of the area of bushy undergrowth and the trees became more stately as they neared the distant keep.

Mouse turned in his saddle to glance at Kat. "I want to remind… ." He stopped as she glared venomously at him.

"I did not intent to remind you of protocol. I merely wished to suggest you wear one of you new leathers when we are called to meet with Murwenna. I believe this will serve us well for you to remind her of your strong resemblance to Rifellan royalty."

"Ah, fine idea."

As they neared the walled keep, similar to the castle-like structure of Eduardo's towers, Kat smiled at the neat farms and plots of land on which grew a variety of vegetables, with fruit trees in full flower dotted in between the crops. Attached to almost every home was a stable large enough for two to three horses. The paths leading between the houses and up to the main gates of the keep were laid with cobbled stones, and the sound of their horses' hooves created a soothing rhythm.

At the gates, two guards stepped forward.

Mouse stopped his horse and slid to the ground. "You are Lord Murwenna's guards?"

When they answered in the affirmative, he walked toward them. "I am Mouse, and this is the Lady Kat. Lord Murwenna expects us."

Kat dismounted and held the reins of her horse, expecting someone to relieve her of them.

Both guards stood a little straighter, and ushered them forward, offering to take their horses to the stable. Mouse thanked them and enquired as to where they would collect their baggage.

The closest guard, snapped his fingers, and a page came running. He gave the young man a few orders, and then hurried off to attend to his duties.

The page addressed Mouse. "Sire, my Lady, as soon as we are aware of which rooms you will occupy, your baggage will be delivered, and you will be escorted to them. I am positive Lord Murwenna will wish you to dine with her for the evening meal, so another apprentice will come for you to squire you to the dining hall. In the meantime, would you please await your apprentice helper in the ante-room."

"Thanks to you." Mouse turned back to Kat. "We will wait in there." He pointed to what resembled a parlor, off to the side of the main hall.

Kat followed him to a small chamber furnished with sofas and comfortable chairs, where they waited to be shown to their rooms.

Kat turned to Mouse. "I'm beginning to realize it's pleasant to be expected."

"In most lands this is true."

Kat peered at him in surprise. *Now what did he mean by that?*

A Message from J. M. Tibbott

Although I acknowledged the main people who have helped me through the process of this book on the pages near the front, I would like now to acknowledge you, as a reader for your contribution.

Like all writers, I adore creating a world with different creatures and people, and I really do all of this for you.

I was fortunate enough to grow up with parents who were themselves readers, and who took me weekly to the library. As a youngster I was only allowed to borrow two books at a time, and as we lived a fair distance from the library (a mile walk and a 35 minute bus ride) we only visited my favorite building every Saturday. Two books could not possibly keep me occupied for an entire week, so I regularly invaded my parents' library, which is why my reading level was way beyond my tender years.

It was the joy I received from books, that prompted me to write my own novel, so that I could foster the same delight among my readers.

So thank you for reading.

J. M. Tibbott

If you have not yet read The First Book, The Arrival Please Go to Amazon.com